Tails of Terror

Stories of Cat-Themed Horror

Brian M. Sammons
Editor

David Lee Ingersoll
Cover Painting & Interior Illustrations

Mark Shireman
Layout & Design

Brian S. Piorkowski & Bill Adcock
Proofreading

Thank You

I would like to thank all of the backers of the Tails of Valor and Terror campaign, whose generous support made this project possible. My thanks goes out to Brian M. Sammons, our fiction line editor, for putting together yet another amazing book for Golden Goblin Press. I am grateful for the amazing collection of authors who submitted stories to this anthology, so to Edward M. Erdelac, Pete Rawlik, Christine Morgan, Brian M. Sammons, Don Webb, Willie Meikle, Glynn Owen Barrass, Sam Stone, Stephen Mark Rainey, Joseph S. Pulver, Sr., Tim Waggoner, Neil Baker, Andi Newton, Lee Clark Zumpe, and D.A. Madigan – you have my most sincere thanks and gratitude. Once again, it is an honor and a privilege to tell stories with each and every one of you. Thank you to David Lee Ingersol for the amazing cover and interior illustrations, and Mark Shireman for his layout and design work. Last, but not least, to our proofreaders Brian S. Piorkowski and William Adcock for helping keep us all looking as good as possible.

Oscar Rios
President and Editor-In-Chief, GGP

Dedication

While this book has more than its fair share of heroes who are cats, this book is dedicated to the heroes for cats. It takes a special sort of person, with an amazing amount of love and compassion to rescue and foster cats. These individuals provide medical care along with a safe place and a loving refuge, and facilitate the cats' arrival at their forever homes. They love and then they let go, and I am sure their hearts break a little every time. Then they do it all over again. I don't know how they manage it, but I'm thankful they can. So, to all those who rescue and foster cats in need, most especially to Andi Newton (one of our authors) and my dear friend Roseanne McQuade (who gave me my beloved tom, Pickles, the inspiration for Pumpkin in my story), this book is dedicated to you.

If you can, please donate to:

ARFP / Animal Rescue and Foster Program (http://www.arfpnc.com/?page_id=181_)
Bobbi and the Strays (https://www.bobbiandthestrays.org/)

Table of Contents

FOREWORD 5

BROWN JENKIN'S RECKONING
by Edward M. Erdelac 7

DERPYFOOT
by Christine Morgan 19

THE CAT IN THE PALL
by Pete Rawlik 38

GHOST STORY
by Brian M. Sammons 48

PALEST OF HUMANS
by Don Webb 55

BATS IN THE BELFRY
by Willie Meikle 62

SATISFACTION BROUGHT HIM BACK
by Glynn Owen Barrass 72

THE BASTET SOCIETY
by Sam Stone 83

THE VEIL OF DREAMS
by Stephen Mark Rainey 96

THE QUEST OF PUMPKIN, THE BRAVE
by Oscar Rios 109

THE CATS OF THE RUE D'AUSEIL
by Neil Baker 121

THE KNOWLEDGE OF THE LOST MASTER
by Andi Newton 132

THE RUINS OF AN ENDLESS CITY
by Lee Clark Zumpe 142

A GLINT IN THE EYES
by D.A. Madigan 155

A FIELD GUIDE TO WANDERLUST
by Joseph S. Pulver, Sr. 168

IN THE END THERE IS A DRAIN
by Tim Waggoner 182

Foreword

It has been said that there are two kinds of people—those who love cats and those who are wrong. It can be fairly assumed—if you are reading this anthology—which group you fall into.

The story of humanity stretches back hundreds of thousands of years, and is richly interwoven with tales of our relationships with the other living beings on our planet. Whether the dynamic is of predator vs. prey on the plains of prehistory, as worshiper and god in the temples of Ancient Egypt, or as human "parent" with beloved pet in the modern day, few animal-human interactions match the breadth and depth of place within the narrative of the human experience than that of the cat.

As with many examples of animal domestication, our bond with our feline friends began out of mutual gain—as humans transitioned from a hunter-gatherer lifestyle to an agrarian lifestyle, mass storage of foodstuffs became critical for the growth of settlements. Large amounts of food—particularly grains—being stored proved to be a hugely tempting target for pests such as rodents. This same dynamic, however, led small cats to those same human granaries, due to the richness and ease of finding prey. When the humans noticed, they tended to encourage the presence of cats in their communities, as it meant that less food would be lost to vermin.

This interconnection between feline and human has mutated across the centuries—humans have gone from seeing cats as a helpful source of pest control, to granting them godlike status in some cultures, to believing—thanks to superstition and paranoia—that they were servants of evil and bringers of plague during the Black Death. Ultimately, our relationship has evolved into the nearly-familial relationships we have with our cats today: that of beloved companions and family members who have distinct and complex personalities. And who sometimes blep.

One needs only to look at the Internet for more than 5 minutes to witness how integral cats have become in the modern story of humanity. One of the failings of humanity, however, is to think that OUR story is the ONLY story that matters. We do this from a personal level to a cultural level—racism, sexism, nationalism, and so many other -isms are symptoms of our sadly all-too-human tendency to focus only on ourselves and our own needs.

Countless tales have been told of how cats, large and small, play parts both meaningful and incidental across the wide swath of human experience. Those tales, however, are almost universally told from an anthropocentric point of view. As humans, we naturally tend to construct our narratives—both fictional and factual—from a human point of view.

What Golden Goblin Press hopes to do with Tails of Terror—alongside the wider Call of Cathulhu roleplaying enterprise—is to flip that narrative on its head, and give our feline friends their OWN stories and their OWN adventures. I firmly believe that every human being could do with more exercises in seeing the world through the eyes of another being. In this instance, those eyes just happen to shine in the dark.

Mark T. Shireman
August, 2018

Brown Jenkin's Reckoning

by Edward M. Erdelac

As some men dream of Dylath-Leen and the marble walls of lost Sarnath, all cats dream of Ulthar, the little cobblestone village on the winding River Skai where no cat may be harmed.

The dreaming cats of Arkham met in Ulthar at the old temple on the hill, in the little stone amphitheater-shrine whose top tier was arranged with graven images of the Elder Gods of Earth. The clowder seated itself before the greening brass statues of their patrons, Uldar, and the cat-headed goddess Bast, to discuss the depredations of the rats of Arkham, which had, for unknown reasons, intensified as of late.

The old priest Atal filled the stone bowls of the twelve respected master cats of the ninth incarnation with cream.

One of the housecats, a regal Maine coon, spoke:

"The rats are on the offensive. Many new holes gnawed in the homes of man, particularly in French Hill. Food stolen. There are even little bites on the limbs of the sleeping children."

Children sometimes wandered into the Dreamlands in their carefree slumber, and it was the duty of cats to guide them out again, to keep them safe from the various minions of the Outer God Nyarlathotep, who would steal them for vile ends. This oath of child-herding extended into the waking world. It was a matter quite serious to the cats, particularly those fortunate to have human homes.

"Why are the mousers not curbing this behavior?" demanded a haughty, fat orange housecat.

"If it is the rats doing these things," said one of the alley cats, a mangy tabby of the fifth generation, "then they are moving by avenues we cannot tell. The humans have not been idle. They've been blowing poison down into the rat nests for weeks. Most of the warrens have emptied into the hills west of town."

"It's not a rat," said a voice from the shoulder of the statue of Bast. "Though I'd be amazed if any fat-bellied housecat could hear a rat lapping from his milk bowl in the kitchen over the sound of their own complacent purring."

A rough-looking tomcat, nip-eared, broad-shouldered, the color of pipe smoke with white socks, jumped down from his high perch on the statue and went to the center of the shrine. He bore some limp, bleeding shape in his teeth, which he deposited on the floor for all to see.

It was a rat, and it had been subjected to such tortures as only a half-feral alley cat can devise. The tomcat laid one paw on its back.

This tomcat was notorious across the neighborhoods of Arkham as a scrapper and a night yowler, a scavenging rover who had sired kittens as far away as Innsmouth. He was also grudgingly recognized as the best mouser in the Miskatonic Valley.

Yet he was also a master of the ninth incarnation, the only one among the alley cats. Only a master could drag the dream avatar of another creature all the way to Ulthar. By their ninth and final incarnation, most cats, having lived several lifetimes of adventures, were content to settle into extended retirement like pampered mandarins, safely exploring their future Dreamland abode from the comfort of some warm human house where they could safely sleep all day, undisturbed in a forgotten hutch.

Not so, this tomcat. His behavior befuddled the other masters, for he had not attended a clowder in the Dreamlands in recent memory. In the waking world, he slashed the knuckles of hands that sought to stroke him, and pissed on proffered bedding. He would rather lie dead in a road than on his back in a soft lap. No one knew where he slept.

Beneath his paw, the mangled rat twitched. The cats licked their chops at its squeal, tasting fear.

"Tell them," the tomcat hissed.

"Brown Jenkin!" squeaked the rat.

The cats stirred uneasily. The reputation of the creature called Brown Jenkin, the prowling monster rat with the heads and hands of a man, vile familiar to the witch Keziah Mason, servant of the Outer Dark, was well known. Keziah and Brown Jenkin, fugitives of the Salem trials, had haunted Arkham from the upper rooms of the Stinking House on the corner of Pickman and Parsonage for three hundred years, stealing out in the dead of night to snatch children to bleed on the altars of the Old Ones.

"The witch is dead, and her pet with her," said the Maine coon dismissively.

This was true. The violet witch light had not been seen in the upper windows of the Stinking House for many months. Even the old landlord had at last abandoned it.

"You're wrong," wheezed the rat, sounding slightly pleased, even in his pathetic state, to know more than the cats. "Brown Jenkin lives!"

"Tell them the rest," urged the tomcat, spreading his claws.

"The witch *is* dead," croaked the rat miserably. "But our master sustains himself with the blood of children, and through the sacrifice of we faithful."

"One of a mischief that lives in the walls of the Stinking House," explained the tomcat. "Fanatics who worship Brown Jenkin as a god. What is your master preparing to do now?"

But the rat would not answer, for all the tom's persistent cruelty.

At last it cried out in hoarse agony:

"The Crawling Chaos comes! Ia! Ia...!"

The tomcat nipped the base of the rat's skull. Its blasphemous hosanna died in its throat.

"I will tell you what he told me when I caught him," said the tom, leaving the bleeding carcass to hop back on the shoulder of Bast and address the clowder. "Brown Jenkin seeks to kill a child this very night. It's the final part in a ritual interrupted by the death of his witch; a spell that will bring his master into the waking world."

Many growled to hear this. As child-stewards and sworn retainers of Uldar, they were directly aligned against Brown Jenkin's master, the force called Nyarlathotep, the Crawling Chaos, and worked always to oppose its machinations.

"Preposterous!" said the Maine coon. "Why would the Outer Gods answer the summons of a rat? Even Brown Jenkin."

A respected old Abyssinian, once a master cat of Arkham in elder days, now a longtime resident of Ulthar, lifted her muzzle from her bowl between the feet of Uldar and spoke.

"Brown Jenkin is no mere rat, and no pet of Keziah Mason. It *was* a rat once, but discontent to live a scavenger's life, it called on Nyarlathotep for power. The Crawling Chaos took it before the Demon Sultan himself. There it was tutored in secret ways, and reborn in the womb of the witch. She was never its mistress, but its surrogate. Its handmaid."

Some of the younger cats looked askance, but others were rapt.

"Something must be done!" cried an overwrought Siamese, thinking of his home and the child who even now slept at his side.

"But what?" said a more pragmatic Bombay. "If this is all true, who here has the power to face an agent of the Outer Dark itself? Can it be harmed by claw?"

Here, the tomcat spoke again, yawning and stretching.

"Well, a few months ago I surprised Brown Jenkin in a dark alley off Lich Street. It had come through the fence of the burying grounds dragging something back to the Stinking House. I thought it was a possum at first, and we tangled. It's when I got a taste of his bitter black blood that I realized what it was. I let it get away from me. He scuttled off between the angles of a shadowy corner and disappeared."

"You are of the ninth incarnation," said an impious Persian who didn't like the authority with which the old beggar spoke, master or no. "Why didn't you chase it? You could have."

"Because I'm not a fool," said the tomcat, grooming his paws nonchalantly, so that the Persian's scruff bristled in annoyance. "What cat alone would follow Brown Jenkin through some portal to Uldar-knows-where?"

"Coward," muttered the Persian.

At that, the tomcat drew himself up and hissed, arching his back. The Persian lowered his head and spoke no more.

"Even if it were true that Brown Jenkin could be destroyed," said the Bombay, "being what it is, its evil may not end there. Killing it might prove an unfettering of the power its body contains."

"We cats may hunt mice and rats in Arkham," said the Maine coon, "but against such a being, what can we do? We cannot defeat it."

"I might know a way," said the tomcat.

He preened a bit more as the clowder hung on his words.

"Three years ago," he said, "I was in Partridgeville. The pickings were slim. I'd been going regularly to the door of a bachelor who lived above a jewelry shop for scraps. One night I was awakened beneath a bush by a hard shaking of the ground. I stole to the bachelor's. As was my custom, I walked the ledge of his neighbor's apartment to get to his door. Through the window, I saw something.

"A man crouched naked in the middle of a room which he had evidently rounded off by hand with a trowel and some plaster. The earthquake had knocked some loose though, exposing a single corner. Through the pane, I saw smoke coming out of a space there, as if something smoldered. No fire, but a stink worse than corpse-rot. Something emerged from that space, from between the angles, something that was all strange, flickering angles itself. It pounced on the man, and tore him apart like paper."

"A creature of angles?" remarked the Maine coon dubiously.

"Of angles, from angles," the tomcat said. "And ravenous-wild. Long and lean it was...with a blue tongue like a toad's."

The cats murmured.

"What happened then?" the Maine coon demanded, blinking its slim eyes patronizingly.

"I didn't stick around to find out," the tomcat admitted.

"Convenient," said the Maine coon, swishing his prodigious tail. "Another fantastic beast you somehow saw fit not to follow."

The tomcat leapt down again and came to stand before the housecat, hissing and glowering, but this Maine coon had spent many years and several lives hunting ship larders and brawling over wharf rats in dark port cities. He was not easily cowed. He lowered his ears and returned the threat in kind.

"Had I thrown my last life away needlessly then, you wouldn't be hearing about it now," said the tomcat.

"Catnip dreams," scoffed the Maine coon, unimpressed.

"No," said the Abyssinian. "I have heard of things, like hounds, which hunt the angles of eternity, stalking the Tindalos, those who pass too far and too frequently through time in the wrong direction."

"If such a thing exists," said the Bombay thoughtfully, "it could destroy Brown Jenkin."

"It sounds like it could destroy us all," one of the strays murmured.

"It only hunts those who travel through time," said the Abyssinian.

"And only along angles," the tomcat added.

"Would it be able to survive long in curved space?" mused the Bombay. "Surely it must devour and depart, or succumb to the physical laws of our plane."

"But why would it hunger for Brown Jenkin?" said the Maine coon.

"I, for one, do not think Brown Jenkin and his witch have lived continuously three hundred years," said the Abyssinian. "They have the power to travel in any direction in time and space along the outrageous angles of the universe, and have done so, moving between the far gone past and the present at will. Their reappearance in Arkham over the centuries has made them seem long lived."

"Then we only have to put one of these things on Brown Jenkin's scent," said the Bombay.

"And how do you propose we do that?" the Maine coon said.

"By drawing one out," the tomcat answered.

"But where do they come from?"

"From before the birth of the first star," said the Abyssinian. "That is where they are said to dwell."

"It would take a cat of the ninth incarnation to physically go there," said the Maine coon. "And if they are as relentless as you say..."

"Yes," said the tomcat, closing his eyes and ruminating.

It would be a suicidal errand. A final sacrifice of existence. There was no tenth bodily incarnation for cats. Cat spirits went to the Dreamlands or beyond, assuming what shape they chose. But if these hounds devoured the self, there could be no transition. No passing on from the life of flesh to the life of spirit.

"I'll do it," said the tomcat, opening his eyes.

"What?" said the Maine coon, almost as aghast at the finality of the prospect as he was flabbergasted by the volunteer.

"It'll require coordination," said the tomcat, turning to address the clowder. "You housecats who have children in your homes will have to keep watch tonight and sound the alarm when Brown Jenkin appears," the tomcat said to the Maine coon. "It will mean staying awake."

"We can surely do that," the Maine coon said, ruffling at the inference of indolence.

"The brothers and sisters in the streets must keep watch, too. The fleetest of our mousers will give chase, but the masters must pursue Brown Jenkin down its escape routes. It mustn't be allowed to leave Arkham. It must be harassed. Herded."

"Herded where?" one of the alley cats called.

"To the Stinking House. We'll converge there. When it's penned in, I'll bring the hound to finish it."

The Maine coon glowered, suspicious now, and said to the clowder:

"How can we trust this stray, who has never shown any loyalty to any cat? The Stinking House is where Brown Jenkin is strongest. Who's to say this isn't some ploy to lure us all to doom?"

"You accuse me of being a traitor, housecat?" the tomcat hissed.

"You are a master, but you root in garbage and are never seen in Ulthar. I've not seen you at clowder since we were both in our sixth incarnations. You live your last days like a cat with no future. We really know nothing about you," the Main coon finished, staring into the eyes of the stray and laying back his ears. "Perhaps you lie dreaming in the Stinking House right now, with Brown Jenkin whispering your words."

The tomcat glared at the Maine coon, but he did not attack. He merely lowered his head.

"You are right to suspect me," he said at last. "I can only tell you this, and you must choose to trust me or not. You ask why a master eats garbage and denies himself a rightful home. It's penance. The alley off of Lich Street isn't the first time I met Brown Jenkin. I was a housecat once, in Arkham, in my seventh incarnation. That old monster and its witch came into the nursery one night and took my charge from her cradle. Where was I, you may wonder? Prancing about the Dreamlands like a kitten, chasing zooks through the tall grass. *Bast and Uldar!*" he cursed. "It was the wailing of her mother that awakened me. I thought a stray cat had got in. Her screeching was like the condemnation of Bast herself. Know this about me, you cats of Arkham: alone among you, I do not live for Ulthar, so you may trust me to die when I must, if it means Brown Jenkin will be no more."

The Maine coon blinked and sat down.

The other masters unanimously ratified the tomcat's plan without argument.

The particulars were worked out in detail, with the masters organizing task forces in each of their neighborhoods, marshaling the strays, assigning them alleys to keep watch, covering every dark corner of Arkham with cats' eyes.

When the sun sank over the Enchanted Wood, the clowder ascended the seven hundred seventy steps to the waking world.

The Maine coon watched the tomcat, pitying him, but now doubly dubious of his mettle.

The Maine coon awoke in his favorite spot underneath the child's cradle, the sunny patch he had reposed in long departed. Feeling a sudden panic, he leapt up to the changing table to peer through the crib bars at the boy-child lying in the bunting, just a peach face taking small, regular breaths through his bow mouth, floating somewhere in the Dreamlands among the gurgling pink clouds of his kind, perhaps drifting over the Twilight Sea.

He went to the window seat to wait for night.

Hours passed, and the mother came to feed the baby. As the shadows lengthened in the back garden, the Maine coon saw a scrawny calico clamber onto the fence. Ordinarily this encroachment would have sent him into paroxysm of vocal outrage, but this was his assigned sentry.

They stared at each other through the pane for a while. The calico was probably in her third or fourth incarnation, aware of the unseen but not yet able to move physically through space-time. She looked too hungry to even contemplate such matters. The Maine coon reflected on his own privilege, and on his previous eight lives. Once he had sat on a fence and looked in at a cat very much like he was now.

Inevitably he thought of the tomcat and his self-imposed penance, imagining the scent of his pain encompassed in the comfortable smells of the house. The tuna in the kitchen bowl. Talcum on the table. *Kapusniak* boiling. Every reassuring stroke of a loving arm the passing of a scourge across his guilt-ridden hide. His own purrs an unallowable blasphemy. Was it any wonder he disparaged the life of a housecat? He knew the dangers of a complacent steward.

The Maine coon blinked his eyes and suddenly it was night. The calico had left her post.

There was an odd sound coming from the baby's crib, and he rose from the window seat and sprang lightly to the changing table.

Looking down into the crib, which was slightly illuminated by the blue moon through the nursery window, he froze.

Hunched over on his child's chest, two of its tiny, repulsive human fists thrust past the wrists into the baby's nostrils, its grotesque bulk covering the child's mouth, was Brown Jenkin. The baby was trembling, in the throes of suffocation.

As the shadow of the Maine coon fell across it, Brown Jenkin half turned, the moonlight catching its repulsive, scraggly-bearded features, its beady black eyes and hooked nose, and the shriveled lips that drew back from jagged yellow teeth.

The cat leapt screaming into the crib, raking his claws down the thing's back, ploughing black furrows. Brown Jenkin jumped away with a muttered curse and flopped over the rail to the floor.

The baby gulped air and began to wail shrilly.

The Maine coon heard the creak of the bed in the next room, the exclamations of the mother and father, and caught the wink of the electric light under the nursery door.

He saw Brown Jenkin scurrying for the corner of the room and jumped down after it.

The monster made for the vertex and wobbled up on two hands, making some furtive gestures with its fore-hands. It uttered something, then fell back on all fours and galumphed into an interspatial passage as it shimmered into existence.

As the door to the nursery flew open, the cat plunged into the portal and vanished.

Through a shifting, disorienting maelstrom of spinning shapes and colors, the Maine coon hurtled in his quarry's wake. The appearance of Brown Jenkin became polyhedral, a strange amalgam of ever-changing shapes, altering at will, apparently to affect its course through the abyss. The Maine coon wondered if this was the true form of the monster, or perhaps an idealized geometric configuration it had devised to best navigate angular space.

The polyhedron turned sharply and tumbled out through some membrane onto the wet grass of the Miskatonic Quadrangle, assuming, in the curved world, the shape of the rat-thing once again. The Maine coon appeared a half second later, still yowling piercingly. As Brown Jenkin scuttled under a bush, another cat's cry sounded nearby, and another further away, and another, and another.

The alarm was sounded. The cats of Arkham were roused. If the plan held, the tomcat would begin his errand, plunging back through time to some ncalculable eternal gulf in search of a monster to kill a monster.

The Maine coon dove into the bushes, expecting to see Brown Jenkin's disgusting tail retreating into another portal, but recoiled as he found the monster crouched, waiting.

They were evenly matched in size. The cat felt the little hands grasp and claw, the jagged teeth bite through his hide. He shook and bucked, trying to slip Brown Jenkin's grip. Hot color exploded in his forebrain as his left eye was scraped free.

Then another cat, a burly, striped Bengal, crashed into the brush and tackled Brown Jenkin. The two rolled away in a ball as the Maine coon staggered away shuddering and bleeding.

The black Bombay he remembered from Ulthar thrust her face into the bush, blocking the only egress.

Brown Jenkin chittered some unintelligible word and suddenly it was gone from the grip of the Bengal. The Maine coon was able to follow its etheric passage with his one good eye. The creature had desperately slashed a hastily calculated gap in space-time and tumbled through. It moved only a few inches, but reappeared in the space occupied by the Bombay. The black cat blew apart in bloody scraps as Brown Jenkin burst from her body.

The Maine coon growled in rage and followed Brown Jenkin out of the bush back onto the Quad as the Bengal matched his speed at his side.

Brown Jenkin corrected its course as four more cats came racing across the grounds, each from a different direction.

It made for the base of the statue in the center of the commons, and once again reared up, preparing to open one of its passages.

The Maine coon and the Bengal were too far behind to catch up, but two housecats followed it through the shimmering gap a moment before it closed.

The Maine coon stopped to catch his breath.

"Are you alright?" the Bengal asked, marveling at his wounds.

"What about that gray tom?" he asked.

"No word. We can only hope he is successful. What now?"

"The Stinking House," the Maine coon said, and broke into a trot headed south towards College Street, flecking the grass with his own blood.

A cool March wind blew down the benighted avenues, and a bloodied, tailless Manx joined them, reporting that another of the pursuing masters had been killed, but three more had taken his place. Brown Jenkin was leaping back and forth across Arkham in harried desperation.

But this pell-mell chase was a deliberately random attempt to exhaust and distract the hunters from its lair.

The neighborhood was like an infection spreading out from the malignant sore that was the Stinking House. The gambrel roofs were decrepit, shedding shingles, the yards overgrown. It was as if the house were a vampire sucking the life from the neighborhood. A half-hearted attempt at stymieing the corruption by the city fathers of Arkham had left a rusting cement mixer on the broken curb.

When they reached the house, they saw a myriad of cats streaming up the vine-covered walls, jumping through its broken windows like attackers through a breach. The Maine coon and his companions gained entry to the second floor, momentarily stunned by the air of decay and rot that permeated the place and gave it its name.

A battle already raged inside between the outnumbered but fanatical rats of Brown Jenkin's cult and the Arkham cats.

Felines shrieked, slashed, and bit, their bodies festooned with clinging, nipping rats who squeaked and gasped as they were picked off and disemboweled with swiping claws. Fur and blood scattered into the oppressive air.

The Manx joined the fight, but the Maine coon and the Bengal went to the uppermost gable room. It was empty.

"Something's wrong," said the Maine coon. "This isn't the place."

The wind howled. The upper floor creaked and shuddered. Concentrating, the cat let his eye go out of focus and scanned the area like a lighthouse lamp, looking for signs of Brown Jenkin in the other planes. To his surprise, he saw the polyhedral shape he had pursued emerge in a hidden room entirely sealed off from the house directly overhead, turn, and decapitate a closely pursuing cat, sending the head spinning into a corner.

"What is it?" the Bengal asked.

The Maine coon didn't answer. He knew the young Bengal didn't have the ability to follow. He sprang into the air and slashed through space, reappearing in the hidden room.

The occult chamber was a jumble of papers, old books, and ritual paraphernalia. Bowls and bells of strange metals clustered about. A repulsive blue idol sat upon a table. Everything was covered in sigils and red geometric scrawls. The nest of Keziah Mason and Brown Jenkin. The dark keep of the house wherein the witch and her familiar had communed with their god.

Brown Jenkin spun at his appearance. The creature held the wicked long knife with which it had dispatched its last pursuer in its two hands like a man would hold a sword. It bared its teeth and circled him warily, inviting him in to die.

He drew himself up and obliged.

Then, from a high corner of the wall, the tomcat shuddered into being and landed full upon Brown Jenkin's back.

Brown Jenkin rolled to dislodge the new menace, and sent the gray crashing into a high stack of arcane papers which tipped and fluttered like pigeons about the room.

The tomcat looked like he had already fought a great battle. His hide was shredded. He dribbled blood from a dozen wounds. His teeth were visible through his drooping cheek. One ear hung ragged.

Brown Jenkin snuffled and backed away, brandishing the knife. Its greasy brown hair was dark with the tomcat's blood.

"It's too late," the tomcat half-wheezed, half-laughed. "I've marked you."

Lightning flashed, blinding in the room, but no thunder followed. From the space where the tomcat had appeared, a putrid black fog began to billow, bringing with it a noisome stink that rivaled even the rot of the charnel house.

Something like an assortment of diamond shards flickered into existence there. Brown Jenkin cowered, the knife clattering from its hands as it looked up in astonishment.

The crystalline 'beak' of the creature forcing its way into the room parted. A thick blue appendage spilled out, uncoiling on the floor before it began to quiver and lash probingly about, overturning the table with its idol, toppling a rick of grimoires.

A gale-force wind assailed the house. The Maine coon had to dig his claws into the rotten floor to keep from being lifted by it.

The tomcat too had hooked his claws into the floor against the sudden blow. He inched towards Brown Jenkin, who had reared up and was fumbling with its hands, desperate to weave an escape.

"No," groaned the tomcat. "No, you can't get away!"

The tom sprang once more on Brown Jenkin, summoning the last of his mortal effort, and bit into its neck. Black blood spurted over his whiskers, and though the foul thing clawed the hide further from his face and roared its outrage, the tom hung on.

The flickering creature fell from the corner into the room with a crash that broke the old floor and the roof caved.

The Maine coon yowled in alarm as he fell through to the floor below.

The battle below ceased at the calamitous intrusion. Those cats not crushed by debris wailed in fright at the sight of the weird abomination winding its blue tongue around Brown Jenkin and the tomcat. Brown Jenkin screamed an unnerving human scream as the thing pulled itself closer to them, its blue maw opening wide, eliciting a series of unnerving, thunderous sounds that further shook the decrepit structure.

"Get out!" the Maine coon yelled, and led the surviving cats out of the shambles, sparing one frightful glance back at the hound, seeing its form bend and contort, birthing anew to the edict of curved space, taking on an appearance not unlike an immense, slimy, decorticated canine.

The cats fled for the windows, leaping down to the bare, choked trees. The thing loped after them on ungainly limbs, dripping vaguely luminescent blue mucus.

In that instant he remembered what the Abyssinian had said about curved spaces.

"There!" he called, and ran for the abandoned cement mixer, scampering up the back and into the blackness of the empty cylindrical drum.

The cats jammed themselves in behind, pressing each other against the cold metal, unquestioning the command of a master of the ninth incarnation.

How long the hound could survive in their dimension the Maine coon couldn't guess. But he suspected in this rusted steel womb, they were safe, should it follow.

There they waited. The wind outside rattled the drum. They heard the terrible booming, and pressed close as kittens to each other until the windstorm overcame all, eventually fading to a comforting drone.

They huddled there all night.

In the morning, there was no trace of the hound.

The upper floor of the Stinking House had fallen in on itself.

In Ulthar, the one-eyed Maine coon accompanied the six remaining masters in a solemn procession to the old temple on the hill.

Old Atla poured them customary bowls of cream.

They insisted upon an eighth bowl to honor the tomcat, and this the priest placed on the shoulder of the statue of Bast.

Ever after, this became the custom when the cat-masters of Arkham came calling.

And nevermore was Brown Jenkin seen, in Arkham or in worlds beyond.

Derpyfoot

by Christine Morgan

Warms. The warms and the purrs. The milks and the licks.

Others. Squirming pile, furry mewing bodies.

The Mother. The licks, wet and rough.

The purrs, rumble rumble, and the heartbeat whump-whumpwhump. Voice and cry, meow, trill, croon. The Mother. Soft tummy, bulgy teats, nipple, push-push-push knead-knead-knead, the milks.

Milks. Purrs. Warms. Licks.

The scruff, the teeth-clamp. Lift. Tuck and curl. Swinging. Squalling. Then drop.

Alone. Cold. New. Strange. Not-fur. Like-fur, not-fur.

Mew and mew, struggle and mew. Legs. Feets. Blunder and bump.

Mother-smell again, fur and milk. The brush of a touch. The Mother comes, the Mother goes. More mewing, more squalling. The Others. One by one. Drop, drop, drop. Roll and squirm. Complaints.

Then the Mother comes, and stays. Curls around. All the warms. All the purrs. Lick-lick-lick. Nose nudging. Milk smells, milk smells. A teat, a nipple, an Other.

Mew. Mew and cry.

Nudge. Lick. Another teat. Another nipple. No Other. Milk and milk, knead-push-purr, milk.

Yawn. Nuzzle. Burrow. Licks. Warm fur-pile, Others, Mother.

Sleeps.

Sounds.

Loud-sounds, strange-sounds.

Strange-touch, not-fur, not-scruff, lift. Cold. On back, belly-up. Mew and wiggle, complain and squirm. Smells, thick not-milk smells, strange.

The Mother, a call-cry, concerned. Mew and mew and mew!

More sounds. Strange-sounds. Not-same-kind sounds. Big thing, strange thing. People-thing. People-thing and people-sounds. Movement, head brought close to warms, to licks, the Mother.

"See? Your baby's right here, your baby's fine. Good kitty, Bella, that's a good mama-kitty."

People-sounds and people-touch.

"How many this time?"

"Eight. Five boys and three girls."

"Eight? Eight more cats? Jesus fuck." Pause. Strange-smells, gusty humid yeasty smell and bitter smoke-smell. "What's wrong with them?"

"Nothing's wrong with them! They're perfect little babies!"

"They don't look right. I seen a shitload of kittens thanks to you, and those do not look right."

"They're fine!"

"And what about *that* one?"

"Runt of the litter, is all."

"Runt, all right. Is all? My ass. Look at its paw there."

People-touch, grab and pinchy. Squall! Bend the leg. Prod the paw. Mew!

"Got one foot a little crooked. It's nothing."

"Nothing? Fucking deformed."

"One little crooked foot!"

"Mutant freak-cat."

"Don't say that! He's a fuzzy sweetie!"

Squall and squall, squirm and mew and squall. Mother-meow, a rustle, the flump and tumble and complaining of the Others.

"Some sweetie. Screaming like the possessed. I never heard no cat sound like that."

"You're scaring him! And he misses his mama. Here you go, Bella.

Here's your baby."

Lowered. The smells. Mother and milk. Fur and purrs and warms. Released. Roll and wobble. No more strange people-touch. The Mother. Lick, lick, lick. Pushed over. Lick, lick, lick some more.

"You ought to drown the whole ratty lot of them."

"Caleb Bodean!"

"What? You inbreed 'em so much, now they're all starting to come off deformed. Like that one big bastard with the damn yellow lantern eyes."

"I din't breed him! He showed up a stray and you know it."

"Stray, whatever. I swear that one ain't right, ain't normal. Bet he's the one knocked up your precious Bella, and now she got these mutant freak-cats. Probably ree-tarded."

"Shut your stupid face."

"You shut yours, woman!"

"I don't have to take this from you!"

"Who the fuck else are you gonna take it from?"

"Jackass!"

"Cow!"

Hissssss. The Mother. No purrs. Fur bristling.

"See what you've done, you're upsetting Bella."

"Fuck Bella!"

"Well, fuck you, too!"

The Others. Mew and mewl and whimper. Crawl. Teats, where? Nipples? Milks?

Hisssss again. A low, drawn-out yoooooowwwwl.

"Listen to that bitch! She's gone nuts!"

"I told you, you're upsetting her! She's a brand-new mama. Never done this before."

"Christ. You and your goddamn cats. I need a beer."

"Then go get yourself one."

"Did I ask you to wait on me?"

"What, you mean you're gonna make your own damn dinner for once?"

"Maybe I'll take myself down to The Wheel for dinner!"

"Maybe you should!"

"Have me a big ol' chili-burger."

"Go right on ahead, and when you get the sizzling shits, don't come running to me."

Stomp-clomp-stomp-thud. A clinky jingle. A slam. A grindy-growly noise.

"Jackass." The people-touch again, stroking the Mother as she settles, brushing over the Others as they clamber and fumble for milks. "There, now, Bella. He's gone. You're fine here with your babies in this nice box, you got your nice towel. That's a girl. That's a good girl."

The purrs. The warms, purrs, and licks. The Others, furry side to furry side, kneady-pushy paws, milk-milk-milk. Lick and lick. Purr, purr, purr.

Sleeps.

Same and same and same.

Sleeps and no-sleeps. Warms and purrs. Milks and licks.

Safe.

The Mother.

Sometimes another Other, an other-Other. Similar-smell but different-smell...*strange*-smell. Fur. Warms but no teats, no nipples, no milks. Curious sniffs and licks, quick hiss-and-swat, louder hiss from the Mother.

Gradual understanding...that other-Other is the Father; there are more other-Others all around but none quite the same. Hearing them. Smelling them. Meows and meows. Scent-marks and scat-marks. Many, many other-Others.

Brightness. Brightness and blur. Light and dark and shape and shadow. Big-shape people-shapes to go with the people-sounds, touches, smells.

Clumsy legs. Wobbly-weak. Tippy. Tip and tumble, roll, wallow. Ears and fur, whiskery noses, eyes, tails. Milk, milk, milk. Little claws, little teeth, more more more and mew-mew-mew when the Mother goes and more more more purr purr purr when the Mother comes back.

Sleeps.

Waking no-sleeps.

People-sounds, people-voices, loud and angry. Slams and shouts.

"—about goddamn *had* it! For fuck's sake, woman! *Look* at this place!"

"You knew I wasn't no Martha Stewart when you married me!"

"I didn't know I'd be living in wall-to-wall cat piss!"

"Oh, it is not that bad—"

More slams and stomps. Hisses, wary snarls. Ears flat. The Mother hunkered over them, the Others crowding close.

"Take a whiff! Cat piss, cat shit, the fucking hair's everywhere, can't walk across the floor without it crunching like a gravel driveway. You said they'd do it outside!"

"I got the litter boxes so they wouldn't have to go out there and freeze in the winter-time doing their business!"

"That's why you had me saw a hole in the damn door, put in that dumb-ass flap that lets in all the cold air."

"Not my fault you're a sorry excuse for a handyman. Speaking of which, when you gonna fix the—"

"I wasn't finished! I'm tired of smelling cat-piss, tired of stepping on their dried turds, tired of cat hair on everything and in my food. Tired of that yellow-eyed fuck staring at me all the time. You've seen the damn furniture, too, clawed half to crap!"

"What are you saying, Caleb?"

"I'm saying I've had it with these cats. One or two, hell, three or four even, that'd be fine, but..."

"You want to get rid of our sweeties?"

"We can't keep 'em all, Doreen. You know that. We can't afford it, especially what with them squeezing out eight and ten kittens at a go!"

"The kittens, we'll find homes for soon as they're weaned. Just like always."

"That's what you said last time and you ended up keeping half of 'em."

"That was Sugar-Pie's litter; it would have broken her heart to let them all go. She's old. She might never have any more."

"Always some fucking excuse. What're you gonna tell me next? That since it's Bella's first batch, you can't bear to part 'em from her? In-bred retards though they are? Even that deformed gimp freak-cat—"

"Don't talk about my sweeties like that!"

"I'll talk about your precious damn sweeties however-the-fuck I please!"

The smells, heavy and strong. Sounds. Shapes, looming.

"What are you doing?"

"Drawing a fucking line in the sand, that's what I'm doing!"

"Caleb! Get away from there!"

The Mother hisses again, yowls.

"Back the hell off me, Doreen!" Shoving movement. Stumble-crash, meaty thud, pained grunt.

"Don't you touch them." Gasping, wet snorts. "You leave them alone."

"Or what?"

Sudden grab. Not-fur. Grime and dirt, bad-smells. One of the Others snatched up, lifted, mewing, thrashing. The Mother screeches. Paw-lash claw-slash. Blood.

"Caleb!"

"Ow! Bitch scratched me!"

"Put down that baby!"

Squall. Struggle.

Snap. Crunch.

People-scream. "Bastard!"

A loose thump as the Other drops. Still. Inert. Head twisted crooked. Tongue poking out.

More screams. More crashes and thuds. Two more of the Others seized. The Mother leaping, a ball of fur and fury, claws, teeth. All the other-Others yowling now, hissing, racing around tails-puffed backs-bristled.

Blood and blood and blood. Thin cuts and deep bites. Screaming. So much screaming, so much yowling and howling and screeching and wailing.

"Fucking bitch-cat!"

Wet cracking sound.

"Bella! Noooo! Bella!"

The Mother, no longer hissing.

The box kicked. The box flipped. Towel whump and darkness, squirming, mewing. Stomp-crunch, stomp-crunch.

"Caleb, stop!"

"Should've goddamn listened to me, huh, Doreen? Bossy cunt!" Stomp-crunch.

"You piece of shit! I'm gonna kill you!"

"Like to see you tr—"

BANG.

Silence.

Silence.

Blood-stink. Smoke-stink.

Sobbing.

"Bella, my poor Bella, my poor sweetie...my poor sweetie and your poor sweetie-babies...that son of a bitch, that murdering bastard! He asked for it. I told him to stop. I told him. He didn't have to go and do that!"

Sobbing and sobbing. Snuffles. Snorts.

The towel, sodden, sticky. Blood. The Others. Squashed, broken, limp, loose.

Heavy-dark-wet towel lifted. "Babies? Babies, you okay? Did he...oh no, no!" More sobs, wails.

Mew?

People-touch. Cradling. Stroking. "Oh you poor sweetie-baby, you poor little thing, oh that bastard I should've shot him quicker, your poor mama, your poor lost little brothers and sisters!"

Mew and struggle.

The Mother! The milks, the purrs, the licks, the warms! The Mother! Want-need-want!

No.

People-touch, rubbing on not-fur, leaky salty not-fur and people-breath, sour-sweet not-milk and the sounds the sounds the sounds.

"It's all right, now, everyone, it's all right, it'll be all right, I'll make it all right, my good kitties, my sweeties, everyone shhh, just hush now, hush now, let's just… come on…here, kitty-kitty, come on kitties, everyone over to the kitchen, I'll open up some cans for you, how about that, nice treat some canned food for you while I clean this mess up, while I take care of it…"

Set down. Cold. No fur, no not-fur, cold and flat, hard, claws tick-tick-tick paws slide around.

"…shot him, shot Caleb dead as the piece of shit he is and what if someone calls the police on me? Nosy neighbors, damn kids! But maybe they didn't hear nothing, maybe they don't want to get themselves involved. No, sure they wouldn't, not all the times they been in trouble with the law. Calling the police'd be about the last thing they'd do."

The noise. The *rrerrrr-errr-err-click* noise, and the smells, and the other-Others meowing, jostling, meowing, demanding.

"Just a minute, yes, that's right, just a minute, let me spoon it out, hey, hey, take it easy, nice kitties, enough for everyone, last few cans but I'll go to the store tomorrow and plenty of the dry left. Oh but what am I gonna do with *you*, poor kitty-baby?"

Lifted again, cradled, cuddled, breathed on, not-licked.

"Nowhere near ready to be weaned yet but maybe ol' Sugar-Pie has some milk left…her litter haven't been off it that long, and she'll take you in, I'm sure she will, Bella's little orphan sweetie."

A Not-Mother. Strange fur. Wrinkled teats, tough nipples, thin milks. Grudging licks. Different scent. Different purrs. Sometimes rebuffing, pushing away. Tired. Warning hisses. Ear-swats and sharp nips.

The New-Others. Bigger. Jumping-bouncing, pouncing, wrestling. Sit on. Flop on. Step on. Bump aside. Knock over, bowl over, run over.

The Father. Different but familiar. *Strange* but familiar. Sometimes let's huddle close for sleeps and warms. Sometimes grooms. Sometimes growls, eyes narrowed. Eyes yellow. Yellow-yellow. Glow-yellow, even in the bright.

In the sleeps, huddled close in warms, the Father-heart makes slow *strange* whumps. The Father-purr rumbles low and deep. In the Father-dreams are big-*strange* places. Sounds but not like people-sounds. Shrill-trill high high piping sounds. Sense of vastness. Sense of space. Colors/not-colors wheeling in a dark, a forever-dark.

And people-sounds.

"...say that we had ourselves another argument, and he walked out on me... everybody knows about his drinking and how he feels about the cats...not much of a surprise, they'll think...he'd just up and take off like that without a word... no job anyhow...probably owes a bunch of people money, too...good riddance, I'll tell them...not like he had any friends, bad-tempered son of a bitch..."

Always the people-sounds.

"...grave for Bella and her litter...complications I'll say, birth defects...all's you got to do is look at you, poor baby with your crooked foot, only instead of being the runt anymore, you're the strong one, aren't you? The lucky one, the survivor... terrible thing but small blessings...who'd have any reason to think otherwise? Been putting my sweeties back there for years, markers and everything."

People-sounds and people-smells.

"...only fair, after the way Caleb treated us. After the way he treated me. All of us. Never was good for a goddamn thing in his life."

Milks...and foods...soft-wet foods, mmm-smack-smack...hard-dry foods, krick-crack-crunch...people-foods, warm-salty-meat-juice and sweet-sweet-milky-cream...lick and lap, lap-lap-lap.

"Always griping at me how much I'd spend, like I was feeding you out of crystal dishes like on those commercials instead from the grocery warehouse... griping how I never changed the cat boxes enough, then griping at me for the cost of the kitty litter when I did..."

Scent-marks and scat-marks. Dirt for pee-digging, for poo-digging, dig dig dig scratch scratch scratch bury bury bury.

"Might as well be of some use now. Might as well give some back, the selfish greedy fucker...and wouldn't he be pissed if he knew? Reason enough right there..."

Not-furs to run on. Not-furs to climb on. Play-toy string ball toy-play swat swat chase, swat-pounce-skitter.

"...cheapskate ought to appreciate it then, me being all thrifty...recycling, like those co-op hippies down the road say we should, them with their organic farm...though this not hardly vegetarian, though, not hardly! Ha!"

Strange-foods. Wet but different. Sloppy-messy. Big chunks. Gnaw-gnaw-gnaw. Strange taste. Less-good.

"...his truck, might be a problem, loved that damn truck...he went anyplace, you know he would've took the truck...have to do something about that...drive it around to the old garage, maybe..."

Itchies. Ear, ear, chin, neck, ear, rump, rump, scritch-scritch. Itchies. Groom-groom-groom. Lick-lick-chew-lick. Itchy furs. Itchy skins.

"...nosy damn neighbors...mind their own business, why can't they? Saying I don't take care of my precious sweeties? I love my precious sweeties! And you love me, don't you? Don't you? We don't need nobody else."

Sounds and smells.

Getting worse. Oily and sweaty. Bad-fish. Sour-milks.

"Eat up, everybody, here-kitty-kitty chow time. Oh, come on. Who's hungry? Eat it up. I'll get out to the store soon, but, look, only a few bags left... good thing I got those gallon-size freezer baggies, knew they'd come in handy... scrawny old shit had some meat on his bones after all..."

Dig-dirt stinky with pee-and-poo, too stinky, too filled, not-scratch, not-bury. Food spills. Food spoils. Spoiled-foods and spoiled food-spills.

"...place getting a little messy, maybe, but so what? My house now, isn't it? All mine and only mine. Told him how I wasn't any Martha Stewart when he married me, anyway..."

Meows and complains. Many-many. All the Others, all but the Father. Who sits. Who watches. Yellow eyes shining-shining. Sit with. Watch with. Hungries but sit. Hungries but watch. Watch and wait.

"...soon as I'm feeling better, I promise...need to get some proper groceries up in here, too...damn Caleb and all his beers in the fridge, not hardly room for anything else...gives me the heartburn...really could use a nice dish of ice-cream, take care of that...'bout out of antacids anyway...so tired, let me just have a nap first..."

People-sleeps.

Foods?

No foods.

Complain. Meow. Others meow. Lots of meow. Want-need-demand.

People-sleeps. Grunts and breaths and sloppy snores. People-sound mumbles.

No foods.

Empties.

Empty where-foods-go. Empty hungry bellies. Growl and snarl. Hiss and fight.

Hungries.

Meows. Yowls. More hisses. More fights. More hungries.

So much hungries!

Then, the Father, no more sit and wait and watch. The Father eyes yellow, yellow glow. The Father high up on the people-bed.

And no more people-sounds.

The Others low-hunker, unsure, afraid. Curious but unsure. Hungries but afraid.

The Father down-hops, scruff-bites, up-climbs.

Mew. Squirm.

Released, high up on people-bed.

Warms, but, fading. People but no sounds, no moves, no touch.

No breaths. No sleeps.

The Father, claw and slice, nudge and push.

Licks?

Tastes?

Mew?

Some Others, boldest, approach and sniff, sniff and curious, sniff and lick.

Foods?

Foods!

Lick and bite, and bite, and chew. Greedy growling noises.

Now all, all the Others, crowding crowding busy claws and teeth.

People-taste. People-taste but hungries, people-taste but foods.

Foods and foods, so much foods, red slick wet yellow globby foods.

Foods!

The Father, the flap-thing. Push and through. Urge. Show. Teach. Push and through, through and out.

Bright-hot hot-bright warms...smells, many-many new smells, strange smells...outside smells! Big air, wide space...the World!

The World but not the vastness, not the strange-space where colors/not-colors, where high shrill high trill sounds in the Father's deep-low-rumble purring dreams.

Dirt-real-dirt for scratch and digging. Grass to chew. Chew chew chew. Hork. Chew. Leaves for chase-pounce. Crawly bugs. Birds whoosh so fast so high! The heat-warms, sun-warms, roll and stretch, sun-warms on the tummy!

The Others climb and climb, trees to climb. Try but no, try but fall, try but some paws claw-catch-hold, one paw not. The Others run and run, dash this way that way spring leap bound around around. Try but slow, try but clumsy-stumble. The Others chase and swat, swat and tussle, wrestle wrestle.

The Father, tail twitch twitch get it get it fierce hunter. Yellow eyes flash and gleam. Lick and groom, curl for sleeps, purr.

Naps in the sun-warms, in the shade-cools. Water water drip-drip-drips from metal faucet-tube plink into basin always plenty lap lap lap drink.

Inside for foods, slimy less-good foods now. Dark, not red, not yellow, dark and brown. Buzz-buzz flies and squirmy grub-worms. Soon be bad-foods, sick-make not-foods, should bury-bury kick the dirt.

Hungries come then?

Empty-belly hungries?

Or more foods?

Eat and eat, gnaw and chew for least-bad not-yet-rot bits, eat and eat. And wash and wash, face wash face wash lick the paw wipe the face. Whiskers. Food-meats stuck in claws, chew and gnaw some more. Lick, wipe, wash, groom and groom.

And push-through outside, for more sun-warms and shade-cools.

Then...sounds.

People-sounds?

People-sounds!

Peoples! New peoples. At the stick-fence, at the yard.

"We're gonna get in trouble."

"Daddy promised."

"He also said, after, that he didn't really mean it."

"Which is a super unfair liar jerkface thing to do. You can't make promises and take them back and be a dirty taker-backer. If he won't get us a kitty, we'll just go get our own."

"Why here, though? This is gross, Hailey. Look at the place, it's trailer-trash city."

"Kim at school told me the lady who lives here always has bunches of kittens, and gives them away for free even."

The Others wary-watching, narrow-eyes, gold and green, orange and blue. Some run. Some slink. Some hiss and hunch and puff the fur.

"Whoa...that's a lot of cats. A lot of mean-looking cats."

"Stop it, Justin, they are not mean. They don't know us yet, that's all." The smaller of the peoples, a girl-people, crouches. "Kitty-kitty, hi kitties!"

The taller boy-people puts a hand toward one of the Others. Hunker, ears-lowered, building rumble-yowl deep in chest. Hiss and claw-swipe. Miss, very near miss. "They're, like, feral or something. C'mon. Let's get out of here."

"But I want a kitty."

"Dad won't let you keep it. Besides, they're all grubby. I bet they've got fleas."

"Ohhh, look, this little grey and white one's got a derpy foot."

Sniff and sweet clean people-smell, and gentle people-touch. Head-pets, soft, nice.

Mew?

"See? This one's not mean!"

Mew and nudge and nuzzle.

"Hailey, watch it, be careful!"

"Aww, Justin, see?"

Hands and lift and hold and cuddle. Snuggle. The Girl!

Another touch, the Boy, hesitant but then under-chin scritches yes yes bliss so good, and purr! "I guess he's not so bad. At least he's friendly. Wonder what happened to his paw."

"Poor little derpy foot kitty, you want to come and live with us now, don't you?"

Purr and purr and purr. The Others still wary-watching, or indifferent. The Father pushes through the flap-thing, messy muzzle, matted whiskers, face-wash time. Stops, eyes yellow, eyes flash, stares and glares and hisses.

"Is that what you're gonna call him? Derpyfoot?"

"Maybe. Hey, he fits right in my hoodie pocket like a baby kangaroo! All snug and comfy!"

Long sighing air-sound from the Boy. "We better go ask the lady who lives here if it's okay. You can't just take him. That'd be stealing, even if she gives them away for free."

Snuggledarks and warms, the Girl, slow-moving, walking.

And the Boy. "Jeez, it stinks."

"Litter boxes maybe?"

"I dunno, worse than litter boxes."

Up and up. Steps. Knock and knock.

Others-meows but no people-sounds.

"Keep trying, Justin!"

Louder-knock. "Hello? Anybody home? Missus…uh…"

"Bodean."

"Missus Bodean?" Loud-hard knock, and creak. "It opened—oh, man! Whew! What *died*?"

"Eew-yuck-gross."

"Hey wait, I see something—"

Then, people-shouts and people-screams. Then, fast-moves run run run bounce bounce claws-dig-in hang on hang on. Screams and shouts and gags and cries.

Fast run bounce jarring jogging claws-dig hang on.

Scared. Scared. Huddle small be small hang on in the soft warm-darks. No purrs. No yowls. Not even mews. Scared and scared, hold on.

Brights. Brights and lights and new smells, new place, new place-smells.

"You brought him *with* you?"

"He was in my hoodie pocket, I forgot!"

"We have to take him back!"

"No no no I don't want to go back there not back there Justin pleeeease!"

"Well…"

"You don't want to either!"

"Yeah, but…"

New place. New sounds and smells and feels. New big clean place. Many smells to sniff, to explore.

"…when Dad gets here, and the police, they can…"

"…but we rescued him, we saved him from that awful…"

Thirsties, and mew, and mew, and water, bowl water wet-cool wet-clear lap lap lap drink.

"…Dad isn't going to let you…"

"…can't send him *back*, there's nobody…"

Foods, hard-dry foods, crunch-crunch-crunch. Tasty hard-dry foods and no pushing-shoving, no shares, no growls, no swats and hisses, no Others.

No Others, but no Father.

"…or as evidence or something…"

"Evidence?"

"…or maybe to the pound—"

"No! Not my Derpyfoot! Not the *pound*!"

Dirt-box, new dirt, clean dirt, no scent-marks no scat-marks, scratch and dig, scratch-scratch, pee and poo, dig-dig-dig bury.

"...and look at him, anyway, he's all dirty; what if that stuff in his fur is—"

"It is not don't you say it don't you dare!"

"Okay, okay, but we at least better give him a bath."

White place. Cold hard white place, slippy under paws, shrieky under claws, can't catch can't hold can't climb want out out-out-out.

Soothy Girl-voice.

Not soothed! Very much not!

Runny runny water! Runny splash! Louder splashing rushing roar water water not drink-water! Wets! Not-cold, warm-wets but still wets too much wets wets all over bad bad bad!

Out!

Can't!

Wail and protest. Wail-wail-wail.

Girl-voice. "Derpy, it's okay, it's okay, Derpy!"

Wets. All the wets. Drenchy splashy wets. Feets in the wets, pick one up, shakety-shakety fast but set down again back in the wets!

Wets and scrubs. Soapy smelly foamy on the fur in the fur scrubby-scrubs fur this way that way wrong way, messed and wet and soapy! The back the legs the tummy the chest the neck-chin-head, the tail!

"...feel *so* much better..."

Suds and tingle, icky smell, icky taste, feets in the wets and cold now cold shiver-shiver and yowly-sad meow.

"...rinse you off and..."

More wets! Wets everywhere! In the face!

"Sorry, Derpy...hold still...almost done."

Miserable long-longer-longest-ever yowl.

"Almost done, promise!"

Drip. Drip. Shiver and drip.

"There we go. Good kitty, Derpy, what a good kitty. Okay. Let's dry you off."

Cloth. Swaddle and cover. Rub, rub, rub. Less wets. Less and less wets. Shake the paws. Step, shakety-shakety, step.

And the brush, nice, nice.

Dry fur. Warm fur.

Soft and clean and nice.

Thing! Thing on the neck! Head caught! Stiff band of smelly thing! On neck! Around neck! Caught, caught!

Back up back up back up! Out, out!

Can't! Stuck stuck stuck! Hind paw, snag and grab, push, push hard. Off-off-off!

"...only a collar, you'll get used to it..."

The Girl, pick ups again, pets. Hugs. Snuggle-nuzzle.

"See? Not so bad. And it'll keep the nasty fleas away."

Hugs and pets. Pet-pet-pet.

Mew.

"It's okay, Derpy. It's okay. You're my kitty now, my good kitty, and I love you."

More sounds, people-sounds. Angry. Loud. Yells and shouts.

"—you'd disobey me like that—"

"—said we could, Daddy, you *promised*!"

Flinch. Bristle. Mew and hiss.

"—told you I'd *think* about it—"

"—means *no*, everybody knows it always—"

"Dad, we only—" The Boy, trying to intervene.

"—start with me, Justin; you're older, you should be more—"

"—not *his* fault; I forgot Derpy was in my pocket when—"

"—your sister to a *crime* scene—"

"—didn't know, and we called the police as soon as—"

"—talking about this; the cat's got to go."

"Nooooo! Derpy's *my* kitty!" Hug, squeeze, hurt-tight this time and more crying, fear-smells tear-smells.

"—with all the other ones they took in as evidence—"

"The ones they didn't shoot, you mean; I heard on the news they killed a bunch!"

"You're not helping, Justin."

"I don't want them to shoot Derpy!"

"Hailey, calm down. They won't shoot him."

"But what if they take him to the pound and gas him to death?"

"—about enough of this from both of you. Even if I was going to let you get a cat, it wouldn't be a...a...*cannibal cat*."

"Jeez, Dad, it's not even the same species, that's not how cannibalism—"

"Damn it, Justin!"

"But it isn't!"

SMACK.

Silence.

No people-sounds. No people-moves.

The Girl, trembling, hitch-hitch-hitch for breath.

"Justin, oh my god, I'm sorry—"

"Don't touch me!"

"Are you all right?"

"I said don't touch me! Hailey's right! *Mom* was right! You're a liar and a jerk and *I hate you*!"

Girl-room.

People-place is quiet. Mad-quiet, sad-quiet. Closed doors and no-talks.

Sad Girl hugs and hugs, pets and pets. Purr, mew, cuddle. Head-boops. Roll over for tummies. Purr and play. String, swatty-ball, feather, crinkly thing! Jump-chase-tumble-pounce!

Finally, happy Girl. Happy-sounds. Laughs and giggles.

Lots of pettings. Lots of cuddles. Warms and pets and cuddles. Purr-purr. Knead, push, purr.

The darks, warm-darks but not all-darks, soft light low and soft pillow-blankie-bed.

The Girl, slow breaths and sweet smells. Sleepy-pets.

Purrs.

Happies.

Sleeps.

Sleeps.

Sleeps and sleeps.

Sudden grab and lift!

Wakes!

Mew but covered, people-hand, big-people-hand, gripping face, squeezing muzzle. Strong-bad smells, whiskey smells, smoke smells, sweat-sour smells.

Squeal, but muffled. Struggle and kick, but held. Scruff. Scruff and collar-thing, tight on neck, tight. Half-chokes. Legs uptuck. Tail undertuck. Ears flat.

The Girl turns, sleepy-mumbles, pillow-burrows, breath-sighs.

Carried fast. Away from Girl. Away from room. Carried fast, doors and doors.

Cool air, night air.

Outside. The World.

People-sounds, slurred, grumbling.

"—*have* to do this...tell her it must've got out, wandered away...upset at first but she'll get over it...buy her that phone she's been wanting...won't say anything if he knows what's good for him...call *me* a liar and a jerk?..."

Outside, the night, the night. Wide vast night alive with noises, alive with scents, rustle-rustle bushes, dirt and trees, away from the people-place, away from the Girl.

"—squirming, you little...*could* just wring your mangy neck...lucky I'm only dumping you...catch mice or birds or something...can't with that foot then oh well...law of the wild..."

Stumble and sway, arm-swing, awkward slip-grip of scruff. No more big hand on face, no more grip-squeeze muffle. Hiss and spit, claws and *swipe*, claws and skin-flesh-snag-drag, claws and *blood*!

"Ow! Son of a—"

Grappling, grappling, caught by tail, caught by leg, wrench-pain, hurts, hurts. But *fight*, bite and fight, screech, claw-scrabble and fight, rip-shred-rip at wrist, teeth sink sharp-deep in soft meat. Sudden taste, people-taste blood-taste food-taste.

Scruff again, held again, clamp-tight fist on scruff, more hurts. More people-sounds, angry-sounds. Faster stumble-walk, stumble-run.

"—ought to throw you against that tree...bash your head in with a rock... look at this, scratches, bleeding like hell...tell the kids?"

Yowl from near.

Wavering, warning, rising yowl from near.

Eyeshine glinting, yellow glow, bright angry-yellow shining in the dark.

People-stops, unsteady, uncertain. "What the...?"

Familiar smell. Familiar shape from the gloom. Head low, body low, tail low. Pad-steps careful. Deliberate. Silent. Placed.

The Father.

Then, more. More-shapes, cat-shapes, Other-shapes...but strange. Limp-drag-slow strange. Made from shadow made from mist strange.

"Psst! Go on! Scat! Psst!"

Surrounding. Closing in.

Backward, people-stumble, clumsy-stumble worse than ever, backward, blundering.

"—the hell *away* from me!"

Reel and totter. Crack-snap, wet bone snap, and people-yell, crazy waving arms, topsy-tumble.

Loose! Loose and dropped, falling, twist in air, land on feet, but leg-ouch paw-bend, oof and thump, mulch-leaves-earth. Grunt-mew.

Bigger thump, louder thump, twig-snap ground-shake thump, and more people-sounds. People pain-sounds, on back rolling, foot crooked, flop-wiggle, wobble-wobble.

"—my fucking *ankle*!"

Helpless, feeble thrashings. A get-up try and fail, more pain-sounds, yelping, word-sounds, swearing.

And here are the Father, the Others.

Not all but some. Many.

Closing in.

Growling.

There are angries, and much hungries.

And blood-smell in the air.

Limps.

Limps and limps.

Limp and hobble.

So far away, so far, when hurt, when scared, when tired. When crooked paw and leg all sore-stiff.

Then, nip and grip, lift, the scruff-carry. No struggles. Hang and rest, swing and rest, sore and stiff and tired.

Through the dark with yellow eyes, glow and shine, yellow through the dark. The Father, carry and purr, low-deep-rumble purr.

To the people-place, to the door left open.

Stop. Un-scruff and down. The Father rough-licks rough-licks and nudge.

Mew?

Nudge.

And go...limp-hobble in. While, below, the Father sits and watches and waits.

Limp-hobble in, limp-hobble up. Stairs stairs stairs, up and up.

To the room where soft light welcomes in warm-darks, where soft pillow-blankie bed rises high up above, so high.

So high, and hard climb, hard climb with bent paw and sore leg, when aches and tired. Hard climb, strain and pull, claw-claw pull and pull.

Until, finally.

Until the slow and sweet deep-breaths, the gentle hand to burrow under, the warms, snuggle-warms. The drowsy-pets and murmurs.

The Girl.

"Derpy, here's my good kitty..."

Mew and nuzzle. Curl up cozy, purr and purr.

A pause, a half-wakeful stirring. "Uck, why's your fur all sticky? Do you need another bath? In the morning, 'kay? It's sleepytime."

Happies, sleeps and sleeps.

The Cat in the Pall

by Pete Rawlik

It was a little more than two years ago, on June the 16th, 1923, that I was brought to the restored house at Exham Priory. Prior to that I had resided in a small cottage on the outskirts of nearby Anchester dwelling with the man that I called Shakes. I had been with Shakes for most of my life, and had lived with him in America in a town very different from Anchester, one filled with factories billowing dark smoke and the near constant sound of machines churning both night and day. In Anchester, Shakes had added eight others of my kind to our household, and these came with us to Exham Priory. They were, in no particular order, a Siamese who preferred to be called Mao; Lady Pyrr, of Persian descent; Katrina, who was Siberian; the Manx Stubbins; and the queer Abyssinian Madame Cassandra. Finally, there were the siblings, two burly British shorthairs named Johnnybull and Jackymac. These were not their birth names, nor were these the names used by the mans, but rather their day-to-day names.

As for me, these fellows called me Mr. Ginger, not because of my color, which back then was as black as moonless night, but because even amongst the tribes of cats I was light-footed. My steps were like a breeze through the grass, and when I ran, it was merely a rush of whispers. We were as most households of our type, a motley crew, friendly as cats go, yet not without our moods and fights, but united when it came to defending our home and mates. Stubbins may have been a foul-mouthed bastard, but he was our foul-mouth bastard, and woe to the stranger who laid a claw upon him.

As eldest, and clearly Shakes' favorite, it was I who dominated our new home. I say new, but that was both true and not true. Exham Priory tasted both old and fresh, and as I explored, I learned that new construction had been laid over old—ancient—foundations. The place reeked of freshly cut wood stained and painted with all matter of solvents and dyes, but also always lingering in the background was the ever present odor of the aged stone itself; stone that had endured centuries of weathering and moss and lichen, and still held the scents of place that such age imbues. It was a large house though, large enough for several temperamental cats, with many high places with which to set up individual dominions and routines without too much conflict. I of course took control of the bedroom in the west tower, where Shakes slept, as well as the library which contained plenty of comfortable couches and chairs, as well as a rather massive fireplace that I knew would be needed to heat the place when winter finally came. Despite claiming these territories, I was a benevolent prince, and allowed the others to share the library with me, but the master bedroom was mine alone.

Shakes and our family were attended to by a pantheon of mans who each specialized in cleaning or cooking or tending the garden, and these were all strangers to us and we spent the first few days learning their personalities and training them in their service to us. Also present in those first few days was a young man whom we called Tubby. I had known him from his many visits to the cottage, and knew from the years that Shakes would often go and visit the man in his own home, or in the village pub. They were good friends, and it pleased me that Shakes had such a person in his life. Once there had been others, but since his wife and son had died Shakes had become increasingly isolated, and at least Tubby was someone to speak with.

It was on the morning of the third day that the first hint of trouble was raised. Stubbins came to me with strange news. He had found his way out the kitchen door, and spent the night prowling, first around the walls of the great house and then later in the garden and woods beyond. But in all his explorations he had been able to catch no sign of any small animals of any kind. There were birds a plenty, but these kept to the treetops or to the edge of the cliff that overlooked the crashing sea. There were no signs of field mice, or voles or moles. There were no hedgehogs, no hares, no shrews, not even a dormouse.

"A bad sign," he muttered. Which was true, but as Stubbins was not the brightest of felines I decided to have someone else look into the matter.

It was two days later that Madame Cassandra came to me with her report. All cats, are by their nature sensitive to the preternatural, we are after all one of the few species able to move—albeit with some effort—between the waking world and that of Dream, but Madame Cassandra was particularly precocious when she came to me in the way that she did, and I fully expected her to speak of something odd found in the stomach of a vole, or perhaps the colors of the intestines themselves were wrong. But there were no intestines to look at, no trichobezoars to marvel over, no deformed baby rabbits to excise from the wombs of their dead parents, no malformed toads with three eyes...indeed there was nothing to look at, at all.

Nothing tangible.

"There is something queer in the grounds." She mewled. "Some of the leaves on the trees and bushes are odd, gray and brittle, and not just the fallen ones. There are berries on the edge of the wood, but I don't know what species they are, and when I slice them open the juice is black and almost like a paste and the flesh is ashy. I've seen no trace of animal life, and yet..." she trailed off. "The ground cover moves. The grass and litter on occasion shudders, as if mice were hiding within it." She arched her back a little. "I saw a whole field come to life, undulating and roiling as if it were full of vermin, and then it suddenly stopped. It became as still as it could possibly be. I crept in, but there was nothing there, nothing at all." She whined a little. "I don't like it, Mr. Ginger, I don't like it one bit." She wandered off after that, as cats do, the issue unresolved.

I was intrigued, but after all my years I had become something of a house cat and I took this to be a concern of the land outside our abode rather than within. It was early on that evening that I was proven wrong. With the sun setting over a calm ocean in a drift glass sky, I myself began to detect something unusual. What it was I could not initially determine. It was a sound, a low annoying drone that set my whiskers to twitching, but the origin of the incessant rustling was unclear. Determined to locate the source of the minor discomfort I roamed from room to room, at ill-ease, constantly sniffing at the walls and columns that formed the outer structure of the edifice. Yet no matter how much I searched, or what I sniffed at, I could find no relief from the murmuring vibration that I could feel even in the very pads of my paws. It grew louder and it seemed to me that it was as if thousands of tiny feet were clawing their way up the outer walls of the building, climbing slowly from stone to stone, moving as a single mass up the towers and into the very sky above Exham Priory. The whole phenomenon lasted for about two or three minutes, and toward the end the demonic marching tapered off at the bottom and then spiraled off into the towers and the sky above.

The mans had not reacted to the event, and as much as I wanted to simply ignore the phantasmal cacophony, I couldn't, and after the mans had gone to sleep I called a convocation of my fellow cats, and all reported sensing the same thing, being equally unable to discover its origin. At the suggestion of one of the younger cats, Katrina, the troop began to systematically explore the house from tower to ground. It was an exhaustive search of the upper levels and extended beyond the rising of the sun and into the early morning. The activity caught the eye of the mans who seemed both distressed and amused at the members of the home prowling about in search of what they knew not.

Our efforts were fruitless, we found nothing of any particular interest, though in the cellar we found a large door that none of us had ever been through, and we were all confused by the minute traces of scent that were both strange and repellant that were leaking out of the small gaps between door and frame. We also sensed a disturbance while we prowled the attic regions, though these were not in the attic itself, but seemed to be in the air above the house. It was something darkly electric, that clawed at the bases of our ancient feline brains and made us as uneasy as kittens in a room full of rocking chairs. It placed us all on edge, as if a great storm were churning into existence right above our heads. Still, the feeling was highly localized, and scampering down just one flight of stairs eliminated all ability to sense the psychic maelstrom.

That night, my normal routine upset, I retired quite exhausted. As usual, I was in the west tower, sleeping at the feet of the man Shakes, comfortable in my slumber. It was therefore surprising that quite unexpectedly I passed from the world and into Dream, rousing at the gates of Ulthar itself. Passage from one realm to another is not uncommon amongst cats, but I had made no effort to reach the virtual world that sat beside ours and was puzzled by the transition. The cat city was abuzz with activity, though I could not say why, but as I prowled its streets I caught sight of cats from around the world and beyond. On the temple road I fell in behind the trail of an otherworldly saturnine feline that stalked down the road and into the conjoined temples of Bast and that of Ulthar, for whom Bast is high priestess. It was a curious thing to see the iridescent hues of a distant cousin as it moved ethereally through our lower gravity and paid homage to our common maker the Q'Hrell quintet known as the Ulthar, but it was reassuring as well. To know that your species was favored by the makers, and that versions of cats existed throughout the universe, more so than any other design, was somehow comforting, in an existential manner. The great candy-colored grimalkin kneeled before the altar of Ulthar and gave obeisance to our lord, and feeling a momentary pang of guilt I followed suit, bowing my head and closing my eyes in respectful devotion. Imagine my surprise when I looked up and found the mysteriously beautiful cat from Saturn standing over me, her mouth open wide and her eyes rolled back in her head. She was flehming, and I held still so that she could assess my status and confirm that I was neither a threat nor a worthy mate I was puzzled why I should even merit her attention.

Imagine my surprise when she finally relaxed and spoke to me, her voice a deep melodic thing, like a dying star. "You have the stink of the Qabba upon you. Why do you reek of such pestilent things tiny one?"

I was deferential, she could have easily swallowed me whole. "Apologies my liege, but I am a simple terrestrial cat; I cannot even say what the Qabba are, let alone why I smell of them."

She sighed, "Do they not teach you the ways of the universe on your tiny little blue planet? On Cykranosh even the milk-fed are taught of the Rats of Qybele, the thin lurkers of the void, children of the dark star-goddess Qybele."

I bowed my head in shame, and being a crafty old cat made up an excuse. "My parents were killed while my eyes were still shut. I was raised by mans and only now have begun to educate myself in the ways of our lord Ulthar." I peeked and saw that she was exasperated with my ignorance, but also was poised to seize the opportunity to complete my education.

"No one knows where the Rats of Qybele originally come from, but they exist in the depths of space between systems, far from any stars, for the pure light of a sun may itself destroy them. They are vast bidimensional things that cross vast distances in instants and drive lesser minds mad with their touch. Only those of the feline variety are swift enough to catch and kill the cosmic vermin, though truth be told there are those sensitives amongst lesser species that might catch a glimpse, but here is where we differ from such creatures. We see them as pests, to be hunted and killed, where others see them as tremendous beasts, draconians of the void, to be feared and fled from."

"But I have never been to the depths of space, I've never even been off Earth, my most excellent of teachers."

"The Qabba lifecycle requires that their young be hatched on worlds with life upon which their enigmatically colored offspring can feed. Woe to those that dwell in the land infested by the Qabbalin, for the energy that binds their very molecules together shall be torn away, leaving nothing but dust behind." She paused and stretched her neck. "The worst of things is that even after the Qabbalin departs for space, it leaves in the land a festering presence, a corruption that effects even the most stalwart. It may linger for centuries, eventually spawning forth yet another child, one that must be nourished foully but which may grant terrible gifts to those who protect it and through it worship the dark mother Qybele. It is the charge of our creators to destroy such things, no matter where they may dwell." She paused and stared at me with those strange purple eyes. "Even now, the Qabbalin comes near to you!"

I woke with a start. Something was moving behind the tapestry, up the walls, through the walls themselves. The noise, it was not just a single noise, but a cacophony, an orchestral chaos of thousands of tiny claws scrapping against the wall. Enraged, I sprang from the bed and onto the vast cloth that concealed the masonry. It collapsed under my weight and fell, revealing nothing. At least nothing visible, but with all my senses I was confronted with the sensation of a horrid vista. It was not just one thing, but a horde of things, spectral memories of a terrifying event that had scarred the very foundations themselves. And then as soon as I resolved what it was, it was gone, vanished, as if it never was. I prowled up and down the floor where the cloth had fallen, but to no avail. I could find nothing, and after a few more minutes of poking and prodding I abandoned my searches and returned to the bed. We are nothing if not a practical species and it seemed that the only thing to do was to go back to sleep. I wasn't even sure if Shakes had seen what I had seen, or he had just been disturbed by my antics. Thinking back to what the cat from Cykranosh said, I wondered if perhaps Shakes was a touch sensitive himself. I had never noticed it before. I tried to fall back to Dream, but that doorway had closed for the night.

Any doubt on what Shakes had seen was removed the next day when we all observed the men moving about the house deploying small circular wire traps filled with bait tinted with a small amount of powder of an unwholesome yellowish green in nature. The cats of the house tried to dissuade the deployment of such things, for it seemed a wasted effort, but mans are not known for their ability to perceive the preternatural, and thus the protestations of the household cats were ignored. Even the west tower bedroom was violated with one of the poisoned contraptions, and though I made my distaste at the situation quite clear, nothing was done to change it.

That night I was once again roused from sleep by a spectral cacophony, but this time of such magnitude that even the great cloth that hung against the wall could be seen to be moving. I howled and hissed enough to wake Shakes, who made the cool light shine so as to allow his weak eyes to better see the source of the maddening sounds. It was a fright to see the tapestry moving in that manner, as if it were a net full of fish struggling to escape. Almost immediately the haunting ceased, and the man poked and prodded the wall hanging in an attempt to elicit a response, but there was none. The wire trap that had been set in the room had been sprung, but no trace of what had triggered it remained visible.

Unable to return to sleep, Shakes left the room and began to move to the ground level, and I, as is my habit, followed. As we mounted the great terraced slope, both of us heard the unmistakable sound of those ghostly rats behind the wooden panels of the great room. This time as the lights came on the action of that phantom army did not cease but rather continued their mad and maddening frenzy. I, with the help of the light and keen ears, was able to discern that the great horde of spirit rats was engaged in a momentous migration from the upper levels of the house through the ground level, and into the depths beneath the restored domicile. I, and indeed all the cats of the house, careened down several flights of stairs and began yowling at the door to the sub-cellar, a door that had been closed ever since we had taken up residence. We crouched there at the bottom of the stairs for a minute or two, but then the storm of ghostly vermin ceased, and we settled our nerves and dispersed back amongst the upper floors and rooms of the house.

Late in the next day Tubby came to visit, and after a short conversation both he and Shakes descended through the door where they spent several hours out of the sight of me or any other cat. Then in the evening there was a great flurry of activity, and a number of couches were brought down the stairs and set up in a vault deep beneath the house. Shakes and I, along with Tubby, all set forth to spend the night in the roughly built crypt. I took a moment or two to prowl about the place and in doing so caught sight of the human letters carved into the stone. I may not speak any human language, nor can I read the marks they make, but somehow I knew that these dank scratches made reference to the dark mother Qybele and her human disciples. I shuddered with loathing at the thought that this place had been infected for so long that even the man had forgotten about it. Frustrated I found my way back to our small encampment, and it was not long before Shakes was asleep and I was curled up on his chest. His sleep was not sound, and Shakes tossed and turned before waking up screaming. Tubby laughed for a moment, but only for a moment, before both I and Shakes fell back to sleep.

It was hours later that the next wave of the phenomenon began. I woke to the sound of the cats in the upper part of the house howling at the door. The Qabba had returned and I could hear them all around us, moving down the walls of the sub-cellars. I leapt from my place and began frantically running about trying to find the source of the spectral invasion, but to no avail. The rats were still moving down, deeper into the earth and I and Shakes could hear the scuttling claws as they clambered deeper and deeper, far deeper than the sub-cellar. It was then that I realized that what we were hearing were merely the spectral echoes of the monstrous void-spawn clambering in the spaces in between and that we would have to make a supreme effort to reach and destroy the monsters.

Then, all of a sudden, my comrades beyond the door ceased their screeching, but I was suddenly revitalized. I had found a small spot, a hole really, at the base of a stone block that sat in the center of the room. It was from this hole that the last echoes of the verminous horde could be heard, and I was determined to bring it to the attention of the mans. Finally, after nearly a minute of frenetic pawing and scraping, Tubby brought his portable flame towards the crevice and discovered the slight draft emanating from the minuscule crack.

We spent the rest of the night on the brightly lit main floor. Shakes and Tubby talked incessantly well into the morning, and I listened intently trying to discern what they were saying, but to no avail. While cats may have made some progress in understanding the language of canines, even the greatest of cat philosophers has failed to make sense of the guttural sounds that emanate from the mouths of the mans. Oh we understand them plain enough, about as much as they understand us, but it is a crude sort of communication, and only the basics are ever conveyed. All I know is that later that day Shakes packed a large bag and left the house. Tubby was waiting for him in a car, and together they drove off into the setting sun.

The next day I called for a conclave and informed my colleagues of the situation and of my visit to Ulthar and the words of the Saturnine Feline. Mao was skeptical, but Cassandra simply nodded as if she had known these things for all her lives. Together we nine came up with a plan to deal with the terrors, the enemies of our Lords Ulthar. There was dissention. Lady Pyrr would at any opportunity, launch into discourse on the idea of moving, suggesting that we should abandon the man and the house he had built, in favor of one of the neighboring manors or farms. It was an interesting proposition, but I was too old to find a new master, and while Katrina, Stubbins, and the twins might be able to earn their keep as working cats, Madame Cassandra had always been a house cat, and Lady Pyrr herself was not the most comfortable moving about the wilds or even the alleyways of a town or city.

It was two weeks after they had left that Shakes and Tubby returned, and they brought with them five of the strangest people I had ever seen. One was definitely sensitive for he seemed the meekest of all of them, and yet there exuded from him a kind of palpable fear, but also understanding. Johnnybull hissed at him, but Lady Cassandra approached him with reverence and would not leave his side for the entirety of that afternoon. Even at dinner she stayed by his feet. It was my fear that his presence and her infatuation with him might derail our plans. I confronted her later that night, but she assured me that all was well and that she merely sought to protect him from what she felt was an impending doom.

She was of course most prescient on that point.

Late in the morning of the next day, Shakes and his cohorts gathered together a small quantity of equipment and began to gather at the cellar door. It was a surreal sight as the wooden gate was unlocked and the expedition to the lower level filed in. I was calm in the arms of Shakes even as the door was barred behind us and for the full hour it took for one of the party to pry up the altar stone and reveal the horror that lay beneath. There was a passage leading downward, steps worn so badly they were scarcely more than an inclined pathway, and lined as it were with all matter of bones. Most of these were easily recognizable as belonging to mans, though many were marked by the evidence of inbreeding and poor diet, for they showed greatly diminished brain capacity and even queer alignments between the bones of the arms and legs that suggested the gait of a quadruped rather than an upright stance. Also present was a second shaft, this one much smaller than the other, large enough for a cat or small dog to fit through, and it sloped upwards and from it issued a gentle breeze of cool air. With the air came a raft of odors all of which I recognized, and I immediately realized that this shaft must work its way through the very walls of the house, perhaps even up to the towers, acting as a kind of natural ventilator, but also as a passage for the Qabba to make their way from the upper levels into the catacombs below.

I will not bore you with the details of what the expedition found in the vast dimly-lit caverns at the base of those stairs, but I will say that it not only sent Lady Cassandra's favorite into catatonia, but it drove Shakes into a violent rage. He attacked Tubby with his hands and teeth, frothing and raging in the most terrible way. I scratched him across the face, and the others had to pull him off his friend and restrain him. It took an hour for the party to make their way back to the wooden door in the sub-cellar, during which time Tubby whose throat had been torn open, slowly but inevitably bled to death. As the gate to the upper world opened Shakes began to struggle violently, screaming and frothing at the mouth. I think it was only he that caught sight of me and the others on the floor there, and he called my name. He screamed it actually, over and over and over again, but I was too busy. In all the madness it was only the madman that saw the household cats stream through the legs of the expedition and vanish down into the depths below. It was only the madman who saw our plan begin as the door to the netherworld was slammed shut behind us.

That was two years ago. Down we ran, down past the tumbled altar stone, down past misshapen skulls and tunnels of bone. Down past a twilight tableau of ageless horrors, of pens and abattoirs where mans and things that had once been mans were corralled and fed and slaughtered to feed those who once dwelt in this place, and the vermin that haunted the darkness beyond. Down we plunged into stygian darkness. Down into the abyss itself, warriors in pursuit of prey that itself crawled ever deeper into the unending caverns below.

Two years. We lost Mao first. She died the first time we caught up to them. They hadn't known we were in pursuit. But even with the advantage of surprise we were only able to destroy a hundred or so of them, and they killed Mao. She thought she could hide in the dark, that her color would protect her. But the natural place for the Rats of Qybele are the places between stars. The darkness only makes the Qabba stronger, and we, limited as we are to feeding on fungi, worms, and grubs, have become weaker with time. Stubbins and Jackymac were killed in a rock fall, a year or so in. Johnnybull wandered off a week later, delirious with grief. I still hear him, or at least I think I do, howling in pain, out there in the dark.

Two years, and you my son are the firstborn of our first litter, and now old enough to lead our clan in pursuit of our quarry. Listen to your mother, Lady Pyrr may not be as perceptive as Madame Cassandra, but at least she hasn't been driven mad yet. I'm too old to go on, too old to keep the pace, to chase the draconian darklings that must be defeated. I was never much good at it anyway. You were born here, in the black, in the pall of the earth. You will lead your mother and brothers and sisters, and the rest of the clan to victory. I know that for a fact. Madame Cassandra has foretold it. She may be mad, but she still can catch glimpses of the future, and of the world we left behind.

Go now, do what I could not. And if in your quest you hear caterwauling in the distance, if you hear a lost grimalkin calling out in the endless night, it may be Johnnybull, but it may also be me. Tired and slow, but still there, still in pursuit, still hunting in the darkness for the Qabbalin, the Rats of Qybele, a lone and lonely cat in the pall.

Ghost Story

by Brian M. Sammons

Ghost sat on his throne and surveyed all that was his.

The fact that the throne was an old blue pillow on one end of a worn leather couch did not matter to the cat. Everything the light touched belonged to him, such was life, such as it should be.

Ghost blinked slowly and yawned. His human had been gone for a long time, now. Many days-to-nights and nights-to-days. Not that Ghost cared or missed the human...much. Another human, older, plumper, smelled nicer, and whose touch was softer, came around every so often whenever Ghost was left to rule alone. This one was a female and she would clean Ghost's dirty sand, give the foods, and stroke his gray fur, when he deigned to allow her to do so.

His human was often gone for long periods of time. He would come home, smelling of strange places and foods, and often smelling of blood. Sometimes the blood was his, and the human's normally sure and graceful (for a human) movements were stiff and pained. Sometimes the blood was not his; tthese scents were always faint and masked by the bitter thing the human would often wet and rub against his paws. But though the human was infrequently present, Ghost considered him a good human. He would come home, give the foods and the pets. Ghost was a predator, it was in his blood from a long line of peerless hunters, so the cat could sense another killer when he saw one, and so Ghost knew his human was a predator as well. But when the human was with Ghost, giving the pets, the foods, or the playtime, he sensed a change in the human. His body softened and he made all the human happy sounds, and that made Ghost happy.

The cat was a benevolent monarch, after all.

But despite all the happy, sometimes the human would make the fear noises in his sleep, for his trips to the dreamlands were often not pleasant. Ghost would sometimes look for the human in his own dream wanderings, as dreamers often passed through many worlds of slumber in a single night. Only cats were aware of this simple truth. Humans were ignorant of the fact, like they were about so many things. Ghost never found the human in any of his nighttime sojourns. The cat thought that the human must go to far darker places when he slept than the bright, green meadows where the feline played at night. Ghost often wondered why the human would want to visit such places, for surely he could control his dreams, couldn't he? Or was that another area where humans were so completely helpless?

Ghost yawned again and was giving some serious thought to standing up for a big stretch when he first heard the sound. It was a faint, whispery, sibilant hissing. If the human was here he could not have detected it, but Ghost did and was instantly on guard. The hisses were not random sounds and they slithered into words from an ancient tongue. The cat could not make sense of the whisper, but he recognized: it was spellspeak. Ghost did not meddle with the dirty magicks of the ancients. No cat worth his whiskers would. Cats had their own eldritch gifts bestowed by the Old Gods, but all felines, whether on their first life or their ninth, knew of magick. Knew enough to fear it.

Ghost crouched down, blending into his pillow, as his head slowly swiveled to pinpoint the sound. There! In the room with Ghost's big, high, soft bed that he allowed his human to share with him. The hisses concentrated, coalesced, and the cat knew they were taking shape. The bane of cats the world over, curiosity, was upon him, so Ghost sprang from his throne, hit the floor without a sound, and crouch-ran to the open archway of the sleeping room. Peeking his head in, Ghost zeroed in on the sound, and there he bore witness to the birth of an unnatural thing.

Motes of dust swirled about taking a long, sinuous form. Tendrils of shadow crept out of a darkened corner of the room, giving the creature flesh, bone, and muscle. Ghost sensed the invocation bringing something into being out of nothingness, and he took advantage of the creature still transforming from thought to form to spring onto the big sleeping bed to get a high view of what was happening.

The sibilant sounds caused the fur along Ghost's back to stand up. Recognition burned in the cat's mind as the shape solidified at last into a snake. Specifically a cobra with gleaming fangs and a white crescent moon on the back of the serpent's unfurled hood. It was a Scion of Yig, an Ancient One that ruled over all serpents. Yig was once worshiped by the reptile race that preceded humans on the Earth, and was still deified by insane and misguided humans today. A Scion of Yig was extremely dangerous and was sent by the snake god to kill when someone had angered the ancient power. The conjured cobra lived only as long as it took to strike its victim, and one bite was always deadly.

Ghost watched as the cobra slithered underneath the bed in complete silence. Then, there was nothing, no sound and no sight of the serpent. There it would wait, not sleeping, not eating, not moving, not even breathing, until its chosen victim arrived. Ghost knew the cobra had been sent for his human, just as he knew how things would unfold upon the human's return. He would come home smelling of strange scents and weary from his travels. He would call out to Ghost for the pets and the foods, but he would be heedless to any cry of warning from the feline. Humans were just too dumb to understand such things. He would then go into the strange rain box in the back room to have the waters fall all over him. Ghost didn't understand why the human didn't properly wash as he did, but he knew the human always used the rain box before lying down for sleep. And there, as the human walked towards the bed Ghost allowed him to sleep on, the cobra would strike. The fangs dripping venom would burrow into the human's meaty hind paws, and that would be that. Death would not be swift, for the snake god wanted those it smote to suffer, but death would be inescapable.

Right then Ghost made a decision: his human would not die to this snake. There was no doubt the cobra was conjured to life by Yig, but Ghost had the blood of Bast in his veins, and the royal bloodline now boiled with rage. How dare this invader come into Ghost's kingdom and threaten the life of his loyal and faithful human. Humans were no match against such things, so it was up to Ghost to handle this incursion, and so handle it he would.

The cat softly prowled to the other end of the bed and dropped to the floor. Slowly creeping under the bed, his unmatched night sight easily spotted the cobra in the gloom, wound in a tight coil, motionless, ready to strike. Ghost had strategized well, for the head of the serpent faced away from him, allowing the cat to carefully close the gap between them. When the cat was within pouncing distance, it got low, wiggled its ackside as its paws gripped the floor tight for a perfect jump. When all was to Ghost's liking, he tensed up then shot forth, all claws, fangs, and fury.

All four paws landed on the snake and Ghost instantly dug his claws into the cold scales of the serpent. Ghost bit down, his mouth on the back of the cobra's moon-crescented hood and this was vital. If Ghost could maintain this bite and control the head of the snake, then it couldn't turn back around and bite the cat. That was the feline's theory anyway, but the Scion of Yig was not going to make things easy for him. Almost immediately the snake uncoiled and began to thrash about. It made no noise in doing so, as a natural thing would; it was just a jumble of twisted bending and rapid rolling to get the cat off of it.

Ghost bit down harder as the cobra's gyrations caused everything to turn upside down and he was slammed against the floor, the wall, and the floor again. Ghost's forepaws were on either side of the serpent almost as if he was hugging it, while his hind legs rapidly raked through the scales and into the meat beneath. It was those back claws that would have to do all the work in killing the cobra, everything else Ghost had went into holding on tight.

Around and around the pair went, thudding and thumping against the floor. Ghost had expected the taste of blood in his mouth from where it had latched on to the cobra, but there was no rush of fluid, only the staleness of dust, as if he had bitten into some desiccated husk. Likewise, his claws didn't feel wet as they dug into or ripped apart the body of the snake. Only filth and foulness jammed between his toes and smeared the pads of his paws. Ghost could feel his back claws rake against something hard within the cobra: its bones. Cats can't smile, especially not when biting something for dear life, but if Ghost could, he would be. He knew the day was won, it would be only a matter of time until the thrashing serpent was still and dead. He would pull the cold, limp thing out from under the bed so that his human could see what a great hunter he was. Then he would get lots of pets and—

With a bone-rattling thump the serpent slammed Ghost against the wall with far more force then the cat had thought possible. This caused Ghost to open his jaws in surprise and pain, that caused his front claws to come sliding out of the reptile, and soon his back claws were raking only air. Ghost hit the floor with a thud but quickly recovered and sprang to his feet.

The Scion of Yig, now free of the cat, had slithered around and regarded the feline in silence. Ghost could see scales and flecks of meat fall from the serpent. They came not just from the wounds the cat had inflicted, but dislodged and fell from all over the snake. The conjured snake was coming undone, returning to the shadow and dust that had born it, but not quick enough. There was still plenty of fight left in the serpent and it still posed a deadly threat.

The cobra lashed out, fangs first, at Ghost. The cat leapt, avoiding the strike, and felt the serpent's passing on the short whiskers on his front legs, just above his paws. Ghost landed and barely had a fraction of a second to reorient himself before he had to dodge another strike. Coming down again, he saw the snake rear back for another lunge, and Ghost knew he couldn't keep dodging the lightening-fast strikes forever, so he beat the cobra to the punch and lunged forward himself. If he could grab the snake by the neck close to its head, he could control where its deadly jaws pointed and keep the serpent from lashing out until the Scion of Yig completely dissolved.

Ghost's fangs struck true. He guessed the snake of shadow and dust wasn't used to being the one on the receiving end of an attack. Not being a real creature of nature, that probably had never happened to it before. The shock of Ghost's fury startled it long enough for his mouth to get a firm grip on the serpent just below and left of the jawline. The cat sunk all his claws of all four paws into the cobra, then pulled his head, and the snake's, backwards as far as it would go. The cobra's long, lithe body thrashed about, leaving more shed parts of itself as it came undone, then wrapped around Ghost constrictor-like, but there was little strength left in the beast. In a few beats of the cat's pounding heart, even that was gone and the summoned assassin was still, limp, dead.

The cat let the cobra drop from his mouth as he withdrew his claws. He wiggled out of the serpent's coiled body that was rapidly returning to nothingness. Ghost felt wild, alive, exhilarated, in touch with the proud line of cats that came before him. This was him in his purest form. Even with all the comfy beds, the good pets, and foods he didn't have to hunt down before eating, this was the essence of who Ghost was. He thought of his human, how he was a predator too, but right at this moment, despite the vast size difference, Ghost knew he could have bested him in mortal combat. After all, he had killed a Scion of Yig and—

Ghost turned to regard his fallen foe, only the cobra wasn't fallen. It was coiled and it struck out one last time at the unprepared cat. Even as it fell apart to nothing, its fangs were still intact and it was still fast. So very fast.

Jordan slowly walked up the front porch steps to his house. It felt like every part of his body ached and he moved as a stiff-legged marionette with poor rigging. He turned his keys over in his palm until he found the one for the front door, wincing as he did so.

For fuck's sake, even my fingers hurt, he thought as he slid the key into the deadbolt and turned it. *How did my fingers get hurt?*

He tried to recount his injuries and the last few days he had spent in Louisiana as he opened the front door. He had spent three and a half weeks casing a cult of crazies that played at being old timey religious nuts. The kind that had tent revivals, spoke in tongues, and danced around with poisonous snakes to prove how in love with Jesus they were. But if all they were was fanatical Christians not hurting anyone but themselves, Jordan would not have been sent down there to assess the situation and take care of things if need be.

Jordan worked freelance for the CIA. More to the point, he killed for them. Even more, more to the point, he took care of the weird cases no one else wanted and no one else could do. He had a gift for dealing with such strange things. He believed the doctors called it borderline sociopathic tendencies. Whatever the reason, he was good at his job, but that didn't mean that he didn't catch a beatdown from time to time. Like what happened on the last night in the bayous with the snake dancers.

Wouldn't you know it, those kooks actually were religious nuts, but they worshiped something a couple dozen millennia older than Christ. At least that's what the old, dusty books claimed, the ones his handler back in Langley consulted after Jordan had phoned in his last report. Jordan didn't put a lot of faith in those old books. Mostly because he didn't want to believe in all that they had to say. He didn't have to believe to be an effective wetworks operator. In his line of work, believing in too many strange things could lead to trouble. But all that was rendered moot anyway the night he saw them stringing up some kids they had abducted in order to sacrifice them to their real god, some snake-headed thing they called Yig.

Once inside, Jordan kicked out of his shoes without untying them. Doing that would have hurt too much. He looked around his entryway to a half wall on the left side that marked the beginning of the living room. That's where Ghost always sat when he came home, being so cat-like and pretending not to care, but pawing at the man if he didn't stop and give the feline some neck scratches and just-above-the-tail pats as soon as he got through the front door. Except now, his fat gray cat wasn't there.

"Ghost? Here kitty, kitty, kitty. Where are you, buddy?" Jordan called out as the back of his mind played through the events of that last humid night in the swamp: the suppressed M4 bucking in his hands; the blood-crazed cultists reacting, some trying to flee, but the lion share coming right at him, charging a man with a fully automatic weapon, armed only with knives and clubs and the faith that snake daddy Yig would protect them. Well, he didn't. Sure, one big Cajun swamp-rat had gone at him with an old, rusted wrench, whacking him a few times all over including once in the hand to get Jordan to drop his rifle (ah-ha, that's where the sore fingers had come from, lucky they weren't broken). In the end, a Ka-Bar knife in the ear had dropped the Cajun, just as all the snake lovers that had rushed him were down. As for the few that had fled, well Jordan had first taken care of their rusted out Bondo buggies and even the old airboat they had out back. They weren't too hard to track down, sloshing and splashing through the swamp as fast as they could go through the waist-high water. No matter how hard they pushed it, they couldn't outrun a bullet.

When that was all done, Jordan had returned to the tent to cut the kids down. Saving them wasn't part of his op, he was only there for the cult, but come on, they were just scared little kids. So he saved three young lives and that made him feel pretty good. But the Yig worshipers had strung up four kids that night.

Three out of four wasn't that bad, right? Jordan told himself, and he so badly wanted to believe it. "Ghost, where are you? Come on." Jordan called out, a note of desperation in his voice. While he would never admit it, he needed the cat when he came home from the field. It grounded him. Petting Ghost helped him to forget at least a little bit, and feeding the cat made him feel a little less like a monster. *A real monster wouldn't take care of a cat, right?*

He called for Ghost again but there was still no answer. Jordan, who killed crazies and sometimes less human things for the government as a matter of course, felt the first pangs of fear starting to creep over him. He turned to walk past the half wall into the living room and stopped cold.

There Ghost sat on his favorite old blue pillow on the couch. Eyes closed, head down, not moving.

"Ghost? Buddy, you alright?"

The cat lifted his head, opened his eyes, and meowed regally at him, then gave a wide yawn.

"You lazy, fat cat, you had me worried," one predator said to the other. Then the human plopped down on the couch, picked up the cat, and placed it on his lap. Immediately the CIA assassin started scratching around the cat's neck, forgetting about his sore fingers and his other pains, both physical and mental, as the sound of deep, throaty purring, and the occasional laugh, filled the room. For a brief moment, each warrior found peace.

Palest of Humans

by Don Webb

I never did him any harm. The male human. Nor his wife. Nor the big and stupid dog. Nor the rabbit. I did have plots against the goldfish. I did not understand why he hurt me, but it is often in the nature of humans to hurt and regret and hurt again. It is in their nature to be two creatures living in the same pale skin. One a sensitive creature of love wounded only by harsh sensations, the other an imp of perversity that seeks only to ruin his life and the life of such humans that fall within the gravity of his orbit. Because these two creatures seldom do any deed save for the brief war that marks a human life span, humans live but once and are forgotten. They expend much energy in the building of things thinking that they thereby gain life after life. And when such buildings prove themselves temporary, ruined by fire or flood or simply time herself, they bemoan their status. When he found me I lived behind a public house. I lived upon the mice and vermin that delight in human filth. Often the men were in their cups, the loutish creature in such men is stilled and their gentle side will exalt itself. They will sing to me and offer me bits of sausage and meat pies. There is another sort of human, one that is gentle when sober, but vicious when drunk. I knew that he was such. I have lived many times and one learns the habits of mice and men.

He took me home, for in his gentleness he was lover of many creatures. The dog, the fish, his uncomplaining wife. She, however, looked at me in fear. For it was the nature of some of the white-skinned humans in those days to think that we cats born wholly black were witches in disguise. Humans in those days believed that some of their kind possessed a singularity of being that allowed them to change the order of the world. I have never met such humans in all my lives, but I have not met many of this too populous race. To jest with her, he called me Pluto. In this I knew his other self, the imp of the perverse, was drawing near. She ceased to fear me after her mother paid a visit. A fat old woman with a nut-brown face, she smelled of three cats, and during her brief stay doted on me. She watched the husband closely, she could see the imp in him, too.

He was paler than most of his kind. As a child, perhaps he had been deemed sensitive and meek. And he was a small man with smallish hands and a quiet, cheerful voice. He gave much hope to his wife, for in her past she had been badly used by men. She was young and by their standards pretty. The only men she had known were coarse men, men who only grew gentle in spirit when overcome by drink. This unfortunate past would lead her to an unfortunate future, for such is the way of the hairless apes that their past is their future. Such is true of us as well, but we are given more choices in this. He was fond of thinking himself a protector. He worked at something away from the home, I know not what, nor do I fully understand the ways of humans. I only know that they will feed us, and this means much in the uncertainty of the world. In those days women and cats were bound by the same law.

Each day he rose shortly after the sun. He would feed me and the rabbit and the dog, who gave the slavish display that marks their kind. Off he would go, petting my head and telling the dog that he was handsome. She rose soon after and gave more food to the dog and turned me out into the yard. I would spend my days in sleeping and dreaming and the joys of hunt. Dusk would come and he would return and often brought tasty scraps that he would give the dog and me. He would eat what his wife had made and they would speak. In that first year, they would snuggle and even mate, although these frenzied efforts led to no hairless kittens. She would look at him with love, but I had the eyes of Bastet and I saw the gleam of his imp. Its redness showed against the snowy whiteness of his skin and his wispy blonde beard. So, I knew It waited. His last deed every night was to blow out the candles and the whale oil lanterns that lit the home, then (if it were winter) bank the fires and retire to bed.

Then in the second year he began to visit the tavern where he had found me. I knew its smell and so I knew what was coming.

He would return with the greasy treats I remembered well. Some nights his steps were unsteady, and some nights he would find that his wife had gone to sleep. His words became less fair, and on occasion he kicked the dog, which merely made it more slavish. He took to petting me with a rough hand, so I began to avoid him at night. Some nights he would forget to extinguish the candles and they would burn to nubs. One night he came home to see that his wife had gone to sleep with a face wet with tears. This gave him pause. He was angry at the tears, and in the obscure way the human mind works saw me as the correct object of his anger. He called for me, but I knew it was the imp's voice. I sought to run beneath the bed but he caught me with his strong small hands and he carried me downstairs. He shook me and said many things. His mind was cloudy and I could not grasp his anger. He pulled forth a small blade. I fought to get away, but he held me strongly with his left hand bruising my ribs. I bit him and clawed, but as the drink had lowered his sensitivity to pain he held me. He took his small knife and pushed it into my right eye. He pulled some of my eye out and I screamed with all my might. He released me laughing. My screams awoke his wife. He called out to her. She saw my face as I tried to hide behind the cold stove.

In the days that came afterward, his wife came to dote upon me as her mother had. I know that she found the offending blade the next day, and as she was not stupid I know she knew her husband had blinded me. My skills as a hunter were lessened considerably. I would leap at a mouse and land nearby. I knew that I could not survive away from humans, but the wife began providing me great saucers of cream and petted and played with me constantly. My days were bright. For some weeks, my ruined face banished the imp and he became loving but sad. I knew this was a bad thing, for humans can stand anything but guilt.

The trips to the tavern returned and his arrivals at home grew later. Some nights he didn't return at all. The love play with his wife ceased, but on occasion he would mount her—although her smell clearly showed she was not in heat. I avoided him at night because the merest glance at my ruined face would make him angry. He now never blew out the lantern nor banked the fire. On most mornings, he would feed the dog and me. The dog became greatly sad, for such creatures need love. He would whimper and abase himself—and was often kicked for his trouble.

Early one morning, he had a sly air about him. By smell I knew that the drink of the night before was still upon him, but he moved like a hunter. I had never seen a human hunt before and my curiosity became my downfall. He called to me as he sat out a little bowl of cream. I am quite fond of cream, and I was surprised as he never gave me any. I darted to the bowl. He said my name with great sadness I could hear his good being leaving his body with my name. Straightaway he fell upon me, grabbing me with both hands. I struggled, scratching him mightily, but he quickly placed a looped cord over my neck. He threw me away from him, but the cord tightened around my neck. I could not breathe. I began choking. He carried me suspended by the ever-tightening knot and hung me up in a tree outside his home. My body hung close to the plaster of the outer wall. I began feeling my life leave my body as it had many times in the great cycle of my life. I let go and went into that Other Place, and my last thought was a desire to hurt him for what he had done to me.

It is of course from our last thoughts we remanifest. All cats know this, just as they know how to land upon their feet. I don't know how long I was in the Other Place, but I found myself staring at a smoke-stained wall. It was all that remained of the humans' house. The house which his sober self had so strongly sought to protect each night had burned down. By some freak of chemistry, my hanging body had cast a shadow on the wall. There was a solid white cat hanging from a noose. I assumed that he and she and the dog and the rabbit and the fish had perished in the blaze. I mourned her passing and even that of the stupid dog, but I had hoped the man had suffered. The grim memorial of his crime in some way had affected my new body. I was still a large black cat, but now I had a white spot on my chest. I had not simply returned as a kitten, so I knew some of the rules of the Other Place clung to me as they sometimes do.

I knew not what I was supposed to do. These things arrange themselves, but as I had died hating the pale human who had killed me—and as his home was gone—I didn't know what to do. I felt that I should hang around the spot of my return.

Nights passed and days and I hunted and scavenged, and then one night I heard his voice. The sweet voice, not the voice of the imp, but of the man who had played with me. I leapt upon a barrel. It was he. He walked over to me. I head-butted his hand and purred and used all the charms my race can use against his. His good self not understanding that I had returned—for the pale-skinned humans do not know of such things. I looked much as I had looked before. I was a big and elegant Tom, strong of muscle. He saw me as a second chance. He took me home as before. His new home was not as large as his old, but did have a basement. His wife had lost some of the liveliness that she had had. I assumed the fire had destroyed much and humans need their possessions. The dog and the rabbit were nowhere to be seen. Nor was the goldfish. She was immediately in love with me and pampered me even more richly than before. I grew fat under her care, which was my downfall.

He would put me out at night. The other Toms in the neighborhood had established territories. I began to carve out my own, but my sleek new muscles soon became greatly softened by the unending bowls of cream and the fatty tidbits she would procure for me (from wherever it is humans get food). A fat tom is a slow tom and I fared badly in fights and lost my right eye. Now I looked very much as I did before, and this frightened the man so he returned to his drink. I took again to hiding when I smelled it on him.

She began calling me "Pluto." She clearly knew I had returned to them. She would pat my belly and mutter something about him. Sometimes I can understand humans when their minds are clear and they speak to us. But most times their alien thoughts are babble. I know she was doing something called prayer, where humans speak to an Invisible and ask for things. I do not know to what Invisible she prayed, nor do I understand why humans think they are so special enough to gain attention. But every day she rubbed my white belly and slowly the spot on my belly changed shape. She would call it guillotine. And sometimes she would call me "my little guillotine."

She grew fearful of her mate. Perhaps she had begun to see him clearly as had her mother. Some mornings I would see that her skin would be marked with bruises. He would strike her in the night, but I was a bad hunter once again with one eye, and although I know not how she hunted I assume that she hunted badly. Neither of us dared to flee the man. She drew great comfort in looking at my spot. I do not know what a guillotine is, but I imagined it to be a hunting device. As I wanted to hurt the man and I felt that she wanted to hurt him, I began to lie on my back and show her the guillotine, and this was a bad habit.

One day when he had drunk late into the night, he did not go to whatever place he went to hunt. This happened from time to time. He would lie in bed the first part of the day and moan and complain of sounds or light. I had forgotten that he was at home that day. I was lying in her lap with my belly to heaven, when he walked into the room. He looked at my stomach and he grew even more pale. He yelled something that I could not understand, save that it had my old name "Pluto" in it. He fled the house and she looked upset. He did not return that night.

When he did come back I tried very hard to win his affection. Whenever he was sober I would rub against him and purr and use all of my feline wiles, but this seemed to fill him with greater fear and guilt. How could a human, even a small human, be afraid of me? He grew even more pale and his eyes developed a film. Sometimes behind the film, I could see the red glow of the imp. I knew this was a bad thing. The imps of the perverse lead humans to their doom, but they are ever glad to hurt as many living things as they can in their exit. He began studying me. I tried hard not to let him see my belly for I knew fear is bad for humans.

As for myself I was greatly fearful. Fat one-eyed hunters do not fare well in the world. I also had grown quite fond of the human woman as well. I knew that she should fare badly if he cast her into the world—and I did not understand the human world well enough to know what would happen if he were to die. I resolved to make my exit, yet each day she would pet me and feed me and my resolve would fail. Of course, we hang on to our lives less closely than humans hang on to their single existence.

He began to act very solicitously. He brought flowers for his wife and small cakes. He would sing little songs to her as he had in the early days when I had first lived there. His film left his eyes and he acted like a new man. I went from his house to the site of the old home. The fragment of wall that recorded my demise had been torn down and a new home was being built. Perhaps all was well. I returned home. I could feel no conflict in him. He even bought me fragments of meat pies. Thus, warning fears are easily bribed into sleep for both cats and women.

That night, he came home earlier than usual. It was at dusk, when the welcoming shadows of night begin to lengthen and provide great hiding places for hunting. He asked something of his wife; I could not catch the words. She assented and left the house. He offered me a bowl of cream—not in my usual place near the fireplace, but downstairs in the basement, near the niche which lay underneath the fireplace. As I lapped the glorious rich cream up, I heard the basement door close gently. I looked up. He was coming for me with an axe in the dim doom, its sharpened edge throwing back the dusk-dimmed light of the small window near the roof of the cellar which showed the garden. I scrabbled away, tripping on an old ratty rug. He swung at me but hit the floor. I heard the basement door reopen as I gained traction. I ran around him while he was lifting the axe. She had returned carrying a long loaf of bread, fresh with smells. She dropped the bread, I sprinted toward the door. He turned to swing. She cried out. He jumped at the sound of her voice and changed the arc of the axe. She bent toward me, and his axe hit full in her head, slicing her open, ending her scream, and filling the basement with the smell of fresh blood. Her body, which was rapidly becoming her corpse, fell fully atop me. I froze, caught by her weight. He bellowed in fear or anger. It was the full cry of the imp. The gentle man I had known died at that moment. I made myself as small as I could and hoped her body would shield me. He was running about the cellar, swinging his blade, overturning the rude furniture and wood stored there. I knew he was looking for me—wanting to kill me again, to mingle my blood with she who had saved me. The sun continued to sink and the cellar went dark. He went to the door and closed it tight. I remained hidden shielded by her cooling corpse.

He began to drag her along the floor past a pile of lumber that had long lain in the basement. I scurried/swam/crawled beneath her corpse. There was a niche in the west wall, directly beneath the fireplace above. Perhaps it was the space of an old chimney. He forced her to stand in the dark in this place and the lack of light enabled me to hide under her skirts. He pushed a big piece of lumber across the gap. Then I smelled the sulfur of a match. I could press myself against the wood he had placed across the open side of the square niche. If he did not look inside of the box he was making, I would be safe. Rapidly he began nailing the wood in place. Soon he had made a wall across the niche. Then he went away. I could hear him close the cellar door. He had boxed me in with the corpse of his wife. I scratched at the wood to escape, but to no avail. He returned so I became silent. He was mixing something outside of my prison. He began to spread it on the other side of the wood. It smelled of the white paste he had made once to fill in mouse holes in the old home. In a few hours, he was done, and I knew that I would pass my life trapped with her corpse.

In the hours and days that followed I licked at her blood. I climbed atop her to feed at what had been her brains. I knew I could live for a space of time. I smelled the beginning of decay. I tried as much as possible to sleep. I heard vague sounds from above. He lumbered about. Other humans came. I could hear him crying and maybe a feast. Then two days of silence. I grew sick from my diet and lack of space.

I heard the cellar door open. Several humans came down into the basement. I could hear fear in his voice. His voice grew loud, the other humans, all males, grew quiet. I could hear his words and his intent made them clear. He was yelling about the walls of his home. How strong they were. How old they were. He began knocking on the walls of my prison. I could take it no longer. Even if he tore the wall open to beat me to death, it was preferable to laying atop this decaying corpse, my fur clotted with drying gore. I yelled. I yelled and screamed with all my might.

Suddenly the axe crashed through the wall. The room was filled with policemen. They were holding him. He screamed about Pluto and hell. I jumped off her body and scrambled into the cellar. They were dragging him away. He was yelling about the guillotine. The police were laughing, tapping the sides of their heads. I never saw him again.

In the next few days her mother arrived. She took me home. Her old cats had gone to the Other Place and she wanted new companionship. She named me Polyphemus, which had something to do with my missing eye and a cave. The spot on my chest soon became a blur; at first, she would show it to visiting humans, but eventually it lost its fascination.

She gave me cream every day.

Bats in the Belfry

by William Meikle

Christmas Day had been a quiet time for me, being a bachelor and with no living relatives, save a married sister in Yorkshire who celebrated the festivities with her in-laws in the north. So it was that I was more than ready for some company the following Friday, and was most happy to receive a note of invitation to Cheyne Walk from my good friend Carnacki.

It was one of those crisp winter evenings we do not get nearly enough of in the city, and I had a most pleasant walk down to Chelsea as fine, delicate snowflakes drifted down to give everything an icing-sugar dusting. I was, for the first time of the season, feeling quite festive by the time I arrived at Carnacki's door.

The other chaps were already gathered around the fire in the library, and greeted me warmly with best wishes. Carnacki then provided us with a feast of a smoked salmon on toast starter, a fine, succulent goose with all the trimmings, and a steamed pudding that was so rich I was quite stuffed by the time we retired to the parlor for drinks and a story.

Carnacki got his pipe lit to his satisfaction, waited until we were settled, and began.

"My tale this week is a festive one, as befits the occasion," he said. "I had planned to pass the period in quiet contemplation in my library, and I was not intending any kind of celebration at all beyond perhaps raising a glass or two of single malt to the continuing good health of our fellowship.

"It was two nights before Christmas, or rather, it was early evening, and the last thing I expected was a knock on the front door. At first I was not even sure I had heard it at all, for it was little more than a light tap, and a tentative one at that, as if my visitor was not quite sure of wanting the door to be answered at all.

"I waited for several seconds, listening, then heard the knock again, no more firm than the last, but enough to get me moving. I opened the door to find a distressed young lady on the doorstep. I could tell from her clothing and the cut of her jib that she was from a rather well-to-do background, and probably unused to calling on strange gentlemen after sundown, so I was curious as to what had brought her to my door. Unfortunately, I was not to learn anything immediately, for she burst into tears as soon as she saw me.

"You all know me well enough to realize that a chap can get quite flustered in the face of such things, and I did my best to console her without being overbearing. I brought her into the library beside the fire, and made a pot of tea; I might have attempted to calm her with a spot of sherry, but I did not wish to appear too bally forward. Thankfully, by the time I returned from the scullery with the tea and some shortbread, she appeared to be much recovered, and very apologetic as to the manner of our introduction. I got her tale out of her slowly over the next few minutes.

"'It's my husband, John,' she began. 'Sorry, Reverend Wilkinson, I mean, of St. Botolphs on the Green in Beckenham. He's not been right for some time, and I fear, what with the Christmas sermon coming on and everything else, things are only going to get worse.'

"'What kind of things are we talking about?' I asked.

"'Your kind of things, Mr. Carnacki. I heard from a family friend how you dealt with the matter of the old oak in Chislehurst, and I thought right away, there is the man for the job if anybody is.'

"'And what precisely is the problem?'

"'Bats, Mr. Carnacki. Black bats in the belfry, hundreds of them.'

"'I'm afraid that sounds more like a job for a local tradesman, or a specialist vermin exterminator, perhaps?'

"'No, you don't understand, sir. They're not real bats. I'm not even sure they're there at all. It's only John that sees them, you see? But he sees them all the time, and I fear they are driving him quite mad.'

"Of course, it's not the done thing to agree with a lady when she suggests that her husband has gone off the deep end. But I knew that a country vicar's job is often one with its own peculiar stresses and strains, and one that has sent many a fine chap to the bottle, or worse. And the lady was still in a most distraught state, so I did the gentlemanly thing, and agreed to look into the matter.

"She then, on the spot, just as she was taking her leave, invited me to the vicarage for Christmas, and it would have been dashed churlish of me to refuse.

"So it was that, instead of sitting in my library with the Sigsand manuscript, I found myself on the morning before Christmas taking a midday train down to North Kent. I lugged my box of defenses with me, as I've found it is better to have them and not need them than the other way around. The lady, having spent the night in town at her sister's place in Kensington, joined me on the train and kept up a constant stream of chatter; now that she had my attention, she had no intention of letting me escape. I did garner several useful points of information, the most pertinent, it seemed, being that the church in question was by some way the oldest in the area, and had been built atop a much earlier structure, the details of which had long been lost to history."

"The vicarage, Gateside Cottage, proved to be a most delightful thatched dwelling situated just across an unmade road from the old church itself. To my jaundiced eye there seemed to be a sense of foreboding hanging over the old steeple, but that might just have been the lady's story playing havoc with my nerves, for once inside the house I could not have asked for warmer or more agreeable accommodation.

"John Wilkinson was not the nervous wreck of a man his wife had led me to believe, although he did not rise from his armchair to greet me on my arrival. Instead he berated his wife, albeit gently, for involving a stranger in their business. As for myself, I did not approach him to shake his hand, for his lap was occupied by a large, old ginger tomcat that gave me a baleful look every time I moved, as if to warn me off from encroaching on its territory.

"But once the Reverend got used to the idea of my presence, he proved to be an erudite and passionate conversationalist, especially on the subject of the church, and the belfry in particular.

"'The bell tower is Pre-Reformation, bu t the old walls are far older than that and date back to the earliest Norman period at least. Much of the stonework was obviously borrowed, or stolen, from an even earlier structure, for there are carvings and glyphs there depicting a range of figures that I believe to be pre-Roman, etched there by some of the original inhabitants of these lands in those distant days. Some nights I can almost feel them with me when I am ringing the rounds.'

"I almost hesitated in broaching the next subject.

"'And the bats? Your good wife seems most concerned on that score.'

"His voice went hushed, and the tomcat perked up its ears, as if expecting to hear something useful.

"'It's not bats, Mr. Carnacki. I'm not entirely sure what it is, but it most certainly isn't bats.'

"He wouldn't be drawn any further on the subject at that juncture, for his good lady arrived just then with tea and toast, and talk turned to more mundane matters and the small everyday goings on in a rural parish. It was only as the big clock in the corner turned toward midday that I was able to make headway on what, after all, was supposed to be an investigation and not just a pleasant sojourn south of the river.

"The vicar made to rise from his seat. The tabby thought twice about allowing this slight to its comfortable position, but gave way, although I got the baleful stare again as it strode at Wilkinson's heel.

"'I am off to ring the lunchtime round, Mr. Carnacki,' the vicar said. 'You are welcome to join me, but I am not sure you should expect anything. I'm the only one who sees them, you see.'

"I joined him in the short stroll across the road to the bell tower. The cat came with us, although it walked on the far side of the vicar from me, as if in disdain of my company."

"As it had on my first viewing, a feeling of trepidation swept over me on approach to the old tower, the old familiar tingle that told me I was in the presence of some part of the Outer Darkness. The vicar's wife had been right to call on me, whether the man agreed with her or not; there was something at work here that was not bound by the practices of his calling.

"The tower itself felt cold when the vicar showed me inside, but he showed no sign that he noticed anything untoward, and went straight to where two long cords hung from somewhere high above. The next few minutes were both a lesson to me in the art of church bell ringing, and an indication as to just how much trouble the vicar might, unwittingly, be in.

"It began simply enough, with the vicar dancing to and fro between the pulls as the chimes called out all around us. It was only during a brief pause that I spotted the large ginger cat stood up on its back legs, pawing at the air, as if trying to catch something speeding across its field of vision. If we were out in the garden

I might have suspected butterflies or sparrows, but here in the bell tower the only other thing that was moving, as far as I could see, was the vicar himself.

"And then I heard it, far off, like a train chugging in the distance, a rhythmic beat of a great drum being pounded, accompanied by a high-pitched, tuneless flautist.

"The cat stopped pawing, the vicar stopped ringing and ever so slowly the sound of drum and flute faded away entirely. But it was with a heavy heart and distinct lack of Christmas cheer that I returned to the vicarage.

"You see, I now had a dashed good idea what I was up against."

Carnacki paused to knock out his pipe on the fireplace and get a fresh one lit.

"It is no coincidence that the lovely vicarage is named Gateside Cottage.

"I have spoken before to you of the places where the veil between ourselves and the Outer Darkness is so thin that passage may be had. People have long searched for a way through to the other side—whatever their idea of that other side might be. It is only logical that over the course of those long millennia, from primitive tribesmen, through great civilizations and all the way up to my own most recent forays against the dark, that some have succeeded, in some small part. The gate is there for any that want to look hard enough. And where there is a gate, there is, of necessity, a gatekeeper.

"I have seen it before. And there in that belfry, I found it again. The vicar has opened an old passage, just a fraction. Part of our place here, our Microcosm if you like, has no doubt gone over there to the Great Beyond—just as part of something from that side has seeped over here. The poor vicar was feeling the effects, or at least seeing part of the dark trying to make its way here.

"The gatekeeper has many names, in many cultures. The ancient Persians called it Darban. Primitive cultists knew it as Yog-Sototh, and you may have heard me call it The Opener of the Way.

"Whatever the name, I knew only that there was a gate in the belfry. And I had to persuade the gatekeeper to close it, before the dark came through to engulf us all."

Carnacki got his pipe lit to his satisfaction, and resumed his tale.

"Over afternoon tea I attempted to explain what I have just told you to a skeptical vicar. He was bally nice about it, being an agreeable chap, but he refused to have anything to do with what he considered to be pagan nonsense. The old ginger tom sat in his lap the whole time, nodding its head as if in agreement.

"I did, however, manage to get Wilkinson to allow me to set up an experiment—I thought it best to describe it as such—in the bell tower. After tea I dragged my box of defenses back across the road and began to set up my protections underneath the bells.

"I hoped—it was my only hope—to pit my color theory against the opening gateway, to send a message to the gatekeeper that the gate must be shut. I only hoped that someone—or rather something—might be listening.

"I set up a pentacle of the colored valves, the circles encompassing most of the area of the bell tower floor, and hooked them up to my large battery. I was almost ready to begin, but at that very moment the big tomcat decided to take note of me, and became very curious as to what I was up to. It came over and had a good sniff around the battery, was not at all impressed when it licked the connecting clips, and showed special interest in the pulsating valves as the pentacle warmed up and came to life.

"I did my best to shoo the creature away, but it seemed intent on staying in the tower with me. I could not allow that, for it might break the circles at the worst possible moment and doom me to a terrible fate, so I bodily transported him outside—much to his chagrin—and closed the large oak door against him. I could not lock it from my side, but it seemed sturdy enough, and although the cat mewled piteously on the other side, its entreaties did nothing to dissuade me from my course.

"It was time to begin."

"I had set the valves to a rotating color scheme of red, blue, yellow then green, and had my small control box at hand should this permutation prove ineffectual. The valves hummed and threw washes of swirling color and shadow on the old walls—but there was no feeling of a presence, no distant drumming, and I felt quite alone, and, if truth be told, slightly silly, standing there in the cold.

"A chill wind blowing through the tower quickly changed my circumstances.

"The heavy oak door blew open with a slam, and the ginger tom strode in, slowly, as if making a grand entrance. He walked up to the edges of the outer circle, sniffed the air then, with an elegance belying his bulk, nimbly leapt over both that and the inner circle to join me in the interior.

"He looked up at the bells high above, then looked at me, then back and forth several times. I had the strangest feeling I was missing something, and whatever it was, it had the cat somewhat exasperated with me. He sniffed, contemptuously I thought, then leapt up to swing on the nearest of the bell cords. His weight was just enough to tug the cord downward. The bell above chimed loud in the quiet evening.

"The response came equally as loud.

"The valves of my pentacle flared and whined.

"A drum pounded in the distance and a tuneless flautist joined in off the beat."

"The air above between the pentacle and the bells thickened, as if beset by a sudden fog. My green valve pulsed, faster than the others, and I took that as a sign. I turned the dial, brightening the green above the rest, and washing the whole bell tower with its warm, almost verdant, color. The cat sat up on his hind legs, expectant, as fluttering shadows came down from on high.

"The vicar had been right; these were no bats. They most closely resembled silk handkerchiefs, dark as the darkest night and caught in a whirling wind, but they dived and swooped as one, united like a murmuration of starlings, keeping time with the great drumbeat even as my green valve synchronized its pulsing with the pounding.

"The turmoil set the bells to swinging, the tolls almost deafening inside the tower. The swirling, flittering shapes dropped lower, and the cat pounced, snatching the lowest one out of the air and swallowing it down. I swear the bally ginger tom had a smile on his lips when he looked up at me. But I did not have time to marvel at his perspicacity. Something else was happening, high in the bell tower.

"The fog immediately thickened and became almost palpable. A black tear opened in the air above my head, accompanied by what sounded like the ripping of paper. A single black egg, no bigger than my thumb, hung there.

"The egg quivered, a rainbow aura danced over it, and ever so slowly it became two, oily sheen running over their sleek black surface. They hummed to themselves, a high singing that was taken up and amplified by an answering whine from my crystal valves.

"As two eggs became four, the whole bell tower rocked from side to side in rhythm.

"The dance had begun.

"The eggs hung in a tight group just under the bells, pulsing in time with the distant drumbeat. Colors danced and flowed across the sheer black surface; blues and greens and shimmering silvers that were all too familiar; we were now in the presence of the Sototh, the gatekeeper.

"The eggs calved again, and again, and again.

"Thirty two now, and they had started to fill the tower with a dancing aurora of shimmering lights that pulsed and capered in time with the drumbeat and the whine of the green valve whose color was quite swamped by the light show above us.

"The black murmuration swooped ever faster, ever lower until it was so close I felt the air moving in my hair as they passed overhead. The tomcat proved himself to be remarkably agile by leaping high once more and landing, perfectly stable on his feet inside the circle, with two more of the shadows between his teeth. He smacked his gums as he fed.

"The shifting egg formation beneath the bells pulsed, their numbers uncountable, and more of the swirling blackness came down as a mad flautist went into a frenzy of trilling notes. Something from the Outer Darkness was making its way through, and the black shadowy handkerchiefs coalesced, clumping together into something with intent on becoming solid. I had mere seconds left now to try to persuade the gatekeeper that the way should be closed.

"But my green valve was not up to the task. It whined loudly, popped with a crackle of breaking glass and went dar.

"The bat-like shadows sensed their moment had come and one made a leap downward, intent on reaching the floor where I stood, but fortunately for me the remaining valves still provided a defense, albeit a weakened one. A black, almost oily sheet hit an invisible barrier above my head and slid off to one side, a glistening, fluid pool coalescing on the flagstones beyond the circle.

"Meanwhile overhead the mass of pulsating eggs danced ever faster, thousands of them now, filling the tower with a pounding beat, the crazed flautist providing a high, tuneless accompaniment that grated and put my teeth on edge.

"I had to get the gate closed, but the black pool on the floor was already starting to take shape, thickening in the middle and taking on definite form. A thin ridge split and opened. A white, lidless, eye the size of a dinner plate blinked and stared straight at me.

"I almost took a blue funk at that, and might well have done so had I been standing alone in the circle.

"The bally cat saved me."

🐾 🐾 🐾 🐾 🐾 🐾

"He gave a pointed look at the controls in my hand then walked over to step, forward and back, between the blue and yellow valves. One more pointed look, then, as gracefully as before, he bounded out of the circles without touching the lines, heading straight for the black pool of goop that now writhed and seethed as something fought to be born from within.

"I had to lower my eyes to the controls; the cat's instruction had been clear enough, it was something I should have thought of myself, had I not been so bally taken by the funk. I turned up the power to the blue and yellow valves. A green wash flowed over the walls and, high above, the dance of the eggs slowed and the drumbeat faded, not by much, but it was a start. I turned the power up another notch and the green wash grew in strength.

"Out beyond the circle the cat tore into the black goop in a frenzied, yet completely silent, attack, ripping great gouges on the oily material and chewing it down with a relish that was all too clear. The beast looked bigger, almost tiger-like, although that may just have been a function of the swirling color and shadow that filled the tower. What is not in doubt was his sheer animal ferocity. Within seconds he had reduced the blackness to little more than oily scraps of torn flesh, and even they were chewed down until there was little left but rainbow sheen on the floor.

"At the same time, my green wash was now proving most efficacious against the dancing eggs of the Gatekeeper above, and it too quickly departed from the scene. The mass dwindled down: sixteen, eight, four, two then a single, oily egg that popped and was gone, leaving the bells in the tower to toll, just once, then fall silent.

"When I lowered my gaze and looked down, I was all alone in the quiet bell tower. The cat had taken his leave. I waited for several minutes to ensure nothing was going to return from beyond, then began the task of dismantling the pentacle.

"It seemed the job was done."

"It was only after I'd returned to the vicarage and was being plied with a hearty supper that I thought to ask after my savior.

"'I must say, that cat of yours is a dashed intelligent beast,' I said.

"The vicar and his wife looked at each other in puzzlement.

"'We don't have a cat, Mr. Carnacki,' the lady of the house said, and the vicar shook his head in agreement. I could scarcely call them liars over their own dinner table so I let it lie, but brought it up with the vicar himself later over a smoke and a glass of port.

"He went quiet when I told him about the ginger tom he'd had sat in his lap, and quieter still when I related the events that had taken place in the tower.

"'I think we had better take a walk, Carnacki,' he said. 'There is something you need to see.'

"I followed the vicar across the road again, and back into the bell tower. He had to use a lantern to show me what I'd been brought to see, but even the flickering candlelight was enough for me to make it out, although the carving on the old stone right at the floor level was old, and crudely wrought.

"A group of men cowered beneath a mass of bubbles in the sky. Between them and the darkness stood a large cat, up on its rear legs, pawing at something that was coming down from the open gate above it. I couldn't tell whether the cat was ginger or not, but I recognized only too well the baleful stare that looked out of the stone and looked straight at me."

Carnacki stopped, his tale done, but Arkwright was having none of it.

"Dash it, man, what was that all about? Was the damn cat a ghost or what?"

Carnacki took his time in replying.

"No, I do not think it was spectral in any way. But neither do I think it was entirely corporeal in this realm. Remember, chaps, that many gates swing both ways. And as a result of my sojourn to Beckenham, I am starting to wonder whether there might not, in such circumstances, be a gatekeeper for each side.

"Now, out you go," Carnacki said, and showed us into the night.

Satisfaction Brought Him Back

by Glynn Owen Barrass

As soon as Tiberius awoke, he sensed something wrong in the air. Beyond the windowpane he sat upon, in the park across the street, a group of curious humans had gathered to stare at something strange. He found it strange, too. Past the glass, past the space between Tiberius's home and the park's wrought iron fence, a group of pigeons performed a circling procession. There were fifteen birds in total, bobbing their heads as they plodded in a clockwise movement. At the center of their group lay a prostrate feline, a tabby by the looks of it. Had it died? And if so, how? Weakness and exposure, Tiberius guessed, for there were no visible wounds.

A closer look was required, but could he get outside?

Tiberius sat up, stood on his hind legs, and examined the top of the window. It was locked tight. The human he lived with was out, so this was probably the same for the other exits. He sat down, quickly licked an itch on his left paw, and closed his eyes for a few moments.

Get outside: daylight and too much visibility.

Run across the street: cars to avoid.

Enter the park: dog, possibly human threats.

He reopened his eyes. No...daytime was risky. He could wait till later, when darkness fell and Jasper was home...

His curiosity wouldn't allow for that.

No, it would take an excursion to another realm to get outside and investigate; there was no way around it. Tiberius leapt from the windowsill to the Oriental rug below, stretched and released his claws, then curled up in the meditation position.

He imagined six symbols in the black backdrop of his mind's eye, one for each realm the Dreamlands Elders had taught him. He moved two of the complicated, shimmering snowflake shapes together, rotated them, and a flash of light later, he was floating above his body.

The world looked strange now. Everything throbbed at the edges, colored in monotone shades of white and blue.

A weird feeling of displacement followed as he saw his prone, sleeping body. He hated leaving himself so vulnerable, but the house was empty, and secure enough. There wasn't even another feline living here to bother him, although if there had been, he could have asked it to watch over him.

No time now for procrastination, though, Tiberius realized, now he had gotten this far.

He willed himself towards the window, and felt a slight resistance as he passed through the glass.

The street before him was busier now, the Astral Realm bearing host to many more beings than the material realm held.

Human spirits walked the streets and park, earthbound beings in various stages of incorporeality. Some were little more than transparent wraiths; others were solid and nearly whole. He felt a chill as he passed a pair of them, and a transparent claw reached out and brushed his tail.

He shivered, and felt himself twitch and growl in his earthly body.

Soon enough, Tiberius was floating over the gate, examining the scene as he approached.

The eight humans watching the pigeons were more solid than the ghosts, but still resembled wavering phantoms. They weren't all human though, and this made Tiberius pause in his flight. One was black, indicating a black soul, possibly a vampire, or a human possessed by demons. Another had a shimmer to it, shiny dots sparkling across a diaphanous white form. An Angel? Perhaps one of the Faerie Folk.

Tiberius gave the group a wide berth as he continued towards the birds. The bird's forms were white, of course—no black souls in the animal kingdom. They chattered incessantly as they circled the tabby's grayish form.

"Guard the soul, guard the soul," they chattered, and Tiberius guessed the tabby had cast a ward, something to stop its soul from departing too soon.

He floated to the gray form, lowering himself before it.

The cat's soul was a glowing jewel, shrinking rapidly as it dissipated into nothing.

Tiberius leaned towards it, and heard a tiny voice.

Tried to reach you...

This body...

Old...

Starving...

Cold got to me...

He recognized this soul, the sound and the feel of it. It was an old cat general from Ulthar, in the Dreamlands Realm.

The words were diminishing to squeaks now, and Tiberius moved closer till his ear was beside the pin-sized jewel.

Dark shadows...something evil, coming for your human friend, Tiberius... Beware—

And then, the soul disappeared.

He died to warn me. Tiberius felt an overwhelming sadness. He blinked, shedding invisible tears.

The soul's disappearance released the pigeons, startling them into flight, their wings whistling loudly in alarm.

The sounds of human voices followed, gibbering in outburst. He turned from the corpse, and saw, amongst the humans and not so humans, a pair of glowing red eyes. They met his own, glaring from a black, man-shaped silhouette. There were no smells in the Astral Realm, but Tiberius sensed that if there were, that being would reek of rotten flesh.

Tiberius returned home with those eyes burning into him, his thoughts filled with worry concerning the departing soul's final words. Once across the street, he passed through the same window as earlier. Descending into himself, he opened his eyes.

What to do now? Tiberius had more questions than answers, and it appeared a trip to the Dreamlands was in order. What could be coming for his human companion? Jasper was an Occultist of sorts, more of a dabbler really, and wrote articles for a local magazine. Perhaps he had offended someone...a sorcerer maybe?

His thoughts continued on these lines for some minutes, but he couldn't pinpoint any recent occurrence that equated to the tabby's desperate warning. Just as he decided on a trip to the Dreamlands, he heard footsteps he recognized on the sidewalk beyond the house. A rattle of keys followed, then the front door opened. Tiberius turned to watch, knowing it was Jasper by his familiar sounds and the smell of his pipe tobacco.

A gust of air followed the man through the doorway. The air was littered with odors, and Tiberius sniffed exhaust fumes, freshly mown grass, and a smell of dog urine. And...was that an odor of rotted flesh? If so, it disappeared when Jasper closed the door.

"Good day, my fine feline friend!" Jasper said from behind the pipe clenched in his teeth, and looked down on Tiberius with a smile. He held a large, flat square object under his left arm, wrapped in brown paper. He patted this with his free hand before continuing, "Fruitful day, oh yes my."

Jasper bent his knees, reached out.

Tiberius made a show of striding forward, rubbing his head against the proffered hand. He took in the smells of his companion, searching for anything unusual. There were just the scents of tobacco, and mild soap on his hand. The object in the brown paper package smelled of wood, and dust. But there was something...something gave him reservations.

His companion gave him a final, encouraging scratch, and stood. Jasper removed the pipe from his mouth, pocketed it, and headed past Tiberius to the room he referred to as his study.

Curious, Tiberius padded behind him, waiting as Jasper took a key fob from his pocket and unlocked the door. This room was locked when Jasper was out, probably because during his wilder kitten days, Tiberius had damaged some things while exploring.

Jasper walked inside, his quiet footsteps replaced by louder ones as his shoes left carpet for varnished wood floor.

Despite that he was over his wilder, chaos-causing days, Tiberius was only allowed in under supervision. He followed Jasper, stepping on the floorboards and smelling varnish and dust, old bones and dried flesh.

The study had been heaven to a curious kitten—its walls lined with musty books, skulls, and dead things floating in jars. A large square table centered the room, with a chair tucked under it. Beyond that, beneath the study's only window, was a chair and writing bureau, the latter holding Jasper's typewriter— something that had fascinated, and terrified Tiberius during kittenhood.

"Come to have a peek, yes?" Jasper said, noticing he was being followed. He paused at the table, put the square object on it, and pulling back his chair, sat.

Tiberius paused, measured the distance from the chair to the table, and leapt, landing perfectly a moment later.

Jasper held a penknife now—and was using it to cut string from the parcel. While he took his time opening it, Tiberius inspected the table's other burdens. It held a pile of books, a cow's fetus in a murky jar, and a yellowed human skull.

With the paper unwrapped, Jasper revealed his new possession, holding it up like a prize.

At the sight of the painting, Tiberius felt his tail fuzz up.

"Ugly little fellow isn't he?" Jasper said. "It's called 'The Gabriel Hounds.' Painted in Wales in the 18th century, apparently. Can you believe it came all the way from there, then Innsmouth, then to here in Arkham? I got it in a public auction today."

Tiberius held back a growl.

Within a frame of darkly varnished wood, the image portrayed a pale creature resembling a dog, its white muscular body tinged in blue and pink. It had the head of a human infant, with large white globes for eyes. The background consisted of swirling crimson shades.

"As soon as I saw this in the catalog, I knew I wanted it." Jasper continued. "It was recovered from that federal raid on Innsmouth a few years back, but I'd heard of it before." Placing the painting on the table, Jasper lifted a book from the pile to his right, a yellowed tome with a red velvet cover. He placed it before him and flicked through the pages. Finding the one he desired, he moved his finger down the aged, yellow paper.

"Ah, here we go," he said, and began reading from the page. "'Gabriel Hounds. British—A Northern English version of the supernatural Hellhounds, that fly across the heavens looking for the souls of unbaptised children. Some legends link them to the Hounds of Tindalos of blasphemous lore. The sound of their diabolical yelping can indicate a pending death. They are said to travel in pairs, and described as having the body of a dog with the head of an infant.'"

They travel in pairs, Tiberius thought, and wondered why the painting only depicted one. This time, he didn't hold back his growl.

"What is it, puss?" Jasper raised his hand, patting him on the back. Tiberius didn't reciprocate; rather, he just stared at the ugly painting. Jasper returned his attention to it, staring in admiration rather than with Tiberius's troubled fear.

"I must write this up in my journal." Jasper lowered the painting to the table, and with a scrape of his seat, stood and stepped towards the bureau.

Tiberius followed the man's every movement, watched as he opened a drawer in the bureau and removed a large red leather book. The presence of the painting pulled at him though, teasing him to stare at it. It must have had a similar effect on Jasper, for he grunted and turned back to the table.

"Think I'll stand this on the sill," he said absently, and leaning over, lifted the painting and took it to the bureau. Once there, he placed it on the windowsill.

Tiberius didn't like what he was seeing, not at all. The painting had a draw to it, some spell, or curse. The Dreamlands might have the answers, and with this in mind, he gave the painting a last, suspicious look, and jumped down, heading out of the study.

After leaving the study, Tiberius padded up the stairs to the first floor. He entered Jasper's bedroom and jumped onto the large, sheet-covered mattress. This was a comfortable, safe place, the white, flower-patterned sheet holding the odors of both him and his human companion. He paced about a little, kneaded the sheet, and curled up upon it.

Tiberius invoked the symbols, then drew three of them together. A feeling of weightlessness followed, but he remained in his body. Being a Dreamer of veteran years, he could pick the place he wanted to arrive at, if he concentrated hard enough.

This Tiberius did, picturing the suburbs of Ulthar in his mind's eye.

And then he was there, standing upon Ulthar's cobbles and looking around in some wonder.

He was surrounded by cottages, their red peaked roofs overhanging narrow, cobbled streets. The sky above held a large, lazy sun, filling the rooftops and streets with a strong but diffuse light. The many cats here always gave him pause, and there were hundreds, thousands even, sunning themselves on rooftops and laid out upon the narrow streets.

This was so different to the Waking World—that place full of dangers from vehicles, people, and other predatory animals. Here, a cat could live without fearing anything.

Tiberius knew where he needed to go. Up ahead, beyond the small, quaint cottages, was the Temple of the Cats. Here he hoped to find the information he required.

He strode forward, heading along a cobbled street with an upward slope. Some cats raised their sleepy heads, nodding at him as he passed. As he neared the top of the slope, a pack of inquisitive kittens attached themselves to him, asking questions as they frolicked and jumped.

Not having time to answer, or stop and play, he ignored them. The temple stood directly before him now anyway, centered upon a wide grassy field.

The Temple of Cats was a grand affair, a red stone step pyramid of three levels, the top of which bore a golden, cone-shaped dome. Large golden urns, filled with multicolored flowers, stood on each corner of the steps. The grassy field surrounding the temple was, of course, covered in sleeping cats.

A central staircase was built into the front the temple, with a golden arch standing at each large step. Tiberius left the cobbles and headed across the grass towards it. The pursuing kittens lost interest in him when they noticed a pair of butterflies flapping about the field, so when he reached the staircase, he was alone.

Tiberius rushed up the stairs, passing under three golden arches and quickly nearing the final one fronting the dome. At the top of the stairs, just beyond the final arch, he received a pleasant surprise. It was the tabby from the Waking World, standing tall and venerable now, wearing a brass studded collar of rank around his thick neck.

Tiberius felt so heartened at seeing him again—once dead and feeble, now whole and strong, a permanent Dreamlands resident since his death.

"Greetings," the tabby said, and lowered his head.

"Thank you for your sacrifice," Tiberius replied, stepped forward, and nudged the tabby's head with his own. This mark of respect finished, the tabby turned and headed between the temple's gold-edged doorway.

He followed him across the temple's stone flags, his escort bouncing up a flight of steps before entering a doorway covered by a hanging, yellow muslin sheet. Tiberius ducked his head beneath it, and found himself in a large, circular room littered with jewel-studded cushions. The ceiling loomed high above him, for this was the inside of the dome.

There were scores of cats here, lounging on the cushions, mostly older than Tiberius but some younger ones, too. Many purred, and few paid Tiberius any attention. To the left and right of the doorway, two temple priests, white of beard and dressed in yellow satin robes and pointed black hats, crouched in obeisance. Each held a large but delicate white paper fan, which they waved gently towards the cats. A circular window, covered in a silver grill of delicate design, faced the door and poured light into the center of the room. The light shone upon a pile of cushions atop which sprawled a gray kitten, shorthaired and with the largest ears Tiberius had ever seen. It looked to be asleep at the moment, basking in the sunbeams.

"This is the Mystic One," the tabby said, and lowering his head performed a bow. The gray kitten remained unmoving, and the tabby said, "Ahem."

A sleepy blue eye opened on the kitten's elfin face, then another. It yawned, stretching its paws. A moment later the kitten leapt down, landing in front of Tiberius. The pair shared a head bump greeting.

"You assisted my grandmother and her army against the unclean Cats of Saturn," he said. "The Cats of Ulthar owe you a debt, as such."

Tiberius nodded. "I ask only to serve, and to discover the meaning of the portent brought to me in the Waking World."

"Ah yes," the kitten replied, absently licked his forepaw, and continued. "Our human sorcerers, using a scrying window, detected rumblings from the

Realm Not to Be Named. They mapped the echoes of things to come, and they led to you. Your human companion, in the Waking World, is he a sorcerer?"

Tiberius groaned inside. "Hardly, more of a dabbler really."

The kitten blinked. "Then he has surely gotten himself into some deep trouble."

"It isn't the first time. May not even be the last," Tiberius replied.

The kitten nodded. "Protect yourself, the approaching threat appears insidious, to say the least."

Tiberius felt perturbed—he needed more than this. "Can I have help?" he asked. "I know our friend here sacrificed himself already."

The kitten turned to the tabby. "General, can you assemble some cats?"

"I can get a group together, yes, but it may take a little time," he replied, then turning to Tiberius, "How soon do you need us?"

"As soon as you can," Tiberius said, and realizing he had probably been away from home too long already, decided to end the meeting.

"Thank you for your help," he said, addressing both the gray kitten and the tabby. "I should get back to the Waking World and make my own preparations."

The kitten nodded, turned from him, and leapt back onto its cushions, curling up a moment later as if none of this had occurred.

Tiberius turned, headed from the room with the tabby at his side.

"Thank you, General, any aid would be greatly appreciated."

"I will post cats in the Waking World and the Astral," he replied, and soon after, they were leaving the dome.

"I'll get started, good luck, and be seeing you," said the general, and a moment later he took flight, heading across Ulthar's sea of rooftops and issuing a call to arms to whatever cats were willing to join the fight.

Tiberius paused, taking a moment to examine the beautiful vista before him: the sun-drenched rooftops, the green fields, and farms beyond which flowed the serpentine River Skai. This would be a good place to retire to, when his time was ready. Good enough.

When Tiberius opened his eyes in the Waking World, he felt his hackles rise. There was a chill in the air, an unnatural one, and jumping from the bed, he ran down the stairs, rushing towards the study. A grim apprehension filled his gut when he entered the room. The study was littered with shadows now, but his pupils dilated, making vision clearer. Although he had expected something of the sort, it came as a nasty surprise to see Jasper still at the bureau, sitting mesmerized by the painting.

He sat down, closed his eyes, and configured himself into the Astral Realm. When he materialized above his body, Tiberius suffered a second shock. His companion's astral form, seated before the painting, should have been bright, glowing with life. Instead it was dull, throbbing weakly, with, to Tiberius's horror, a black umbilical connecting it to the painting. The painting itself was a black void, possibly a portal, leading to places he dare not consider.

Tiberius shook his head, floated forward, and paused near the calf fetus. He had spoken to the calf's tiny soul in the past, and addressed the glowing spot in the jar now.

"Little soul, I need your help, please awake and help me."

There was silence for a while, and then the spot flickered, followed by a squeak.

"I would have your assistance," Tiberius said with more urgency, "defending this place from an approaching horror. In return, I will do my best to free your soul."

More squeaks followed, more flickering, and then a shape formed above the jar, a small, pale, diaphanous double of the fetus.

Its eyes opened, and glowed with white fire.

"Thank you," Tiberius said. "Now wait here and alert me if anything happens." Then he turned and floated back through the study door.

Things were growing critical. He couldn't assume the approaching doom would appear from the painting. Tiberius couldn't assume anything now.

He floated swiftly through the house and exited through the window. Here he paused and examined the scene.

The Astral Realm was empty, eerily so. The glowing forms of humans were visible, two walking across the street and more in the park, but as for astral forms? Tiberius had never seen it like this, so devoid of souls.

They know something's coming, he thought, *but where is my backup?*

He didn't want to wander too far from the house. *Perhaps I should go as high as the roof, circle round?* After considering this a few moments, and deciding it was a good idea, Tiberius was about to ascend when the astral sky turned dark.

Thunder rumbled above him, and then the street between him and the park was no longer so empty.

A black figure stood upon the opposite sidewalk, staring from eyes of glowing coals. Tiberius, recognizing the dark entity from earlier, shivered in both his astral and earthly forms.

The black soul strode forward. Tiberius braced himself, worried over what he could do against something so seemingly powerful.

The figure paused in the middle of the street, and a glowing slit opened beneath its fiery eyes. The wide 'O' that mouth formed grew larger, impossibly so, for the head bearing it. Then something burst from the mouth, a hideous birth of a blasphemous thing.

This new horror had a head of a human infant's, with white, saucer-shaped eyes. The body of a dog hovered behind its ugly visage.

The Gabriel Hound's mouth opened, and a piercing scream issued from its cruel lips.

Tiberius shuddered and felt his form begin to dissipate. This monster was banishing him from the Astral Realm!

With a hiss of anger, he shot towards the Gabriel Hound. At the same instant, a tear opened in the air above the black soul. This portal spilled out a horde of howling astral cats, led by his old friend, the tabby.

His allies' yowls quickly canceled the Gabriel Hound's spell. Feeling whole again, Tiberius breached the final distance and gripped onto its face. He growled and shrieked as his claws attacked the unclean thing. He bit down on its forehead, tasting foul, greasy flesh.

Below him, the cats had the black soul pinned to the floor, were tearing at it en-masse.

The Gabriel Hound tried shaking him off, failed, then shrieked again, so close and so loud that Tiberius felt himself dissipating almost to nothing. His attacker darted through his wavering form, and Tiberius had to concentrate all his willpower to remain in the Astral Realm.

The Dreamlands cats continued ripping up the black soul, strips of its silent, struggling form coming off like oily black smoke.

Tiberius turned and sped towards the house, a thunderbolt of rage that his enemy had bested him. Through the window, then towards the study he charged, hearing screams and bellows as he passed through the door.

The source of the sounds made him pause.

A massive being centered the room, the pale fetus small no longer, but rather a huge, bellowing bull, standing on its hind legs as it bashed hooves at the Gabriel Hound's shrieking form.

Tiberius watched with admiration, then saw beyond the battle, to his companion.

Oh damn, no! Jasper's head was lowered to the table, his body so transparent now that he could see right though it. The picture however, shimmered with brightness, the umbilical still attached to Jasper's prone form. The man's soul, a white blob of fire, glowed at the center of his chest, defenseless—an easy morsel for the Gabriel Hound.

Tiberius had to think fast. They were being attacked on two fronts. Could he stop the painting's attack? Possibly, and an idea came to him that he executed a second later.

He opened his eyes in the Waking World, stood, and flexed his limbs. The room was oddly quiet, after the cacophony of sounds in the Astral Realm, but was still filled with danger. With a single bound, he landed on the table, rushed past the fetus jar, and leapt towards the bureau. He landed on Jasper's back with a 'thump,' but his companion didn't stir.

A growl formed in his throat as he locked eyes with the painting's hideous, grinning visage. The growl grew into a roar, and Tiberius leapt, his claws slashing into the painting. He ripped through the paint, finding the canvas beneath and tearing into that, too. The painting fell forward during his furious, desperate attack. Now that it was face down, he continued wreaking clawed havoc into the painting's rear.

Tiberius was panting by the time he was done. The painting lay in ruins at his paws, slivers of shredded canvas stuck between his toes. Had it worked though?

A groan from Jasper was an encouraging sign, but just to be sure, Tiberius closed his eyes, quickly configured the symbols to enter the Astral Realm.

Jasper's body was already starting to fill out, to grow more substantial. Beyond him, the Gabriel Hound was gone, as was the fetus's astral form. Had the latter prevailed over their enemy? There was no glow in its jar. Perhaps it had transitioned to a happier afterlife. He hoped so.

A movement below returned his gaze to Jasper. He was stirring, and when Tiberius hurried back into his body, he looked down to see Jasper shift and moan where he lay.

He was getting better! Love and relief filled Tiberius's chest, for despite his annoyances, and follies, Jasper was a good man.

Tiberius looked at his paws, at the destroyed painting beneath him. Jasper would be annoyed to find his new prize so brutally destroyed. But wait...there was a letter opener on the bureau, and if Tiberius placed some of the shredded canvas near it, then went upstairs and feigned a deep sleep?

This would save him a scolding, but Jasper would be thoroughly confused when he awoke. Still, better confused than dead.

Tiberius shook and gnawed the shreds of canvas from his paws, then proceeded to plant the evidence.

The Bastet Society

by Sam Stone

"You never know if you like something unless you try it," Skye said.

She held out a fork of mushy-looking haggis but Kurtis shook his head.

"It's not for me, thanks."

"Vegetarian then?" she asked, viewing his plateful of pasta and vegetables.

"Nope. But I don't eat the innards of things. And that," he pointed at Skye's plate, which was full of neaps and tatties, as well as the offensive haggis, "is innards."

The bell rang, Kurtis grabbed his plate and, without even saying goodbye, moved on. He almost stumbled in his haste to get away.

They were "Speed Dating with Food"—it was a new fad. You were judged by the food you ate as well as the conversation. Skye had known that she was not Kurtis's type, and it wasn't the food she was eating that turned him away.

She just had no luck whatsoever with men. Despite the fact that she was attractive, something about her always put them off. She didn't know why. Maybe it was her over-pale skin. Perhaps they realized that the caramel highlights in her white hair was not a quirk, but was the only color that would retain in her albino hair. They saw the taint she carried in her blood line, no matter how she tried to hide it. She was fortunate that her eyes were blue and not pink, or that would have made her lack of pigment more obvious.

Skye put her fork back on the plate as the next man sat down at her table. As she looked up, all thoughts of the black, sleek Kurtis, went completely from her mind.

"I'm Tadeo," the man said. His voice was smooth with the hint of an accent that Skye couldn't place. "I was born in Egypt."

Skye found herself smiling back at Tadeo's perfect white-toothed grin. He was certainly striking—with warm golden skin, which looked as though it had been freshly touched by the sun.

"I think you and I are going to get along," Tadeo said, and he dipped his fork into Skye's haggis, scooping up a mouthful, which he ate with obvious enjoyment.

She responded by trying his food. It was black pudding, one of her favorite breakfast dishes.

"I think I've found what I was looking for," Tadeo said.

They left without finishing their food and before Skye said a word.

Three weeks of sex, booze, and carnivorous food blurred into heady obsession. Tadeo was in Skye's thrall.

"I want you to meet some of my friends," he told her as he fell back against the sheets, soaked with sweat from their exertions. "I think they'll like you."

Up until then, their relationship was based on sensation: food and sex. Friends, family, and day jobs hadn't come into it. Skye assumed Tadeo had a job, but liked the mystery of not knowing what. Equally, she never discussed her dull day life.

Now, Tadeo's suggestion that she meet his friends threw Skye into a state of confusion tinged with panic. What did Tadeo think their relationship was about? Skye herself saw it as a sexual fling that probably wouldn't last, but Tadeo's invitation changed things.

She had never said "no" to anything he had suggested, and this was such a minor thing—compared to his usually inventive depravity which included biting her neck at the same time as vigorously fucking her from behind— that she saw no need to refuse. Even so, as she agreed to go, she couldn't help shuddering with an odd excitement as she replayed his words about his friends: *I think they'll like you...*

Skye knew Tadeo was too good to be true. She had been let down so many times that she couldn't help being cynical about relationships. Often her lack of trust was instrumental in the ending of them. That was when the man stayed around long enough after their first casual fuck. The Tadeo *obsession* wasn't burning out, and this would normally be the moment for Skye to back away, excusing herself from becoming part of his life on a more permanent basis. Like a rabbit caught in headlights, Skye would run for the trees, escaping commitment in the nick of time. This time, however, she didn't feel the urge to flee.

Before he left, sometime after midnight, Tadeo left a card at the side of the bed. "The address."

After he left, Skye picked up the card. No name. Just an address.

The house was in Hammersmith, an expensive part of London. Tadeo arranged to meet her there at eight in the evening. Skye caught the Hammersmith and City line to Hammersmith station, then took a short taxi ride and found herself on the front steps of a palatial old house.

This place must be worth a fortune, she thought. She looked at the card again, checked the address which was printed in a handwriting-style font. Italicized. *Fancy.* She should have realized that Tadeo's secret life would be extravagant. He didn't have the tastes of a man who worried about money.

At the top of the steps, Skye noticed there was a bronze plaque on the wall beside the door. It read THE BASTET SOCIETY.

So this is some form of club then...

The door opened and Skye looked up at a tall man who was wearing a formal dinner suit. Skye was in jeans—even though they were designer—and a white crop top: she was clearly underdressed. She experienced a momentary feeling of annoyance that Tadeo hadn't advised her of a dress code.

"You must be Skye," the man said in a clipped English accent. "Tadeo has told me a lot about you."

"Really? He's told me *nothing* about you..." Skye bit her lip. Sometimes she had no filter.

"I'm Sebastian. Do come in."

Skye followed Sebastian into a large hallway. "I thought there was a party here tonight?" she said.

"There is a...gathering," Sebastian said.

They walked through the silent hallway. Skye had expected to hear music, laughter, the sound of other people in the house. She began to feel peculiar about being there, especially if she was alone with Sebastian. Had Tadeo somehow set her up? After all, she really didn't know him at all, did she?

"This way..."

A nervous anxiety pricked at Skye's skull as she followed Sebastian past a wide staircase towards a door at the end of the long corridor.

Wait. I didn't ring the bell, she thought.

"Where *is* Tadeo?' she asked.

"Downstairs."

Sebastian opened the door to a grand parlor. The room was furnished with plush sofas and chairs positioned before an ornate fireplace.

"Wait here." He pointed to a small round table where a glass of red wine was poured. "For you."

Skye took the seat next to the table but ignored the wine. She wasn't comfortable in this ostentatious house, or club, or whatever it was. She had the suspicion that all was not as it appeared to be, and that wisdom brought about a physical, rather than mental, urge to run.

To distract herself she looked around the room. The walls were full of old paintings of men and women in old fashioned clothing. One she recognized as Elizabethan style because of the rigid collar that the men and women wore in that period. One particular picture looked a lot like Queen Elizabeth I: a red-haired woman wearing a dress with broad puffed out sleeves and a stiff round collar circling her throat. This woman wasn't the former queen, however. She was far more attractive, and somewhat feline—perhaps even decadent—in her posture. The woman intrigued her and she studied this picture for quite a while before becoming bored.

The other pictures made her nervous. Even as she stood and moved around the room, those ancient eyes bore into her. Watching her. Judging her from their dust-filled graves...

Skye tried to shake away those morbid thoughts. It wasn't like her to *think*—she wasn't normally so inventive. She tried to laugh at the cliché she was building in her mind; her senses still screamed at her to leave. All humor fled from her mind.

Now and again she glanced at the door, expecting Sebastian to return with Tadeo, but the house remained silent. Skye's nerves became fragmented. She was twitchy. And the paintings became a source of intimidation. Fifty pairs of dead eyes sucked at her soul. They weighed her down until she sank back into the chair and just stared at the door, willing it to open.

More than half an hour passed before Skye decided enough was enough. Perhaps this was one of Tadeo's games. She was being tested in some way, and suddenly she didn't like it, didn't want to play.

She picked up her purse and walked towards the door determined to leave even though that would probably mean the end of her relationship with Tadeo. Perhaps that was for the best anyway. It had gone on much longer than it should have.

The door opened as she reached for the handle.

"There you are!" said Tadeo. "I did say eight. It's now eight thirty-five."

"I've been here for over half an hour," Skye said.

"Oh?"

"Your friend Sebastian let me in."

"You *saw* Sebastian?"

"Yes. He told me to wait in here."

"Next you'll be telling me these paintings are all of people," Tadeo laughed.

"What do you mean? They are..."

As Skye turned around she saw that the paintings had changed. Where the Elizabethan woman had been, a pretty ginger cat lay across a plush chair. Her eyes flicked over the other paintings. All of them were of cats—not people.

"Is this some kind of joke?" Skye said. Somehow they had been switched when her back was turned...

"Come and meet the gang," said Tadeo.

"Gang?"

"My friends. They are waiting to meet you in the entertaining room."

Skye followed Tadeo from the parlor, glancing back at the paintings again as she left the room. She would question him later on his joke. Now was not the time.

In the corridor she could hear music and laughter and the blur of conversations behind dense walls. Tadeo opened up a double set of doors and walked into a huge room without looking back.

"Everyone...I'd like you to meet Skye Silver. She and I have been *involved* recently."

"A little subtlety would be nice," Skye muttered, but she had no time to complain further about his introduction because she was immediately surrounded by men and women who were eager to introduce themselves. After they said their name, they kissed her on the cheek and walked away. It was the oddest experience Skye had ever had. It was like some form of initiation that she didn't understand.

The evening passed by in a haze after that. Skye accepted a glass of wine from Tadeo and she found herself enjoying the company of his unusual friends. She even spoke to a woman who looked a lot like the one she had seen in the painting in the parlor. For the first time, Skye was curious about Tadeo beyond her sexual fascination with him.

🐾 🐾 🐾 🐾 🐾 🐾

As the last of the guests dispersed, Skye stood in the doorway of the entertaining room and watched Tadeo close the front door. It was difficult to imagine that just a few hours ago she had entered this house for the first time, knowing nothing about his life outside of their relationship.

"This is your house, isn't it?" she said.

"Yes. I run the Bastet Society."

"And what exactly is the Bas...tet Society?"

"An ancient religion you might say," Tadeo said. "The ancient Egyptians worshiped Bastet. She was a beautiful cat goddess."

"You don't seem the religious type," Skye said. "Let alone someone who would run a cult."

"We prefer society or religion to cult. *That* word has been associated with many strange faiths. Ours is a meeting of like-minded people. We believe in one Goddess, just as western culture believes in one God."

"I'm tired," Skye said. "Could you call a cab for me?"

"I thought you might stay the night," Tadeo said.

"I have work tomorrow," she lied.

Tadeo stared at Skye for a moment. He appeared to be on the brink of responding. Perhaps he was even going to beg her to stay. Skye wondered how she might feel if he showed any desperation.

A black tuxedo cat slinked into the room distracting them both from a potentially awkward moment. Skye bent to stroke the cat.

"Where have you been hiding?" she said as the cat rubbed itself against her hand.

"Sebastian doesn't like crowds," Tadeo explained.

"Oh! He has the same name as your friend. Where did *that* Sebastian go? I didn't see him again."

"The only Sebastian in this house this evening was this one," Tadeo said.

Skye's head began to hurt as she looked down at the cat. He appeared to be grinning back up at Tadeo, as though the cat and the human shared a private joke.

"I need some sleep," Skye said. "I'll catch a cab outside."

"Skye?" said Tadeo.

"Yes?"

"Did you *like* my friends?"

"The evening was a bit...odd. I'm not sure what to think."

Without waiting for his response, Skye let herself out of the house and walked down the steps. She had seen a side of Tadeo that she had never wanted to see. He was successful, rich and he ran a cat cult. It was all just a bit flaky and weird for her liking.

The kink of Tadeo biting the back of her neck as he rode her from behind now made sense. She really didn't want to make the association beyond their actual fucking...But he did have a thing for cats...

I have lousy luck with men. Why couldn't he have a normal job? A delivery guy, or taxi driver...

The evening had raised more questions about Tadeo than she wanted answers for. To get those answers would mean more commitment and allowing their relationship to grow. Skye didn't want that. Commitment was something she had never done. She liked the idea even less now that she knew more about Tadeo. What kind of *man* ran a "society" that worshiped cats? It was just too creepy.

She glanced around the quiet street. She would have to make her way back to a main road in order to find a black cab. She glanced at her watch; it was two in the morning, and the tube service ended at midnight and didn't restart until about five. She would have to foot the bill for the cab fare all the way home.

She felt a tinge of resentment that he had expected her to stay in that disturbing house, with those old paintings and a cat that leered at you with crafty intelligence.

Skye pulled her mind back to the moment. She glanced back at Tadeo's house. It was in complete darkness now, blacked out and empty-looking. As though no one lived there. She walked away, down to the end of the street, and glanced down to the junction beyond. The roads were quite empty. Skye had never been out this late alone before. Late nights were spent with girlfriends in nightclubs, picking up the occasional casual fling, or eating alone, with a bottle of Jack for company. She glanced back down Tadeo's street, the house stood out by its sheer lack of any light. Even the streetlight shunned it, casting its light in a sideways glow towards the road and away from the pavement.

"My imagination is running away with me," she murmured. The sound of her whispered words carried into the night. It chilled her to the bone.

Skye hurried on towards the junction because it was the most likely place to find a cab.

I could have stayed a few more hours at his house, she thought, regretting the decision to leave. *Only three more hours until the tube station reopens after all!*

A cat hissed from the steps of a house as she passed. Skye jumped and then glared at the creature as it stared at her from the shadows, eyes reflecting the streetlamps, revealing its position.

"Stupid cat!" she said.

At that moment a black cab turned the corner and headed towards her . The "for hire" light was on.

"Thank God! Taxi!"

She waved her arms and the cab driver saw her and drew into the curb. "Where to Miss?"

Skye moved through the dark hallway towards her lounge door. There was a glow coming from the room through the partial crack of the door. She must have left her lamp on before leaving the evening before and she was now grateful to see that warm light welcoming her home.

"What are you doing here?" she said. Her voice trembled.

Tadeo was sitting on her two-seater sofa: this was freaky, even for him.

"Sit down," Tadeo said. "I've something important to tell you."

When Tadeo stopped talking, Skye ran a hand over her forehead. She was tired, drained, and concerned that the man was a complete stalker and nutcase.

"I know it's difficult to take in," he continued. "But every few hundred years Bastet is reincarnated, and I am always there to facilitate it."

A feeling of *déjà vu* made Skye feel dizzy. She felt she had heard these words before, but didn't know when or how.

"I'm too tired for this shit tonight. This has all been some freaky game to you, hasn't it? And it's not funny. I need to sleep and I want you to leave."

"The process has already begun," Tadeo said. "At the initiation this evening."

"What are you talking about?"

"The cats accepted you. And you accepted their kiss."

Skye's mind wobbled between the memory she thought she had and the idea that Tadeo's words conjured up. In a flashback, she saw herself accepting the rough-tongued lick of one cat after another, ending with the one called Sebastian.

"That's what really happened today," Tadeo said, reading her mind. "You met the family."

Skye slumped back into her chair. She was exhausted and couldn't think straight. His insane words rang in her head.

You are Bastet. You will remember your calling.

She woke in an unfamiliar bed. A large four-poster, with thick drapes hanging from each corner. There was an old-style lamp beside the bed. Skye saw the antique furnishings, beautifully preserved objects, and knew that she was back in the Hammersmith house. Maybe she had stayed here after all and everything else had been a dream.

The lamp beside the bed contained a candle-shaped bulb that made it appear to be a real flame, and not electrical lighting.

Skye slid from the bed and caught sight of herself in a full length mirror that stood beside the wardrobe. Hammer horror movie female—victim or seductress? She could be dressed as either. She was wearing a long, sheer nightgown with a plunging neckline which accentuated her small breasts.

What was I drinking last night?

She went to the window, pulled back the corner of one drape and looked out. The street was still dark, dawn appeared to be hours away. If anything, by the movement of people and traffic outside, Skye would place the time at around eight at night. But which night?

She glanced at her wrist but her watch was gone. Of course it was! Along with her own clothing, which another quick look around the room revealed was nowhere in sight.

She sighed. Tadeo and his games...

She found a white robe thrown over a chair and she pulled it on over the nightdress. It had long medieval style sleeves and a hood—probably some sexual fantasy of Tadeo's. She smirked but it was humorless.

Tying the robe belt securely around her waist she left the room.

Downstairs she heard a regular ticking and noticed an old grandfather clock by the door. She hadn't noticed it before, but didn't worry too much about it as she looked at the time. It was eleven thirty, later than she had guessed it was.

She tried to open the front door to look outside, but discovered it was locked. There was a mortise lock and no key. Perturbed, she walked down the corridor and began opening doors to see what was inside each room. On one side she saw the doors to the entertaining room. She knew that this big space stretched from the front of the house and most of the way back. On the other side there was the parlor, a study, and the third door led to a short corridor presumably towards the kitchen which was sited at the back of the house. There was also a door under the wide staircase that she hadn't previously noticed.

"Tadeo?" she called.

It didn't surprise her that there was no reply. The house was a vacuum, devoid of human presence other than her own.

She braved the corridor to the kitchen, but then a noise behind her drew her back to the hallway.

The door under the stairs was now open. The flickering of candles reflected on the walls of a stairwell and cast shadows into the hallway.

"Tadeo?" she said again, but his name came out as a mere whisper.

Skye was drawn to the door, legs moving despite the feeling that she really wanted to run in the opposite direction. She passed over the threshold as though floating. She was unable to stop herself.

A wooden staircase wound downwards, curving left. Skye followed and walked down for what felt like an impossibly long time. Every few steps she encountered a well in the side of the wall, with a lit candle nestled inside. This was the light for the stairway and it was sufficient and atmospheric. Eventually the wooden steps gave way to concrete, leading ever downwards.

Okay, so he's into even more kinky shit than I realized, Skye thought. *Perhaps this will be fun...*

The stairwell opened out onto a short platform, and then the stairs curved down in the opposite direction. Skye had no concept of how many steps she had already traveled down, but she had the feeling it was many. She had started to count them, but lost count several times in the hypnotic monotony of the descent. Perhaps it was in the region of the steps that led down to the catacombs that she had once visited on a trip to Paris. That was years ago now, and she hadn't enjoyed the experience of dead skulls and bones laid out in artistic patterns in some bizarre Parisian underworld.

She became aware of the change in the steps after the platform. The ones before had been regular concrete, these were now cut stone, ancient, and with worn indentations from the passage of thousands of feet over thousands of years.

Then, with abrupt finality, the steps ended.

Skye was facing a rock wall. There was no basement. The candlelight from the alcove opposite danced over the wall.

"What is this shit?"

Skye reached out and touched the wall in front of her. It was cold but not damp. Then it began to move. The wall slid left, disappearing into the rock at her side.

The radiance from hundreds of candles illuminated a stunning room. The floor and walls were made of polished beige-toned marble, which shone like gold wherever the light fell. There was an unusual pattern carved into the floor. A diamond shape, overlapped by a circle.

Skye looked at the floor markings, and realized that there were symbols and shapes engraved all over it. Symbols that almost formed into words—a language that she didn't understand but seemed to hold meaning for her nonetheless.

"Your parents taught you nothing did they?"

Skye turned to see Tadeo. He was lying on a red velvet *chaise longue* at the other side of the room. Skye could have sworn that the room had been empty when she entered.

"What would you know about my parents?"

Tadeo sat up and stared at her, his brow furrowed. "I see. You were adopted. That explains a lot. But not why they gave you up, and didn't prepare you for today."

"I'm not playing your games today, Tadeo. Of course I wasn't adopted!"

"This isn't a game, Skye. This is my destiny. It is what I live for, reincarnation after reincarnation."

"Where are my clothes?"

"You'll have new robes once you are transformed..."

"Okay, I'm out of here..."

Skye turned back towards the stairs only to find the doorway full of cats, their eyes fixed on her and glinting in the iridescent candlelight.

"Bring her in," Tadeo said.

Skye saw one cat, Sebastian from its black and white chest, creeping forward. As she watched, the cat stretched out along the marble floor. He was impossibly long. He extended his front paws, fingers grew from the clawed toes, and a fifth, a thumb, broke through fur. Sebastian's transformation from cat to human took no more than a few moments, but in that time, Skye saw the torturous remolding of flesh, the shrinking back of fur on his body—turning into a black tuxedo suit—and the folding back of ears as human hair and skin replaced fur. Sebastian's face became clean shaven, but Skye knew this was no parlor trick. Sebastian had shape- shifted. Were they Werecats then?

She took a step back from the former cat as Sebastian lifted himself up from the floor onto his back legs. He was very much human now, no one would think otherwise, except that Skye could tell by his eyes that this human form was the unnatural state for Sebastian.

Sebastian grabbed Skye's arm and pulled her into the center of the circle.

"Let go of me, you dick!" she struggled against his formidable strength.

Skye became aware of the other transformations as more hands grabbed her. She was pulled down to the ground, stretched out and held and by virtue of her horizontal position she found herself staring upwards.

A blaze of stars scattered the black ceiling of the chamber. A constellation which Skye had no knowledge to identify, and even if she had, this arrangement was not one that current technology had even seen.

"M'Lyhr A'Ranoth sumoni Tadeo," Tadeo said.

Skye heard the words but could make no sense of them. He repeated the phrase over and over until the stars above began to move. The alignment changed and then Skye could distinguish Earth's solar system.

The first pattern approached, then overlaid the second, and like a zoom tool on a computer screen the Earth came into solid focus, with the strange diamond and circle patterns embellishing the planet's surface. The zoom-in continued, and Skye saw London, just like on Google Maps, and then Hammersmith and finally the house she was in.

Her mind made sense of it: it was a giant screen—attached to the ceiling.

The marble room trembled, a crack appeared in the image above Skye's head, and then it opened up. This was no screen, no hoax. Something real and terrifying was happening.

Skye screamed in terror as a shadow came through the cosmic portal.

"Open your eyes," Tadeo said.

Skye shook her head. She was terrified. Her bladder had turned to mush and she felt the warm damp patch of urine seeping through the robe and nightgown, filling the grooves in the marble floor beneath her.

"Open your eyes and see your god, M'Lyhr A'Ranoth: the Queen of Cats."

Skye's eyes opened. She cowered in her own puddle, small and frail. The cat-humans that had held her had all fallen back. She stared out from her white fur-covered face not understanding that the entrance of M'Lyhr A'Ranoth had brought about her own transformation.

"There, there," Tadeo said. He stroked her head and back, and Skye felt the rippling sensation of fur being moved.

She opened her mouth but only a small "meow" came from her throat. She licked her lips and felt the sharp feline teeth that filled her mouth. Then she flexed her paws, extending the claws. She swiped at Tadeo, leaving a furrow of claw marks across the back of his hand. She jumped away from the circle with a sideways hop, back arched, hissing in terror. Then she came face to face with M'Lyhr A'Ranoth.

The shadow had fleshed out into a black form. Skye slunk back, the creature before her was a giant. A cat's head on a muscular female human body.

The shock once again triggered a transformation, and Skye stretched out, taking on her human form once more. She collapsed down, exhausted as M'Lyhr A'Ranoth approached.

The creature hissed at Skye as she cowered, submissive. Then its giant paw swiped the air; Skye threw her arm over her face to protect her eyes, but the claws didn't tear into her flesh as she expected.

She felt a sting as her flesh was pierced by the tip of one of the creature's claws.

Fire surged into her veins. Skye looked down at her arm and saw a black line burning through her flesh. Her skin blackened as it burnt from the inside out. She screamed.

As the cosmos realigned, Tadeo kneeled before the throne.

Bastet was in her rightful place. The transformation from good soul, to pure evil, had once more been achieved.

On the outside Bastet resembled M'Lyhr A'Ranoth, for she was remade in the cat god's own image. Inside she burned, the last vestiges of the personality of Skye were steeped in agony. For no deal with an outer god was ever painless.

Tadeo hoped that this reincarnation would last longer than the previous one. There was only so much pain a cat could endure before completely losing its mind. And once Bastet was lost, her power would fail the society, too.

Tadeo bowed his head in supplication.

Fire burned through Skye's body as the power of M'Lyhr A'Ranoth coursed through her. Her skin and hair had turned black as the ancient goddess took possession of her. She screamed in her own mind as the pain washed over and through her soul, tearing her apart. But then...it subsided.

Skye felt control returning to her. The ancient and unknowable presence of the cat goddess was receding...

Skye shuddered and drew in a deep breath. She still had control of the power, but the alien presence was being shed. She opened her eyes and saw Tadeo kneeling before her. She looked down at her arm which was rippling with colors like the skin of a tone-changing squid, the blackness faded and changed to brown and then caramel, then white as Skye's unique pigmentation threw off the blackness of the alien and reasserted itself. Color had never stuck to her before, so why should it now?

As the darkness retreated, so Skye felt the pain lessen until there was nothing but power, nothing but herself. Skye. Bastet. What did it matter what they called her? She was the queen of the cats and now ruler of this little moment in space and time.

She laughed and looked down at Tadeo. Reaching out one hand/paw she lifted his head by his chin to look at him. Her eyes sparkled blue and bronze, flecked with green and a hint of darkness as her slit irises observed that the man was scared of her. And so he should be. For she was Bastet, and he was her toy, her plaything.

The other cats had backed away and were scurrying back up the long staircase to the world above. Taking the message. Letting the world know.

Bastet was back!

The Veil of Dreams

by Stephen Mark Rainey

Since moving with his wife to Munising some six months earlier, Charles Becker had developed an intimate, nightly companionship with vivid, horrifying nightmares, which frequently jarred him awake, upsetting him so that drifting back into comfortable slumber was out of the question. No doubt, sleep deprivation was behind the frustrating mental dullness that had set in and shortened his already too-short fuse, to the point he feared it was affecting his relationship with Anika. This was all the more maddening because they both otherwise loved Munising, set on the shores of Lake Superior in Michigan's upper peninsula, its picturesque setting and small-town character tailor-made to their tastes. For over two decades, Becker had held a satisfying and lucrative position as planning supervisor at Dow Chemical in Midland, but internal shakeups the previous year had eliminated his position. However, with his severance package, his army pension, a robust savings account, and a wife more than willing to leave her local accountant's practice, he had managed to buy a quaint little Munising motel that did brisk business, particularly during tourist seasons. They both enjoyed the more laid-back lifestyle, the friendly if rather quirky locals, and the invigorating seasons. For a time, it had seemed that life might be out to do them well after all.

But these night horrors—holy God. Every night for months they had come, so that he now dreaded going to bed. Most remarkable to him was the consistency of theme and detail in the dreams: inevitably, he was wandering, lost and alone, in a forest so dense and dark it might have been on another planet, searching not only for a way out but also for Anika, whom he knew to be in danger, even if he didn't comprehend the specific threat. He was also aware of something else in the forest, watching him, stalking him. Most notably, certain ever-present sounds dogged him—a distant but constant chorus of piping, buzzing, and rumbling, ominous yet strangely alluring, setting his nerves on edge so that he sometimes woke up trembling and sweating.

His restlessness had disturbed Anika to the point that most nights she would get up and leave the bedroom, sometimes even the house. More than once he had risen to find her dead asleep on the living room couch, and two days earlier, she had come staggering in just after sunrise, not drunk but exhausted. Worst of all, she claimed she could not remember where she had been. And he believed her.

Something was going terribly wrong with both their lives.

It was a Saturday in late September when he woke from an especially unsettling nightmare: the forest had been alive with scuttling, whimpering, yowling sounds, and in the endless darkness, he could glimpse myriads of glowing green eyes peering back at him. Those, however, upset him less than that same something he had sensed in other dreams—a huge, unseen entity— moving toward him, crashing through trees and emitting irregular droning noises, like the buzzing of a gigantic hornet modulated into unintelligible speech. Behind it all, he could hear a human voice, ringing out in agony or abject terror.

Anika's voice.

He wanted to reach her, to bring her back to safety, someplace lit by ordinary sunlight, yet his muscles refused to obey his commands, permitted him only to retreat in horror from the advancing, unknown thing in the darkness. For God's sake, in real life, he had taken gunfire during his military service, and of course he'd been afraid, but somehow, even that fear of physical harm paled beside the acute, nameless terror these dreams inflicted upon him.

An array of white-gold sunbeams streaming through the half-drawn blinds indicated it was mid-morning, far later than he was accustomed to sleeping, even for a weekend. Next to him, the bed covers rustled and he felt a touch of relief, but when he rolled over, rather than Anika lying in her customary place, he saw only Grinder, the portlier of their two housecats, eyeing him with that accusatory look that meant their breakfast was late.

"Oh, hey, tubbo," he muttered. "Didn't your mom feed you already?"

Grinder, an orange tabby so named because, as a kitten, he had eaten an entire smoked turkey grinder from Mancino's, offered his distinctive, broken purr: "Uh-prrrr, uh-prrrr, uh-prrrr."

A second later, Barrington, solid black from nose to tail, but with the cool sapphire eyes of a Siamese, hopped up beside Grinder, and piped in a sing-songy, tenor voice, "Hi, Mr. B! You'd better hurry up, time is wasting!"

Becker stared at the cat in wordless disbelief.

No, surely, that was just Anika, maybe in the bathroom, pretending to speak for the cat. She did that sometimes. He was only half awake, and his brain wasn't registering sound properly.

But it hadn't sounded like Anika. More like Neil Young.

He must still be dreaming. He didn't feel as if he were dreaming.

"No, you're not dreaming," Barrington said, his little cat lips enunciating the words clearly. "But you need to be."

Becker stared a few moments more and then pointed to Grinder. "Does he talk, too?"

"No, Grinder is an idiot."

Grinder squinted at him. "Uh-prrrr, uh-prrrr, uh-prrrr."

He thought back to the previous night. He and Anika had enjoyed a couple of martinis at The Whitefish Pub, as they often did on Friday evenings. "Did somebody spike my drink last night? Is that what's going on?"

"If so, it might explain why you slept so late, but that's about it. Now, Mr. B, I really must insist we get going."

"Going? Where?"

"Balustrade."

"What is Balustrade?"

"Where we're going."

"And you called Grinder an idiot."

"However, before anything else, I'd like some breakfast," Barrington said. "Pasties from Muldoon's, I should think. I prefer chicken to beef."

"That's not breakfast food. And you can't eat a whole pasty."

"I can too."

"I'll get you some treats from the kitchen."

"Treats are acceptable."

"After I've made coffee."

Barrington gave a little sigh. "Ms. B understands priorities far better."

After most of a pot of coffee, he couldn't be sure he wasn't still dreaming. Or worse, that insanity hadn't come calling.

Behind the motel, an old, disused path led into the woods, though he had never explored it very far. To the best of his knowledge, the path petered out after a few hundred feet. Beyond that, there was nothing but miles of dense woodland. Becker, lacking any alternative but to reflect in solitude on the collapse of his familiar reality, had agreed to follow his heretofore linguistically challenged cat into the woods.

"You're saying Anika is gone. Away."

"She's where you left her in your dream."

"That's crazier than a talking cat. So where are we going now?"

"Mount Balustrade. It's this way."

"There are no mountains here. Just big hills."

"Trust me."

"Have you always been able to talk?"

"Not in a way you would understand. Only since we moved here."

"Why? How?"

"Because we're near to what's known as the Veil of Dreams. On the other side, the world is different. Sometimes, things from there spill over to here. I don't really understand it. But after I started going over there, I came back changed, more like the cats on that side."

"You go back and forth?"

"They have better treats."

"But what about Anika?"

"Those dreams you've been having are real, Mr. B. In your dreams, you've also been going over to the other side, even though you don't remember. But Ms. B came this way and crossed the physical border."

"Veil of Dreams, Balustrade, talking cats. This all sounds like some kind of weird Yooper folklore."

Barrington stopped, turned around, and peered at him with his inscrutable sapphire eyes. "This is a rescue mission, Mr. B. You need to know that."

"And you're the brains, is that it?"

"Why, yes."

"She's really in danger?"

"Yes."

"What about me? You? Us?"

"Yes."

"And those things I've seen in my dreams. They'll be there, too?"

"Probably."

"But why would Ms. B—er, Anika—why would she come out here? That's not like her."

"Because it called her. Just like it called you, in your dreams. When it calls, most humans can't refuse, and she couldn't. In the dream world, you knew this and went looking for her. At the risk of offering you an undeserved compliment, you did not to succumb to its call. If you had, it would have you now, too."

"'It.' Just what is this 'it?' And I sure as hell don't remember being 'called.'"

"Humans block what they don't want to remember. And you don't want to remember it."

"And it calls us—why?"

Barrington stopped and gave Becker a long, acerbic stare. Then, with a little "poof" that Becker took as something akin to a derisive snort, the cat lifted one of his back legs and began to chew on his toes.

"Why do you do that?"

He paused. "Why do you use little metal clippers to trim those pointless flat things on the ends of your fingers?"

A pattering sound came from behind them, and Becker turned to see a familiar orange shape bounding up the trail in their direction. He heard Barrington mutter, "Oh, no."

Grinder came up and rubbed against Becker's leg. "Uh-prrrr, uh-prrrr, uh-prrrr."

"So, he doesn't talk."

"Nope."

"What about other cats around here? And people? If being near this 'Veil' affects us, what about everyone else around here?"

"It's different for others—cats and people, both. Your motel is closest to the Veil, but other people are affected, mostly in such little ways they don't realize it. You call them 'quirky.'" He started moving again. "Come along, please."

Becker glanced down at Grinder. "'Come along, please,' he says in his little Neil Young voice, like he's the boss of the world. He's a cat, and I'm following him." Grinder's big green eyes beamed back at him. "And I'm talking to you like you have a clue."

"Don't get your hopes up," Barrington said.

After a while, Becker asked, "So, do you guys really like belly rubs and head scratches and all that?"

"Do we act like we like it?"

"Yes."

"Then we like it."

"But I don't think I want to scratch your head anymore."

"All the more reason to rescue Ms. B."

As they pressed on, the hillside grew steeper, the trees lusher and larger—too large, Becker thought—their trunks thick and covered in scaly, brown bark, the dense canopy obscuring the sun so that the woods ahead seemed darker than night. Michigan trees didn't look like these. Hell, no trees ought to look like these. Before he knew it, he was huffing and puffing, the hillside growing steeper with every step, the air turning cooler and thinner. After a few minutes, he saw patches of dull gray mist creeping like huge, sluggish worms through the trunks on all sides.

"We're passing through the veil," Barrington said, his tenor voice somber. "Once on the other side, we must be quiet. Don't speak."

"Shouldn't I have a weapon or something?"

"If something has a mind to eat you—or worse—there's no weapon that will save you. Just stay close. And don't trip over Grinder."

He glanced down at the tubby orange one, who was trotting along close to his feet.

"You sure are fat," he said.

"Uh-prrrr, uh-prrrr, uh-prrrr," went Grinder.

Ahead, Becker could see a break in the trees, which revealed—to his shock—a deep, midnight blue sky with a few crystal stars sparkling above. But here, along the path, it was still daylight. He glanced at his wristwatch and noticed it had stopped at precisely noon.

"Time is not the same beyond the Veil," Barrington said. "On the other side, cats get four dinners a night."

"You eat four dinners every night."

"It's time to be quiet."

Now even Grinder was slinking along low to the ground, eyes wide and ears laid back. A few steps more, and the woods opened to a rocky outcropping that overlooked a vast gulf of pure blackness, from which he could hear distant pipings, buzzings, and rumblings, blending in weird, musical harmony—just as he recalled from his nightmares. Above, a galaxy of stars speckled the deep violet sky, and he realized he could not pick out a single familiar constellation. As his eyes began to adjust, he made out the silhouettes of incredibly tall trees towering above the rim of the gorge.

From the edge of their precipice, a series of stone columns formed what appeared to be gigantic stair rails leading down into the chasm. Despite being unable to see the bottom, he could feel the fantastic heights upon which he perched, and a rush of vertigo nearly swept him off his feet.

"This is Mount Balustrade," Barrington whispered. "We have passed through the Veil."

"My God, my God, my God."

"Hush, Mr. B," came the sharp little voice. "If it finds out we're here, we won't be here very long."

"What do we do?"

"Go down."

"Down that?"

"Your questions are making me tired. Just follow."

Barrington crept forward, stepped over the edge of the gray stone, and merged with the blackness so that Becker could no longer see him. But then a pair of sapphire eyes appeared in the inky sea, beckoning him forward. Becker took a deep breath and tried to steel his nerves. His first halting step forward was the biggest leap of faith he ever took.

A moment later, he realized he was standing on level ground, and he could see some distance around him by the hazy light of a billion blazing stars. Barrington stood atop a craggy boulder at the edge of the dark woods, and a second later, Grinder appeared at his side, eyes roving back and forth, the orange fur on his backside ruffled.

No purring from the tubby one now.

He looked back and up, saw the now-miniscule precipice silhouetted against the starry backdrop. With a single step, he had crossed that vast space.

Insane! Impossible!

But he could not pause to contemplate this new madness, for the cats were moving again, and the idea of being left behind, lost in this unimaginable place—the source of his nightmares—horrified him.

Funny. Since leaving his residence, a cat opening its mouth and speaking to him had become the most prosaic of the day's events.

Barrington was hunched over, sniffing the ground, moving forward at a creep, occasionally swishing his tail in agitation. Becker felt a thump against his leg and then a momentary vibration: Grinder rubbing against him and offering a reassuring purr.

Funny, he had always preferred Barrington's company to Grinder's, but now he wasn't so sure.

The cats froze, and Becker had to perform an awkward dance to keep from tripping over them. As he steadied himself, he heard a heavy purring sound he first assumed to be Grinder, but then he realized it was coming from elsewhere. And it wasn't purring. More a deep, rhythmic pulsing, almost like the muttering of a heavy engine. Taking his cue from the cats, he knelt next to the bole of some enormous tree that vaguely resembled a cypress and scanned the landscape ahead, fearful of what he might see yet perversely eager to glimpse something that could only exist in a dream.

There—a hundred or so yards away, behind a barrier of dark, conical trees that might have been spruces—a bluish luminescence, pale and amorphous, moving slowly from right to left. The vibrations were coming from that.

Above the pointed black crests, something rose into view: the upper portion of a translucent dome, like the bell of a faintly luminous jellyfish, only gigantic—ten, maybe fifteen feet across. Something long and snakelike slashed through the branches, snapping them off in bunches. A tendril.

The thing stopped moving, and the pulsing intensified into a hornet-like buzzing, modulated into something like alien speech. The dome began to rotate, and a pair of globular, copper-colored eyes, each at least a foot in diameter, swiveled into view, their gaze sweeping through the trees and settling on his hiding place. Becker's heart caught in his throat.

The damned thing seemed know he was here.

He pressed himself against the huge trunk until the rough bark bit into his skin even through his clothes. He became aware of a maddening, tickling sensation, like ants crawling over his arms and legs, and he realized it was the vibrations emanating from that monstrous shape. For what seemed an endless time, the creepy-crawly waves washed over him, wormed into his ears, penetrated his skull. By sheer strength of will—or pure terror—he remained motionless, his eyes clamped shut. Yet when the buzzing began to abate, he could not stop himself risking a peek around the tree trunk. The entity was moving again, back on its original course, mostly hidden by the trees. At last it vanished and the vibrations ceased, though his skin still felt tingly and raw.

Barrington chirped a few strange syllables, and at first Becker thought the cat had sneezed. But then, the little tenor voice enunciated, "Tuskachimaqqua."

"What?"

"That's what took Ms. B."

Anika. Where the hell could she be? Was she even still alive?

"That was the most horrible thing I have ever felt. Like bugs all over me. Inside my head."

"It is surprising but good you didn't move. That would have been the end of you."

"Aren't you the reassuring one?"

"For it, humans are a rare delicacy. The local cats try to keep people away for their own good, but sometimes its call is too strong. As it was with Ms. B. She can't have much time left before it gets hungry."

"What about the cats you said lived here? Where are they?"

"This used to be their territory until Tuskachimaqqua ran them out. Most of them, anyway. A few are determined to drive it away or kill it. They can't do it alone, though. It's too strong, especially when it's this close to its lair. That's the center of its power." Barrington trotted into the trees in the direction from which the thing had appeared. "This way. Make haste."

Compelled to follow, Becker tucked away his fear and rushed after the cat, desperate now to find Anika and get her out of this lunatic realm. He didn't even know whether he could find the way back, but he knew that every second they remained here the closer he came to meeting the horror of his nightmares.

There!

Beyond a row of gnarly, skeletal trees, he could see Anika. Silhouetted against a wall of gray stone, hung like a limp doll between two tall pillars of rock.

A series of faint vibrations crept up his spine.

Jesus! The thing must be coming back.

He tramped over tangles of spindly underbrush, pushed his way through spiky vines that raked his exposed flesh, and stumbled over sharp, craggy rocks to make his way to his seemingly insensate wife. She was strung up between the knobby stone pillars by some kind of thin, phosphorescent thread, no doubt produced by the hovering horror.

Trapped like a fly in a monstrous spider's web.

"Anika!" His voice was a hoarse whisper. "Anika, it's me!"

Her head was drooped, and her long sienna hair, usually brushed into sleek, silky waves, hung in filthy disarray over her face, obscuring her eyes. A harsh moan escaped her lips, and her head rose enough for him to see that blood, now dried, had run down her forehead and cheeks. Her eyes, showing little cognizance of her surroundings, shifted back and forth, radiating pain. Her arms wriggled back and forth in a brief, futile struggle with her bonds.

The vibrations became a sharp, agitated droning. Tuskachimaqqua was approaching, surely aware of his presence here.

Fifteen feet of open space separated him from his wife. The moment he attempted to cross it, he would be fully exposed to the monster.

He glanced back and called, "Barrington!"

But the cat was gone.

"Barrington? Grinder?"

No sign of either of them.

"Boys?"

Now what?

His instincts—and old army training—urged him to find a weapon, however makeshift, so that he might at least attempt to fight the thing. But then he remembered Barrington's warning: "If something has a mind to eat you—or worse—there's no weapon that will save you."

Just to his left, he heard a rustle in the branches, and praying it was one or both of the cats, he turned slowly toward the sound.

"Good Christ!"

Every inch of twenty feet tall, Tuskachimaqqua hung in midair, drifting forward as if propelled by a wind current, its vast, bell-like dome capping a translucent, cylindrical body that tapered to a blunt point, like a huge aqua-blue carrot. A dozen or more tendrils sprouted from beneath the bell, questing and waving, bristling with thorn-like barbs that appeared capable of disemboweling a man with a single swipe.

Becker's mind could barely process what he was seeing. So alien, this thing, so horribly wrong.

A product of an insane reality.

Where the hell were his cats?

The thing floated toward him, its huge eyes fixed on his, seemingly aware of his terror and savoring it, its barbed tendrils spreading wide as if to take him in a deadly embrace. The intense buzzing had begun to affect his equilibrium, and now everything around him seemed to shimmer, to oscillate—much as with the onset of a migraine, which produced a rainbow-like aura over his field of vision.

He had come this far to save Anika from a horrible fate, and now he stood only feet from her, yet as helpless as if an unscalable wall towered between them. A tendril slashed the air inches from his face, and he felt a frigid wind in its wake.

The next one would remove his head.

From somewhere within the woods, a weird, warbling growl, like the cry of some jungle beast, rose into the starry sky, and the droning from the advancing horror abruptly ceased.

A sharp little Neil Young voice rang out of the darkness. "Run, Mr. B, run!"

Before his brain could even register the command, his legs were propelling him back into the darkness of the trees, but a few seconds later, guilt seized him in ferocious, angry talons and sent him stumbling.

He could not leave Anika like this.

He regained his balance and looked back, only to see a mass of barbed tendrils rushing toward him like a roiling wave, smashing through tree branches and sending leafy wreckage hurtling in all directions. At the sight, his autonomic systems overpowered his resolve, and he again broke into a mad sprint, destination unknown, his only hope that he didn't fall or become tangled in the dense vines and undergrowth.

Barrington had urged him to run. What the hell did the cat have in mind?

He chanced a look back and saw in the distance what seemed to be a thousand flickers of light dancing like fireflies on a warm summer night. No, not fireflies—luminous green eyes, moving through the woods and converging on the spot where Anika was bound.

He felt an explosion at his back, followed by a hail of brambles, twigs, and leaves. He could sense Tuskachimaqqua drawing closer, despite his panicked dash.

On and on he ran, seemingly for miles, faster and faster, yet never gaining an inch on his pursuer.

Just as in a bad dream.

Something snatched his feet out from under him, and he planted his face in dirt and detritus. Air whooshed out of his lungs as if he'd caught a baseball bat in the gut, and only with a painful, desperate effort did he manage to twist around so he might get a last look at the thing that was about to end his life.

It was hovering ten feet away, but its glistening copper eyes were swiveling back in the direction it had come, as if something had captured its attention, seemingly uncertain whether to continue after its prey or go in search of the distractor. Apparently decided, it whirled away from him and rushed toward its distant lair, leaving him wheezing and enervated, unsure whether this was a reprieve for him or the end for Anika.

In the darkness, he heard something else crashing through the trees in his direction.

Good God, what now?

With a raucous roar, a huge, orange beast burst into view, gleaming green eyes rolling in his direction.

Grinder.

Grinder! As big as a lion, bearing a slumped figure on his back, slim arms wrapped around his neck, somehow holding on with whatever strength she possessed.

"Anika!"

"Climb on, Mr. B!" It was Barrington, who appeared at Grinder's oversized feet. "Time is wasting!"

Not pausing to voice the first question, he hauled himself upright, leaped for the magically transformed cat, and pulled himself onto Grinder's back behind Anika. She tilted her head back to offer him a brief smile of relief and gratitude.

"Go, Grinder, go!" Barrington cried.

Becker's hands burrowed into the huge cat's luxurious fur and grabbed hold for dear life as off they went, zooming into the darkness like a cyclone, the wind of their passage nearly ripping him from his mount. But above the roaring in his ears, he heard a chorus of screaming—feline screaming—and felt a familiar, evil buzzing creeping from the distance, but this time faltering and irregular.

The cats! The cats from beyond Balustrade. They were attacking Tuskachimaqqua.

And winning. He knew it. He could feel it.

On and on Grinder carried them, until Becker saw, looming above them in new, gleaming daylight, a towering mountain with almost vertical sides, crowned by stone columns that resembled a massive stair railing.

And the next thing he knew, they were once again perched on the precipice overlooking a vast black abyss, Grinder's massive chest rumbling, purring, and Barrington sitting next to him, chewing on his toes.

"You're saying you used me as a distraction? As bait?"

"In so many words."

"Why, you little—"

"Oh, Charles," Anika said. "Barrington knew what he was doing. However he planned it, if it weren't for you—all of you—I'd be dead now. You know that, don't you?"

Becker was sitting in the corner of the living room couch, one arm wrapped around Anika, who lay against his shoulder. She appeared fatigued and wan, with a few lacerations and contusions, but otherwise little worse for wear. Her deepest pain, Becker knew, was regret for having succumbed to the siren song of the thing from the other side, despite knowing that few humans could have resisted it.

Yet he had.

"So is Tuskachimaqqua dead?"

"I don't know that it can really die," Barrington said. "But just as most humans can't resist its will, it cannot resist the compulsion to consume any human that comes into its territory. That was its mistake. The farther it went from its lair—the source of its power—the more vulnerable it became to our power. By coming after you, it allowed the cats to gather in sufficient strength to free Ms. B and attack it in force. Until now, they've never had such an opportunity to reclaim the land that is theirs. Ours, really." He glanced at the now normal-sized orange tabby huddled next him, feet drawn up under his considerable girth. "You, young sir, are a pig."

"Uh-prrrr, uh-prrrr, uh-prrrr," went Grinder.

"He's not going to change on this side of the Veil, is he?" Becker asked with some alarm.

"Probably not."

"Isn't there some way to destroy the passage? Close it off so no one else can be called through it?"

"Oh no, quite impossible. The Veil is as much a part of the world as Lake Superior, or the need for four dinners every night. But now you've learned about the Veil, you will help guard it. In your dreams, you'll know if someone attempts to pass over Balustrade. Then you can stop them. You've heard Tuskachimaqqua's call, and it drew you in but didn't overcome your will. You're on your way to becoming a powerful dreamer. I'll be there to help you. Teach you." He gave the orange cat a disdainful glance. "So will he."

"I don't want to become a powerful dreamer. I want to live here in peace with Ms. B—er, Anika—and run my motel on my own terms. With a couple of normal housecats."

"How humdrum. Just think of all you have to explore, to learn. It'll be a whole new experience for you."

Anika smiled at him. "I think you're finally finding what you're meant to do with your life."

"Please. Don't start sounding like him."

Barrington looked up at him, squinted, and went, "M-rrrrow."

Then he hopped onto Becker's lap and circled three times before curling himself into a ball. Then his sparkling sapphire eyes gave Becker that look.

"You've got to be kidding me," he said, but with a deep sigh, he began to scratch the black cat on the head.

The Quest of Pumpkin, The Brave

by Oscar Rios

My life began from the simplest beginnings, and my earliest memories were of cold, hunger, and plague. My mother, what I remember of her, was a hunter living in the wilds, doing her best to provide for my siblings and me. One rainy day she never returned to us, and with my pack mates, too young to provide for ourselves, we cried for her, endlessly, as the rain fell around us. Days passed, and hunger gnawed at us. Parasites drained our blood, illness wracked us, causing our eyes to swell and close, sealed shut with a burning crust which threatened to blind us. One by one our cries weakened, and began to silence. I could feel the bodies of my siblings grow still, then cold, and all I could do was cry for a mother which, even at that very young age, I knew would never return. And I cried, for it was all I could do in my pitiful state. Of our initial seven only I and one other survived...

🐾 🐾 🐾 🐾 🐾 🐾

In another time...In another world...a young girl ran for her life.

She did not know where she was, how she got there, or how it came to pass that these strange vicious creatures were chasing her. She knew instinctively that if she slowed, or stumbled, they would be on her with sharp claws, plunging fangs, and voracious appetites. Her blood would be spilled and her life would end to sate the creatures' hunger. So, she ran, around wide tree trunks, ducking under vines, and leaping over fallen branches through the dark, shadowed forest.

The creatures were only a little larger than squirrels, with rat tails, and sharp cat-like teeth surrounded by a beard of writhing tentacles. They raced through the branches around her and above her, chittering and scratching, seeming to close in on her from all sides. She had no idea what they were, but they had been chasing her for a long time it seemed. "Please, somebody help me," she cried out into the forest as she ran.

"Gwen! Is that you? I'm coming! Keep calling out!" a voice called back.

Gwen...I'm Gwen! It was only then that the girl realized she didn't know her own name until just now. The familiarity of the word triggered something in her, some lost knowledge, some sense of comfort and belonging. Someone knew who she was, someone who wanted to help her. "Please help me!" she cried, as one of the creatures leapt at her, but missed, tumbling into the underbrush before quickly scrambling back into a tree to rejoin the pursuit. "They are getting closer!"

"THIS WAY! TOWARDS MY VOICE! I'M COMING GWEN! DON'T GIVE UP!" a voice cried out towards her left.

Gwen, because she was sure that was her name now, turned towards the voice. However, changing direction had put her off balance. Gwen fell, stumbling over a depression in the forest floor to sprawl face forward with a scream. She rolled over, scrambling backwards as four of the furry, vicious creatures came rushing in, driving out of the trees towards her. The largest of the fiends was sailing towards her face, claws outstretched, fangs bared, tentacles dripping a bluish saliva.

A small ball of orange fury crashed into the creature, tackling it in midair. The two shapes dropped to the ground, rolling in the fallen leaves furiously. Gwen watched, panting for breath, too unsteady to rise as her legs burned from her long exertion. She heard growling and hissing, and saw powerful rear legs, encased in radiant orange fur kicking over and over, savagely disemboweling the rat-like horror. Her savior leapt away from the slowly dying creature, landing between her and the other three attackers.

It was a cat, a small orange-furred cat, barely more than a kitten. It arched its back, puffed its tail, and hissed fiercely at the strange creatures.

The little cat proclaimed, "Be gone Vermin! I am Myrmidon, Emissary of the White Goddess. This one is under my protection, and while I live you shall not have her."

In another world, in another place, Gwen might have thought this odd, but not today. In this nightmare of strangeness and horror, a talking cat was the least strange and horrifying thing she'd seen so far.

For all the savagery of the little cat's initial attack, and the bravado of its words, the three remaining creatures seemed unimpressed. They began to fan out, surrounding the cat, as the branches filled with more of their number.

The cat turned sideways, arching its back even more, hopping forward and back in rage screaming, "DO NOT TEST ME, SCUM!" Then muttered lower, "Gwen, grab the stick...the stick...Don't run, we're making our stand here."

Gwen blinked in amazement. This talking cat knew her? Was giving her orders? *"Well, okay..."* she thought, *"this makes as much sense as anything else."* She looked around and saw a large branch. She slowly reached out and pulled it to her, taking it up like a club.

One of the creatures leapt at the cat, but missed. The cat jumped straight up in the air, easily dodging the attack to land square on the thing's back, his claws sinking in deeply and the cat's jaws shot forward, locking onto one of the creature's long round ears. It ripped a bloody bite from the ear and tossed the torn chunk into the air as the beast squealed in pain. One of the other creatures rushed forward, biting the little cat on the back and trying to tear it away from its pinned companion. The cat howled out in pain, nearly losing its grip on the creature below it.

Gwen swung the stick, with all of her might, knocking away the creature biting the cat. It flew into the air and sailed into a tree with a thump of broken bones, leaving a smear of blood as it tumbled lifelessly to the ground. Another one of the creatures jumped towards her, but Gwen swung the stick once more, intercepting it in midair. The fiend landed nearby and began whimpering and struggling to crawl away, dragging its rear legs behind it.

The little cat sank its claws deeper into the creature it held captive. The thing squealed in terror and pain but the cat did not deliver a fatal bite to the back of its neck. "Go! Flee you filthy sacks of dung!" The cat sank its back claws into the flesh of the creature, causing it to cry out even louder. "I SAID GO!"

The creatures in the trees slowly melted back into the shadows. The captive creature stopped struggling and laid flat and still. It stretched out its arms in a posture of supplication. The cat, who had called himself Myrmidon, slowly released it. He seemed to tower above his opponent who cowered in fear.

"I know you understand me, so I tell you this. I release you on one condition— you tell others of your kind that we are not to be hunted. We are under the protection of the White Goddess, and mighty warriors in our own right. We demand safe passage through the rest of the Enchanted Forest. If unmolested we will leave in peace. If we even catch scent of another Zoog before then I swear, by the milk of my poor dead mother, I will hunt these woods until I claim the lives of one hundred Zoogs. You understand?"

The creature nodded its head, its tentacles twitching nervously.

"Then go, and do not forget either my mercy or the sharpness of my teeth."

The now one-eared Zoog slunk off, and delivered the message to the others of its kind. In the days to come The Orange Cat called Myrmidon became a legend among the Zoog of the Enchanted Forest. The story was told to young Zoog who disobeyed their mothers to cow them into obedience. The human woman and the orange cat were never troubled by Zoog again.

When the creature was gone, the cat turned to the girl. "Gwen, are you alright? Did they hurt you?" It came forward, its tail slowly taking a more natural appearance.

"N...n...no, I'm okay. Do you know me?"

"I hope so, if you are Gwen of Mineola? Called Gwendolyn by most, but given the name Guwenhwyar at her birth by the White Goddess. Are you her? Please, tell me if you are her."

Gwen thought, and so much of what he said sounded familiar. Mineola...It was a town on a Long Island, where she lived...How did she know this? Also her strange true name, Guwenhwyar, sounded familiar as well. She knew it meant *one who loves to live in dreams*, but how she did not know. "I...I don't know. I can't remember...I don't know who I am. I'm scared." Tears welled in her eyes.

The cat came over slowly to rub its head against her calf. "Shhhhh, shhhhh, it's okay. Just breathe. Even if you are not her, I will get you out of this forest safely. I give you my word. I was told Gwen would know me by my secret name, my true name. Even though we have never met, the White Goddess said that Gwen would know me. Don't think, just speak. What is my name?"

The girl looked at the little orange cat, and a memory came to her. She was sitting in a padded seat, looking out a window as the world raced by beyond it. She held a tiny pumpkin and was speaking to someone, saying that one day she would have a cat this same color. A Halloween Cat, but not black, not a witch's cat. Her cat would be orange, like...

The girl spoke..."Pumpkin...Are you called Pumpkin?"

The young cat shuddered, and then whimpered as tears fell from his eyes. "Yes...yes, I am called Pumpkin, so named by the White Goddess in her mercy and boundless generosity. I have found you, at long last, and you are real. I have looked for so long for you, Gwen."

The girl hugged the cat, and the cat snuggled into her arms. He licked her hand lovingly, muttering. "It's okay...We're both going to be okay. I'm here to lead you home."

Our cries were answered, at least in time for two of us. My sister, with her white paws and belly, and I were taken by mighty beings, who lifted us up from where our mother had reared us. They took us to a place of lights, strange smells, and pain. Potions were pushing into our bodies through sharp needles and down our throats through syringes. Strange chips were jabbed under our skins behind our shoulders, but it was not to torment us. At first we were terrified, but we came to realize that this was a place of healing.

Slowly we recovered, our eyes healing, our strength returning. We mourned our siblings and lost mother, in our own way, but we had each other, and knew we would see them again one day. Life goes on, so we began training with one another for lives as hunters, stalking and pouncing and wrestling one another. For a time, our life was happy; a warm, dry place with food and water, our floor a soft blanket separated from the rest of the world by bars of hard iron. As prisons go this was not so bad, since we were still together.

Until the day my greatest fear was realized.

My sister was taken from my side, lifted up and given over to one of the mighty beings. She cried for me, and I for her, for we have never been apart. My heart broke and I reached for her through the bars as she was carried away. I doubt I will ever see my sister again. Then they came for me. A hand lifted me up, and I was held close to a warm breast, fingers scratching my head. She spoke softly to me, calling me a warrior, a born fighter, telling me not to cry. I was then named, Myrmidon, and I was promised a good, long life if I could be brave and serve her faithfully. I was now in the service of The White Goddess, once the White Queen but no longer. That night she took me to a new place, my last place, called Forever Home. It was a place of many windows, pools of sunlight, food and water, toys and boxes of sand.

I was saved. I was freed. Yet I had a debt to repay.

The little orange cat walked through the forest effortlessly, tail held high, a flag for the human girl to follow. Through the shadows they walked, climbing over fallen trees and leaping across swift cold streams. They kept a wide berth between themselves and the dark caves that dotted the Enchanted Forest. Pumpkin told her dangerous things sometimes laired in such places, and a small cat and lost girl might seem too tempting a morsel to pass up. Gwen held tight onto her makeshift club as they crept quietly around these areas.

Gwen tried to ask Pumpkin questions but he hushed her, whispering, "When we are free of these woods then we shall speak. For now, let us move quickly and quietly, while our luck holds. Lucky so far..."

Luck? Gwen looked down at herself, her dress covered in dirt, tattered and torn, splattered with blood. She looked over the bloody bite on Pumpkin's back as well, wincing at the pain he must be in.

"I'd hate to see unlucky..."

"Unlucky means we'd be dead and that could still happen. Now is the time for stealth, Gwen, we're almost out."

Hours later, exhausted and hungry, the pair exited the Enchanted Forest. Pumpkin led them a quarter mile away from the forest fence before dropping in beside an apple tree.

"We should be safe here for a while. Let's take a rest, clean up a bit, and you can eat something."

The cat began cleaning himself, licking the blood from the wound on his back.

Gwen plucked an apple out of the tree, took a bite and plopped down, exhausted. She was thrilled to be out of the gloomy forest, and the fruit tasted better than anything she had ever eaten before.

"So, can we talk now?"

"Of course."

Gwen wasn't sure where to begin..."Okay, you were sent to find me. Why?"

"Because the White Goddess wanted me to."

"Why?"

"You can ask her when we get there. It's not my story to tell. I am just a cat after all..."

"Why don't I remember anything?"

"I don't know, Gwen, but I think you got hurt."

"Where am I?"

"We are in the Skai River Valley, east of a hamlet called Nir, at the foot of Mount Thurai."

Gwen thought for a moment, then said, "None of those names seem familiar..."

"I'm not surprised; you're not from here."

"I'm from...Mineola...Is that far from here?"

"Yes and no, it's complicated."

"I don't understand..."

"Yeah, me neither sometimes...Luckily, I am a soldier. I don't need to understand, I am on a quest.

Gwen paused and tried to understand, but couldn't.

"So...you're here to take me home?"

"Yes."

"To Mineola."

"That's right."

"Which is and isn't far from here?"

The orange cat stopped chewing the bloody fur on his back to just stare at her for a moment. "I know you're frustrated, but I really am doing my best to explain. It's not like I was born in this world..."

"Wait!" Gwen interrupted. "You're from another world?"

"Well, yes, we both are."

"So we're in outer space?"

"Um...no."

"We're talking in circles..."

"Maybe, but I am answering in a straight line."

Gwen took a deep breath..."Okay, we are in a river valley, near a hamlet, at the foot of some mountain...in a world that neither of us was born in? My world is called Earth...that much I remember. What is this world called?"

Pumpkin took a long deep breath himself. "Okay, this world is still technically Earth, but another Earth, a different one. This is the Land of Dreams."

"My dreams?"

"No...all dreams."

Gwen licked her lips..."So, I'm dreaming?"

"Yes, and so am I. Right now, my body is in Mineola, just like yours. I'm actually lying at the foot of your bed."

"So, if I wake up I'll be back home?"

Pumpkin finished grooming himself and nodded.

Gwen pinched herself, hard, then harder until she had to close her eyes from the pain.

When she opened her eyes, the little orange cat was staring at her. He had climbed into the apple tree and his nose was inches from her own. "What are you doing?"

"I was trying to wake myself up."

"It doesn't work that way. Besides, you can't wake up. You're lost. That's why I am here, I can lead you home."

"I can't wake up?"

"No, all you do is sleep. Keep in mind, I'm a cat. If a cat thinks you sleep a lot, you sleep A LOT. Actually, I've never seen you awake."

"Because I got hurt?"

"I think so."

"And you came to lead me home, to Mineola, so I can wake up."

"YES! That's what I said..."

"No, it's..." Gwen stopped herself, and chuckled. For all his bravery and skill as a guide and warrior, she realized Pumpkin was still a young cat.

"Okay...So let's go."

"Why haven't you cleaned yourself up? Honestly, you look a mess."

"How am I supposed to clean myself up? I don't have any water, or soap, or clean clothes. I don't even have a brush. I just can't lick myself clean, you know."

"Just Dream yourself clean, and Dream up some new clothes while you're at it, and maybe something more formidable than that stick."

"What are you talking about?"

One room of Forever Home was unlike the others. It stank of the healing place I was taken to as a child, with beeping machines and hissing pumps, wires and tubes surrounding a large bed that sometimes moved and took odd shapes. In the bed slept a young human girl, who never rose from her slumber, not even to eat or stretch or scratch the sands.

The White Goddess spent much time there, and shed many tears, and I rubbed against her to give her comfort. She spoke to me, and unlike most humans I slowly began to understand her. She, you see, had spoken to many cats.

She spoke of a fabulous land, of colors and imagination, of adventure and dreams. But it could be dangerous too, with dark places, nightmares, and monsters. But it was a place where cats talked, and she had many friends among them. She said in her youth she had been a Queen in these lands of Dreams, but a betrayal had ended in the murder of her dream self, and she was never able to return there again.

She told me her life in the waking world grew rich after that. She spoke of love and a child. But then the White Goddess cried, and told me that her child was now lost and could not find her way home. She asked me to find her daughter, and lead her home, telling me her name and how she would know me. I began sleeping at the foot of the girl's bed, poor lost Guwenhwyar, beloved daughter of the White Goddess, and I swore to bring her home.

Pumpkin raised his tail and walked forward. "Oh, I see, you don't know. You are a Dreamer, Gwen, you have the power to change things, to make things. Since you're not from here you aren't completely bound by its rules."

"What kind of things?

"All kinds of things. If you can dream something you have the power to make it. It takes time and focus, with smaller, simpler things easier to create than complex ones."

"Okay...How?"

"Use your imagination, of course. Focus on something and push out, reach deep down, with your will."

"Okay..."

For a long time the little orange cat watched the Dreamer learn to unlock her powers. Gwen did small things at first, cleaning herself off, fixing the rips in her clothing, making a more sensible pair of shoes. She struggled and grunted at first, but soon learned how to control her abilities and was doing so effortlessly. By the time Gwen learned to wrap an apple in a leaf, which she changed to a red candy coating to make a candy apple, the cat became bored and hungry.

Pumpkin walked off to catch a few mice, wander down by the river to take a drink, and have a "private moment" in some dead leaves. He was gone for a little more than an hour. When he got back he was stunned.

Gwen was dressed in high soft leather boots, a tunic of blue cloth, and a half cloak of orange, tiger striped fur. She had one large gauntlet like a shield, tipped with three spiked claws. In her other hand she held what was the stick, but was now a spiked club of dark mahogany. The hood of the cape had two feline ears and a half mask of porcelain, painted in white, black, and orange stripes with actual whiskers.

"I wasn't gone long...I see you got the hang of it...Um, who are you supposed to be?"

"I'm Princess Tora, from the Cat Girls Cafe Manga, but the glove is from the Ninja Storm Lions anime series. It sort of fits the motif. Do you like it?"

The cat walked slowly around her, and tried to stay calm. Gwen was an incredibly powerful dreamer, a prodigy. He needed to get her home before someone figured that out.

"I do like it, but I think it is time I took you home. We have two possible paths. One is closer, but I am not sure we want to go that way."

"Why not?"

Pumpkin looked over his shoulder, back towards the gloomy forest they just escaped from. "We'd need to climb a stairway, inside of a tree, in the middle of the Enchanted Forest."

"Yeah, that's not a good idea. What's the other way?"

"We climb a winding stairway up Mount Thurai."

"Okay, lead on, Pumpkin the Brave! Princess Tora is ready to journey home."

I spent most of my time in the Dreamlands, traveling far and wide, following every rumor I could. But my quest met with failure time and time again. Months spent in the Dreamlands would end as I awoke, back in my body, back in Forever Home, at the foot of the sleeping girl, Gwen. My shame grew with each failure. The White Goddess never looked at me crossly, never treated me with anything but love, which made my failures all the more bitter.

Each night in the waking world I slept at the foot of Guwenhwyar, and each morning I awoke with my quest unresolved. Each visit to the Dreamlands was a season of questing, several months of adventures, explorations, danger, and disappointment. Each day in the Waking World was a few hours of eating and playing, comforting the White Goddess, sunning myself, and watching the birds in the back yard through a window. Then when my physical body grew tired, I returned to my place at the foot of the girl's bed, and resumed my search. On my eighty-fifth quest, just shy of the end of my fifth month at Forever Home, I heard the girl crying for help, chased by Zoogs.

Then began my quest to lead her home.

The cat and the human girl traveled for five days, slowly moving higher and higher up the slopes of Mount Thurai. On the third day Gwen made a bow and some arrows out of a pile of sticks and a few bones, weaving them into shape with her mind. She effortlessly took down a mountain hare, which she and Pumpkin shared, roasted over a fire that night. One would think that the girl had been visiting the Dreamlands for years, so comfortable she now seemed here.

As they traveled, Pumpkin asked her about the Cat Girl Café and the Ninja Lions, and Gwen launched into long monologues about each character and how they related to one another. It was a world as fantastic as the Dreamlands, with magical powers and secret destinies, forbidden love, and villainous adversaries.

Eventually Pumpkin said, "You know, for someone who doesn't remember much about their life, you do remember a lot about these books and shows."

Gwen sighed. "I know. When I think about myself, about my life, my head hurts and I just can't focus. But when I think about something that isn't real, like a cartoon, or a book, or a movie or TV show, well, that comes easy. I can tell you all about Princess Tora's mom and dad, but I can't remember anything about my own. I don't know why."

"Well, maybe it has something to do with why you are so good at dreaming. It doesn't matter, because here we are!"

Pumpkin turned the corner and saw, carved into the mountainside, a wide stairway leading up into the mountain. It went higher and higher, higher even than the mountain, vanishing into the clouds. The stairway didn't obey the laws of physics, but luckily those laws were only loosely enforced in this world. "Let's go."

But Gwen stood rigid. "Go where?"

"Up these stairs, of course."

"What stairs? It's a sheer cliff, reaching up into the clouds. I couldn't climb that if I was a mountain goat."

"What? You'd better pick me up."

Gwen picked up the orange cat, and the moment she touched him the stairway vanished, replaced by a cliffside. Pumpkin climbed onto her shoulder and looked out, but the stairs were gone. He jumped down, and they reappeared.

"You still can't see them?"

"What? Stairs? No, this is a cliff."

"Okay, pick me up again."

Once again Gwen picked up the orange cat, and once again the stairs vanished...

"Well...Shit."

Gwen's heart sank and she closed her eyes tightly, balling her fists in rage... and Pumpkin saw the stairs reappear. When she opened her eyes again, they were gone.

"Close your eyes again!"

The girl closed her eyes, and the stairs reappeared.

"Do you trust me, Gwen?"

"I trust you, Pumpkin, more than anyone else in this world."

The cat snorted. "Close your eyes and walk forward. When you feel a step, step up. Walk slowly, and whatever you do, don't open your eyes."

Gwen did so and her feet felt a solid stone step. She stepped up and gasped, as she felt herself climbing onto a staircase she knew wasn't there. She opened her eyes and fell backwards, just a few inches, and found herself facing the cliff.

Pumpkin dug his nails into her shoulder. "Okay, I have a plan, but you aren't going to like it."

For the next nine hours Gwen climbed stairs, with her eyes firmly closed. Pumpkin sat perched on her shoulders or in her arms, telling her where to step. Sometimes they rested, with Gwen resisting every urge to open her eyes. Pumpkin explained, "If you open your eyes these stairs will vanish, and we'll both die. We're almost there, just keep going."

Eventually Gwen felt a twisting and a turning, a dizziness. She grabbed the orange cat, only to feel him fading away. She tried to scream, but all that came out was a moan. She opened her eyes and was blinded by light...

It was mid-autumn when my quest finally ended, and the girl awoke. Her body was not like it was in the Dreamlands. There she was healthy, athletic, with full hair and a bright smile. Here, in the waking world, she was grayish and bald, with yellowing teeth and atrophied limbs. Her mother, the White Goddess, was at her side in seconds. Others rushed in, saying it was a miracle. Muttering things about tumors and cancer and brain death. But Gwen lived, and her mother never left her side. I wandered off, to give them time together. The room got crowded, with many strangers, and I wasn't able to return to it for three days.

I was brought back in then, along with a carved jack-o-lantern, because Gwen asked for both. With what little strength she had left she pet me, and thanked me, said she loved me. I purred, and pushed against her. I resisted the urge to sleep, because I didn't want to miss a moment with her. The White Goddess held one of Gwen's hands, and I pressed my head into the other, as she died.

But that was only the start of our adventures, for The White Goddess informed her that she still had one last choice. Time was short, but her mother taught her all she needed to know. When the time came for her to leave the waking world one final time, two paths opened before her, and Guwenhwyar, heir to the White Queen, chose.

In the floating city of Mitzivador, a young woman from the waking world arrived with one small traveling companion and some incredible claims. Her resemblance to their lost queen was uncanny, but in the Dreamlands such things could easily be faked. The young woman was then tested by the steward of Mitzivador, and when it was over he wept tears of joy. There was no doubt. She knew every secret answer to every riddle, knew the locations of the hidden royal treasures, and the words to the sacred lost oath laid down during the creation of Mitzivador by the White Queen herself.

It was proclaimed that this woman was Lady Tora Guwenhwyar, the daughter and heir to the White Queen. Her people rejoiced and crowned her royal sovereign. Her reign was long and prosperous, thanks in no small part to her advisor, champion, and general of her armies. This was Duke Myrmidon, a fearless orange tom, known only to his closest friends by his secret name, Pumpkin, the Brave.

The Cats of the Rue d'Auseil

by Neil Baker

It was late March and winter was newly retired, having exhaled its last flurry three days ago. Now the weather was in an undetermined state: damp yet bright, and the city was shot through with a crisp haze. Thin cloud cover masked the feeble spring sun and a chill breeze seemed to stalk pedestrians and cyclists no matter where they sought sanctuary. I did not mind the cold, myself. My vast and ancient overcoat, plus a well-earned layer of insulation beneath my skin, ensured that I never felt uncomfortable, and my unfashionably long hair kept my ears warm on even the briskest of mornings. It was on one particularly frigid morning that I would first encounter the cats.

🐾 🐾 🐾 🐾 🐾 🐾

It was early, a good hour before the streets would bustle with workers and school children, all in a rush to get to places they didn't want to be. By contrast, I dawdled, but not because I didn't want to reach my destination. Far from it. I was in love with the secluded area I had found by accident some two weeks ago, a spot I had returned to eight times since. No, I took my time because the change in odors as I traversed the sloping boulevard was intoxicating. The Boulevard du Pont Gris was a flat wedge of cobblestones bordered by bow-roofed buildings.

It commenced with a wide enough girth to accommodate multiple vehicles--this was where the enchanting smells of fresh bread and strong coffee were at their headiest--and then tapered to a narrow passageway before the river's edge, where the comforting morning aromas were quashed by a brackish fog that emanated from the still, ebony waters that lurked beneath the bridge. I loved all of the smells equally; the early ones awakened me, the latter ones inspired me.

As I had done for the previous nine days, I made my way down from the academy lodgings to the crooked gray bridge spanning a shunned length of the waterway that bisected the city, and searched for a new perch on the opposite bank from which I could paint my current state of mind. A student of the arts, I had recently switched from murky pastels to heavily layered watercolors, inspired by the steely landscapes of André Dauchez. However, Dauchez's expansive vistas were far removed from the intimate, closeted inspirations of my own work, and I had discovered that the unwelcoming waters of the river, threatened on both sides by sightless warehouses, were a perfect subject for my melancholy daubing. On my previous visits I had sat close to the bridge itself, on the eastern side. The bridge was very old, its dated stone worn away from years of frost and indifferent mosses that had effaced layer after crumbling layer. It was a good position to paint from; the reflections in the dark mirror were chained to the sun's daily wandering. On this day, however, I decided to sit on the west side of the stone arch. I had not previously explored this region of the southern bank, for it was merely a depot for abandoned construction materials and home for a motley group of miserable shrubs. A half-rotted rowboat had made its home on the muddy bank here, and I discovered that one of its benches was in serviceable condition. The wooden ribcage, its skeleton draped with sagging flaps of bitumen skin, became my new studio.

By mid-morning I had completed four preliminary sketches of the scene before me: a dark mass of water bordered by shattered facades and scrappy vegetation that gave the impression of wiry tourists scurrying through a somber town square. As I took out my watercolor tubes and palette, and clipped the pre-stretched paper to my drawing board, the first strains of low mewling reached my ears and I paused, then turned my head as the chill wind carried a second, rumbling sound. It was throaty and unmistakably feline, and I scoured the bank for the origin of this dire tune.

I would never have spotted the cat had it not shifted its seat on the steps behind me. Indeed, I hadn't noticed the steps at all upon arriving, such was their inconspicuous coloration of wet slate and jaundiced lichen. The gloomy chanteuse was a short-hair, her shade of gray equal to the steps, and she fixed me with one yellow eye, the other long gone judging by the old scar that ran from her ear to her nose. As she gazed upon me with sullen solemnity, she emitted one more, long wail, barely opening her mouth to do so.

Foolishly, I pursed my lips and attempted to coax her from her perch in the hope that she might sit beside me while I painted. It was a romantic notion, and one she utterly ignored. Chastised, I returned to my work, but the paint refused to move across the paper as it shouldnd my concentration was eroded by the presence behind me.

By early afternoon I had given up on producing anything of note, and packed away my supplies, intending to scale the Boulevard du Pont Gris to an exceptional patisserie at its summit, which, by now, would be selling its remaining wares at half price. Apparently, the gray cat behind me had not moved for the entire time I was there, and at some point had been joined by another: a bedraggled old tom missing most of one ear, his patchwork fur matted with mud and blood. The way those two creatures eyed my every move, scoring my exit with growls of disdain, was extraordinarily unnerving, and I traversed the old bridge quickly to the base of the boulevard. I looked back one last time as I started my ascent, but neither the cats, nor the steps, were anywhere to be seen.

The following day I returned to the desolate location as early as possible, foregoing my morning croissant and coffee. The previous night had been a restless one of pervasive dreams that awoke me on more than a half-dozen occasions, gasping, sweating, clutching at sheets. Their meanings were far from decipherable. but a common theme ran through them like a worm trail through an apple. In each of my sleeping visions I stood, knee-deep in gray mud, before the dark river. Tiny eddies swirled lugubriously around a central vortex that sucked down any detritus foolish enough to drift within reach. The water was impossibly black and yet it sparkled with the pinpoints of a thousand stars. Thick tendrils of the foul liquid rose from the surface and reached for me, waving like charmed snakes, and the center of the whirlpool glowed like back-lit amber as the one, yellow eye of the old gray cat formed, fixing me with an evil glare. It was always at the point that the water tendrils were about to caress my face that I would awake, breathless. Despite the heavy portent of these dreams, I had leapt from bed with a perverse eagerness to be back upon the ruined rowboat, inspired to paint what I had seen.

As I traversed the stone bridge I looked west, and could see my rotten studio still abandoned against the mud bank. Squinting, I could just make out the steps behind, and several mottled shapes suggested that the cats were still there, although greater in number. I drew closer, my breath heavy in the dawn chill, and counted nine cats: four on the lower step, five behind on the next step up, with the old cyclopean matriarch in the center. She looked at me as I approached, and I was somewhat unnerved to notice that none of the other cats did likewise. Instead, they fixed their almond eyes upon the black waters. It was then that I saw one of the cats, a robust, marmalade specimen, was bloodied and wheezing, and I spied an obscene gash on his left flank. I felt obliged to reach out, to help the poor animal, but the spotlight gaze of their leader made me think twice, and so I continued to my painting spot.

Once settled upon the rickety hull, I propped my drawing board against the bow and taped a fresh sheet of paper to it before soaking it with a sponge and waiting for the wind to air-dry it tight. This was my second-to-last sheet of cold press Arches paper, picked up on my last visit to the mill in Lorraine, and I feared I would not be able to afford another pack. The pressure was on to make these last paintings sellable, but I knew this would not be the case as I squeezed black, a selection of grays, a dingy ochre, and Prussian blue onto my tin palette. The only customers for these pieces would be manic-depressives, and yet I felt compelled to paint myself into an early grave. Dark slices of dream imagery flashed in my mind as I began to capture the utter despair of the waterway, and I added wash after wash of monochrome pigment to my rendition of the river and its hellish banks until the heavy paper was buckled and threatening to unravel.

After a short while, I saw a pair of shapes bobbing sullenly in the water, previously obscured by the deep shadows of the bridge. Both forms looked like short logs that had broken free of a mooring upriver, but as they rolled and buffeted against the muddy bank, I spotted the triangular shape of an ear here, the sad loop of a tail there, and I rushed over to hook them out of the river with a broken branch. Low wailing commenced behind me as I prodded the bedraggled corpses of two cats, each of them mangled, their tiny bodies hollowed and twisted. Horrified, I returned to the boat, glancing at the cats on the steps. They all watched me now, their eyes slitted, their teeth bared. Deep rumbling groans emanated from their furry throats, but they did not leave their perch. Had the animals raised their hackles or squatted lower as if to spring, then I might have been alarmed, but their posture seemed more resigned, making their unearthly noise resemble a song of mourning.

Were these two sad bodies former companions, or cats from a rival gang? A fight had most certainly taken place the previous night, judging by the wounds and exhaustion of the cats on the steps, and I wondered if I had stumbled upon a power-grab--a feline coup--in progress. I made a pair of shallow holes and was acutely aware of being watched as I buried the dead cats in the bank next to the bridge, marking their pathetic graves with smooth-rounded slivers of driftwood. Suddenly hungry, and with no concern for my painting equipment, I left that little patch of misery, eager to climb the boulevard and spend my last few centimes on smoked cheese and coffee. I did not intend to return until I could feel warmth in my fingertips.

My early lunch turned into an early supper and it was several hours later before I reluctantly decided to stumble down to the river to retrieve my paints and brushes. The sun was setting as I approached the thin end of the road and stepped onto the bridge, and I was relieved to see my equipment and painting were where I had abandoned them, on the boat now swathed in violet light. I was not surprised to see the nine cats still sitting on the steps, but I took a little joy in noticing several paw prints in the mud around the two graves I had formed. Evidently, they had inspected my handiwork.

"I trust you are satisfied with my efforts," I said to them, smiling, the effect of several glasses of sloe gin making this one-sided conversation even more comical to my ears.

A high-pitched, somewhat muffled, wail wiped the grin from my face and then creased my brow as I realized it was not coming from the group before me, but from further up the stairway. I then realized that the sound was not a feline mew, but an instrumental one. A viol. The spiraling strains of an unfamiliar dervish tune floated down, and I couldn't help but wonder if the audience on the steps cringed in their own particular feline fashion as the rosined bow was drawn feverishly across taut strings of catgut. I did not recognize the melody, nor could I discern its precise origin, for the steps ascended into a midnight corridor bordered by crooked houses, and I had no intention of scaling them so late in the day. A sign, half shrouded in ivy, declared this passageway to be the Rue d'Auseil, and that was all I needed to know.

I made my way to the boat and gathered up my livelihood, packing away the tubes and brushes and slinging the board with its melancholy artwork across my shoulders. The air felt ominous; it hung heavy with a brown smell: that electrical stench that results from faulty wiring or burnt hair. The acid in my stomach threatened to rise and I tasted Brie rinds, coffee, and berries in an unholy marriage at the back of my mouth. As I walked back toward the bridge,

I was aware that the awful music from above had grown wilder and louder as if the player had taken to the street, and the cats were all standing now, their lips drawn back, their whiskers stiff, the narrow steps forcing their backs to arch. As one they groaned from within, the tone of their sound echoing the notes of the viol. None of them watched me as I scrambled over the bridge. Instead they fixed their unearthly, glowing eyes upon the dank, dark waters of the river.

That night my dreams were as fantastical and troubling as one might expect after the events on the riverbank, no doubt exacerbated by cheese and gin.

I was the sole, reluctant observer of a macabre performance: a troupe of black cats walking on stage like humans, dancing in pairs to the strains of a tormented viol. The stage itself was a crudely cobbled-together platform of rotten wood, and around the base sloshed foul waters black as tar. Thick worms, formed from the hideous liquid, tested the edges of the stage, and the cats would dance over to them, flamboyantly lowering their partners so that they could grasp the tentacles between their short fangs and tear them apart, spraying purple gore into the air. Their staccato movements, combined with the strangeness of the scene, put me in mind of the popular phantasmagorias of the mad Monsieur Méliès, and I applauded wildly until my hands were red raw.

The following morning I awoke sore, perplexed, and eager to unravel the mystery of the cats. I assembled a sparse kit: my drawing board, the last sheet of cold press, my three favorite brushes, and two tubes of paint: the remainder of the lamp black and a new tube of permanent magenta. I needed neither palette nor water jar, for I intended to use the water directly from the puddles that resided in the hull of the boat.

Upon arriving on the south bank, I could see that I had missed a night of terrific violence. The cats were, predictably, sitting upon the lower two steps of the Rue d'Auseil, their one-eyed leader holding court, but their numbers had been thinned by three, and I soon found their missing companions in gnarled, bloody piles by the water's edge. The two graves I had hastily assembled the previous day had been disturbed, their contents strewn in matted pieces as if a feather pillow had been attacked by an unruly hound. A hundred paw prints and other strange depressions littered the bank, preserved in the chilly mud. I approached the cats and noted that they all appeared exhausted. Their eyes opened and closed sporadically, their pelts heaved--each breath a chore--and many of them bore new open wounds and gashes across their forelimbs and faces. They refused to acknowledge me, so I left them to their convalescences and made my way to the boat, somehow knowing that this would be my last time here and not just because I was on my last sheet of good paper.

As I settled in for a morning of preliminary dry brush sketching, I was struck by the stillness. There were no growls from the feline throng behind me, no musical conversations drifting down from up high, not even the low murmur of the busy boulevard. It was as if I were still sleeping, imagining the moment. A terrible unease washed over me, and I placed my brush on the shelf of the drawing board before pushing back to turn around. The cats could have been alabaster, for none of them had moved a muscle, although I was aware of a new angle to their heads. As one, they had turned slightly to fix their eyes upon one spot in the river, and I followed their gaze to a disturbingly dark area in the water, midway between the shorelines and several feet west of the bridge. Several minutes passed before I fully realized what it was about that spot that seemed unnatural, and I stood up in my broken-shell studio to inspect more closely the uncanny facade of the waterway.

As unmoving as the water was, it still reflected the world above it; the cracked visages of forgotten warehouses stared balefully from the river's surface and wisps of early cloud echoed in the black sheen. The area of the cats' attention, however, was remarkably different. The water at that spot not only refused to reflect its surroundings, but the very surface appeared to be concave and perfectly round, approximately three feet in diameter, a full two inches at its point of inflection.

I stooped and grabbed a handful of gravel from the side of the rowboat and flung it into the water. The tiny rocks rained scattershot upon the river, creating a multitude of tiny splashes, but the ones that landed in the dismal depression merely disappeared into the blackness without a ripple. I repeated this action several times, with similar results, and finally sat down on the bench, confused and aware of a dull ache that was forming behind my eyes. The phenomenon was otherworldly, of that I had no doubt, but to my mind, the strange events of the past few days seemed to justify its existence.

Surrendering to an uncharacteristic curiosity, I set my agenda. I was utterly convinced that this area, the cats and the river, were connected to my dreams, whether they were feeding my fantasies, or feeding from them, and I was determined to understand my role in this perverse performance. I vowed to remain for the rest of the day and paint the waters, to paint with the waters. Then, I would eat supper on the boulevard and return to the bridge in the evening in the hope of witnessing the cats' nightly brawl, perhaps even venture up the foreboding stone steps to the source of the music. All mysteries would be solved in one night.

I emptied both tubes of paint onto the stretched paper and began to work them into the heavy texture with my favorite sable.

By early evening I was nursing a beer and picking at a plate of ham and figs. Roseline's was a popular café, and I had been lucky to secure a small table under the bright red awning. Around me, the world continued to scurry and squawk. Knives scraped on cheap china, occasional bursts of laughter drowned the inoffensive music wafting from the bistro opposite, and vendors proclaimed their end-of-day sales in a mixture of shrill and booming yells. I felt that I should tell someone about the events by the bridge, but the more I chewed upon the thought, the more ludicrous it sounded. So I chewed upon the meat, and then ordered a flask of black coffee and a sausage roll, my victuals for the evening watch. My latest painting was propped against the café wall and I stared at it as I finished my meal. The circle in the center was impossibly black and surrounded by deep magenta swirls that seemed woven together, their dappled hues created by the numerous layers I had put down. My application had been so rough that I had broken down the fabric of the paper to the extent that tiny patches of white pulp now sprinkled the image in complex constellations, and I had chosen not to fix them. They seemed right. Michelle, the owner of Rosaline's, had taken one look and offered to buy it for sixty francs, and I had hastily agreed, eager to be rid of my dream manifestation.

My coat pockets stuffed with bank notes, food and drink in hand, I descended slowly away from the gay lights, toward the pitch maw of the river bend.

It was shortly after eleven, and thus far I had spied nothing out of the ordinary from my vantage point upon the apex of the bridge. I was thankful for a cloudless sky and full moon, for without Selene's silver glow, the tableau would be brutally dim. Picked out in the moonlight were the six unmoved cats, and the edges of the warehouses were trimmed like towering cliff-faces of chalk. The rowboat was faintly discernible further down the bank, and tiny ripples in the water glimmered and danced, except for those within the circumference of the unholy spot that lurked beneath me.

I swigged the last of the coffee, quite cold by this point, and entertained thoughts of retiring for the night. Placing the flask on the edge of the bridge wall, I began to button the thick lapel of my coat across my chest, and then froze, halted by the sound of music. It was a lethargic tune composed of mournful notes being dragged from a viol, and as I listened the melody took on a new form. It appeared to be based upon three chromatic notes, E, D-sharp, and D: notes that had no business coexisting in the same space. As the discomforting music played, the wind blew more viciously and below me the cats leaned into one another. They had started to mew, quietly at first, then their wails matched the sounds from the top of the stairs and I flattened my hair against my ears in a futile attempt to block the insidious composition.

The noise continued unabated for well over a minute, then the felines and musician ceased simultaneously and the ensuing quiet was dreadful. While the racket had split the night, the maligned river bend seemed alive; now all was tomb-like and I became aware of dampness on my skin, despite the dry air that whipped ruthlessly around me.

A loud splash broke the silence and my first thought was that the coffee flask had fallen from the stony crown of the bridge. However, the flask still stood in place, and I peered over the edge into the gloom. I saw nothing. A rippling growl from the cats drew my attention and I looked up in time to see them dismount from the steps and begin to stalk toward the water's edge, their heads low, their Trojan spear shoulder blades stabbing toward the sky.

A new sound emanated from the river and I looked on in horror as the dark liquid circle pulsated with an obscene, sucking resonance. The water around it remained perfectly still as the disk rose and fell, more membranous than fluid, as if the very waterway were breathing, and then it ballooned and continued to rise. I fell back, landing hard on the arched flagstones, as a colossal, shining mass rose up, fully ten feet higher than the bridge itself. Shuffling on my hands and rear to the east wall of the bridge, I pushed my back into the reassuringly solid stone work and drew myself up, at once astonished and mortified by the view. The 'liquid' had formed itself into a perfect column, its surface glassy and pristine. The curved onyx face was blacker than coal and seemed to absorb the moonlight. Even as I watched, tiny pinpricks of light started to form on it, coalescing into speckled bands of star fields. Other shapes materialized, and I recognized the formation of planets and moons, the tiny celestial facsimiles performing orbital rotations. I had visited the academy's makeshift observatory on a few occasions and possessed a basic understanding of the cosmos, but nothing before me bore any resemblance to our own solar system; it was wholly alien in scope and content.

I tore my eyes from the spectacle for a second and saw that the cats were at the river's edge, spaced a few inches apart and hissing in fury at the cylinder.

From high above the Rue d'Ausiel the music had begun once more, the same three notes played over and over, faster and faster, increasing in volume and frenzy. Turning back to the dark column with its hypnotic star field, I suddenly noticed an anomaly. Large sections of the stars and planetoids were winking on and off en masse and it took me a moment to realize that a large object was in fact, obscuring them. The black shape moved slowly around the surface of the shining column, its precise form undeterminable, as an amoeba might change shape beneath the lens of a microscope.

The cacophony of ill-fitting musical notes, deep mewling, and unearthly bubbling from the dank waters beneath me reached a ghastly crescendo and the column began to transform, unfurling like an aged scroll, until it stood in the middle of the river: a vast, square wall. I stepped back and forth, trying to ascertain its dimensionality from the front and back. It was perfectly flat on the side hidden from the bank of cats, and displayed the astral formations as clearly as any conventional map, but the face that projected toward the animals was blistering with bulbous shapes that swelled like grotesque tumors and sprouting flailing limbs. I took a few more steps down the south side of the bridge so that I could more clearly see what was happening and gripped the side, transfixed, as the full extent of the horror was revealed.

The shape that grew from the image of the star field was beginning to take on a recognizable form. It appeared as a bastardization of a familiar oceanic creature, a cuttlefish or nautilus, the bulk of its body made of intricate whorls. Beneath the frontal lid of its 'shell,' clusters of milky bumps rotated around similar, darker polyps, which might have been olfactory organs. An obscenely puckered maw resided in the center of these features, and the thick thatch of tendrils that grew, beard-like, from the base of the 'head' stretched out like lepers' stumps, curling back to the mouth as if tasting the very air they were invading. The scale of this monstrosity was hard to judge, but as it drew closer it was evident that the elongated bumps that now probed the muddy bank were just the tips of the creature's limbs. By this reckoning, it would have been as large as a cathedral.

The music grew impossibly louder and the lumpish feelers seemed to react adversely to it, twitching in the air as if each note were a shard of glass penetrating their dour, gray flesh. Then, as one, the cats attacked, pouncing upon the tentacles, sinking their claws into the slimy trunks and tearing mouthfuls of meat from them. The purple gore from my dreams sprayed once more, slicking the river with a ruddy sheen as the cats scratched and bit with increasing ferocity, their growls barely discernible above the terrible sound of ripping skin. The alien limbs whipped through the air, trying to shake their attackers, and one of the cats lost its grip. It fell headfirst into the mud and started to right itself, ready for another assault, but the thick tentacle slammed down, snapping the poor creature's back. I couldn't bear to hear the cat's wails, but they were soon cut short as curved spines, as long as a gentleman's cane, emerged from hidden slits in the appendage and diced the cat in a flurry of fur and meat.

The battle between the cats and the star beast was mercifully short, and I watched impotently from the safety of the bridge as the felines leapt from the rapidly retracting limbs and resumed their spots on the bank, moaning low as they licked their wounds. The giant creature was retreating now, its bulbous form deflating like a parachute as it grew distant among the stars, and then the entire tableau folded around to become a column once more before sinking back into the waters. The music stopped. The one-eyed leader of the cats sniffed the air and then, satisfied that the intruder was gone, led her soldiers back to the steps.

I gathered my things and prepared to leave with the understanding I had no place here, dreams be damned and unanswered. As I left I turned to lock eyes with the throng on the steps, knowing full well this would be the last time I voluntarily saw them. The honor I felt was immense when the old queen held my gaze, for I realized I was being allowed to leave, to contemplate all I had seen, by these mysterious shades, these Gods of the Ancients, the Guardians of the Rue d'Ausiel.

The Knowledge of the Lost Master

by Andi Newton

The air in Dhingri was still cold in April, and snow crunched underfoot as Stuart Tavish made his way up the mountain. When the wind gusted, rustling the leaves, Stuart could hear them whisper. *You don't belong here. You don't belong here. You don't belong...*

He patted the travel permit tucked into his breast pocket, reassuring himself that it was still there. So far no one had asked to see it, but if they did...

Stuart had spent the bulk of his father's fortune tracking down the Zhang-Ti Sutra. What was left went to securing the permit. Without it, Stuart would have been lucky to make it across the border from Nepal, much less reach this far into Tibet.

As it was, he had sold his own modest estate in Kensington to finance this trip, including hiring Sharpes and Denwoody to accompany him, men who claimed to have infiltrated Tibet before on similar expeditions. If it got him the Zhang-Ti Sutra, and the knowledge the manuscript contained, Stuart was happy to pay them whatever they wanted to serve as both guides and guards.

Up ahead, Sharpes ducked under a low-hanging branch that blocked the path. Stuart did the same. Denwoody, bringing up the rear and nearly a foot taller than either of them, had to push the branch aside. It snapped in his hands.

"I thought Tibet was all mountains," Denwoody said, doing his best to fix the branch.

"It is," Sharpes muttered. He didn't stop to wait for Denwoody, who gave up on the tree branch soon enough so he wouldn't be left behind.

"Then why's there trees here?" Denwoody asked. "I could understand if they were pine or cedar or something, but these are—" He paused to pluck a leaf out of his hair, turning it back and forth in the crisp sunlight to study it. "Maple? No, walnut."

"How should I know?" Sharpes grumbled. "Maybe birds brought them."

"The monks planted them." Stuart had learned the story when he was looking for the sutra. A khan named Yesugei gave the monks at the Tenzin monastery three saplings in exchange for letting his son study there. The trees weren't native to the region, but the khan's son showed the monks how to water them, and trim away weak branches, and to cover the ground around them with pulped paper when the snows came. And when the trees had grown large enough, the khan brought his army across the border and used the cover of the forest to attack the monastery unseen.

Stuart wasn't the first to come to the Tenzin monastery looking for the Zhang-Ti Sutra.

A woman's voice came to them through the trees. "Not long after that, the Panchen Lama closed our borders. Which makes me curious how you come to be here." Stuart hadn't spoken aloud, but it was as if the woman heard what he'd been thinking all the same.

Sharpes froze, his hand dropping to the pistol on his belt. Denwoody continued on a few more steps, enough to put himself between Stuart and whoever was ahead of them on the path. It took Stuart a minute to make out the woman on the other side of the tree line, her features shrouded by the shadows. A wooden cart stood on the path beside her, blocking their way. One long side, hinged, had been let down to form a sort of table or shelf. The woman had draped a silk cloth over poles mounted at the cart's corners, turning it into a makeshift stand like the ones Stuart had seen in Gyantse. The entire surface was covered with statues of cats, some carved of wood, others of rock, a few of an off-white material that Stuart suspected was bone. Each was no bigger than the palm of his hand.

On the other side of the cart, the trees gave way to the entrance to the Tenzin monastery.

Stuart could hear the echo of the forest in the woman's words. You don't belong here.

Sharpes wasn't fazed. "We've got permission. Archaeological expedition. Research purposes." Which was true enough, as far as it went. Lhasa had recently started allowing scientific expeditions into Tibet—it was how Stuart was able to bribe an official to give him a travel permit—and the monastery had been deserted since Yesugei's attack. It was reasonable to expect an expedition to come here.

Stuart reached for the permit, but the woman waved him away. "Makes no difference to me. But you'll want a guide."

Stuart had expected this, as well. He stepped around Denwoody, pulling a wad of srang from his pocket. "Of course. How much?" Stuart had learned this story, too, in his search for the sutra. The story of the cats that guided visitors through the maze of the monastery. And the stories of the people who became lost when they left their guides behind.

The lucky ones died of starvation, or thirst. But the others...

Stuart shuddered, not wanting to remember that part of the stories.

The woman cocked her head, considering, then took the bills from Stuart's hand. "This should do."

"Hey!" Stuart started to object, but Sharpes laid a restraining hand on his shoulder.

"Let it go," he said. "We're not getting past her otherwise."

Stuart scowled, but Sharpes was right. Besides, it was just money. The Zhang-Ti Sutra was worth so much more.

"Do you have a recommendation?" he asked, nodding at the statues.

The woman seemed surprised that he'd asked. She eyed him with renewed consideration, then plucked out one on the third row. "This one." The woman's smile as she handed it to Stuart sent shivers down his spine.

The statue was carved from a dark, whorled wood that Stuart had never seen before, the cat's muzzle, ears, and paws darker than its body. The wood was warm to the touch, and it seemed almost to vibrate, as if the cat was purring. Imagination, Stuart chided himself, then tucked the statue into his bag.

"Oh, no!" the woman corrected him, reaching for the bag before he could close it. "You want to have the shi-mi with you, where it can see the path. How else can it guide you?"

Stuart gave the woman an indulgent smile. Even for all he knew about the sutra and its history, there was only so much credence he gave to local superstitions. Still, he pulled the statue back out of the bag and held it, on his palm, out in front of him. "Of course. What was I thinking?"

The woman smiled. "You were thinking I'm a silly woman who believes in old superstitions. But that does not mean I am wrong."

Stuart blanched, and his bowels gave a watery twist.

"We done here?" Sharpes didn't wait for an answer before he skirted around the cart and made his way to the monastery entrance.

Stuart followed him, as did Denwoody. Just as they reached the opening where a wooden gate had long since rotted away, Denwoody stopped and turned back to the woman. "I gotta ask. You get a lot of customers out here?"

The woman's smile disappeared. "More than I should," she told him. "More than I should."

The Tenzin monastery had originally been a cave, the site where a Buddhist master spent the entirety of his life in meditation. The cave walls had long since been carved into smooth lines and precise angles, the mountain reshaped into a labyrinthine complex on a broad plateau. Brass prayer wheels hung from silk ropes every few feet along the exterior wall of the main temple, and Stuart marveled that they hadn't rotted away. No one had been at Tenzin to repair the ropes for centuries. He ran the fingers of his free hand over the carved symbols on the nearest wheel, making it spin, and the cat statue vibrated in unison with it.

Like the wind and the woman's voice, an unspoken undertone accompanied the sound. *You don't belong here, you don't belong here, leave now, you don't belong...*

"We need to keep moving," Sharpes said. "The daylight won't last forever."

Looking at the pristine buildings around them, seemingly impervious to time, Stuart wasn't so sure. Still, he backed away from the prayer wheels and into the temple's interior.

The temple opened into a single, large room, perfectly square and lined on all sides by racks of small oil-burning lamps, cold and unlit. The room would have been swallowed by darkness a few feet from the door if not for curved windows cut into the stone near the ceiling. Stuart marveled at the engineering that allowed sunlight in while still keeping the cold and snow out. Were they lined with glass? It didn't seem like it, and yet Stuart could think of no other explanation.

Unlike other monasteries Stuart had visited, the walls here were plain, devoid of paint or gilding. The only decoration other than the windows and oil lamps were arched doorways that led away from the room in a layout that had no correlation to the temple's actual architecture. More than half of them should have taken Stuart and his companions back outside, but the temple's exterior walls had been unbroken. Each passage stretched into darkness, whatever it led to lost in shadows.

"Any idea which way we need to go?" Sharpes had joined Stuart in the room while Denwoody stayed by the entrance. Ever the dutiful guards, their attention divided evenly between the world outside and anything that might approach them from the archways.

Stuart had been unable to find a map for the monastery. If the stories were to be believed, it would have done him little good even if he had. Tenzin didn't bend itself to the laws of the physical world. It answered to a much older, much different directive.

Which was why the monks had used cats as their guides.

Stuart walked to the center of the room and turned in a slow circle, holding the cat statue out so it could see each archway. As he did, he whispered to it, "Ma Jhang-Tiko vidhya Sojdiachu, prajnaparamitako sutra. Tapaile malai sikaunuhuncha?"

I seek the knowledge of Zhang-Ti, the wisdom of the sutra. Will you guide me?

The statue remained still, a frozen hunk of wood, for the first turn, and the second. On the third pass, its tail twitched as it approached an archway on the far wall. Stuart stopped and took a step toward the arch. The cat unwrapped its tail from around its feet and held it in a curved hook behind it. This time, Stuart couldn't just feel the statue vibrate; he could hear it purr.

He nodded at Sharpes and Denwoody, fighting to hold back an excited grin. "I believe we need to go this way, gentlemen."

Pulling out his electric torch, Stuart ducked into the passage, leaving the other two men scrambling not to be left behind.

If the main room of the monastery was plain, the passageways leading from it were barren. The further they walked from the entrance, the more rough-hewn and pitted the walls became, without even the red glass of the oil lamps to break up the grey. The darkness became oppressive, almost pushing back at the light from their electric torches, and Stuart found himself longing for the sun.

More arches opened along the passage every ten or fifteen feet. Stuart paused at each one to hold the statue out to it. At some, the cat purred and twitched its tail. At others, it merely sat there, as impassive as the stone around them. Stuart passed by the latter, only taking the passages that the cat reacted to.

After a while, Denwoody offered to take the statue and lead the way. Stuart declined. But when he tripped and nearly sent both his electric torch and the cat statue clattering down the passageway, Sharpes called a halt.

Stuart waved him off. "I'm alright. I don't need a break."

"We've been walking for hours," Sharpes countered.

"And I could walk for hours more!"

Sharpes moved in front of him, blocking the way. "This manuscript of yours has been hidden for over a thousand years. Another half hour won't make a difference."

Stuart started to argue—they were close, so much closer than he'd ever been—but Denwoody laid a massive hand on his shoulder and pushed him gently to the floor. The cat statue, as if sensing it wouldn't be needed for a while, curled up in Stuart's palm, one paw over its eyes.

"You hungry?" Denwoody asked, sinking down next to him. He pulled a sandwich out of his bag and began to unwrap it. Stuart tried to remember when the big man could have bought it.

Still, the smell of cheese and meat set his stomach rumbling. "Yes, please," he said, reaching out for the sandwich.

Denwoody tore off a corner and handed it to him. Without waiting for a thank you, Denwoody took a big bite of sandwich and began to chew with enthusiasm.

Sharpes sighed and shook his head.

"What?" Denwoody asked, crumbs spraying from his mouth. "I only got one."

"It's fine," Stuart said, risking a tentative bite of the sandwich. It was good, goat meat and sharp cheese and thick, dense bread.

Five sharp pinpricks dug into his forearm. Stuart looked down. The cat statue had uncurled and was staring up at him, the claws of its left paw pressed into his skin.

Startled, Stuart dropped the sandwich. The cat leapt onto the floor and devoured the meat and cheese. It ignored the bread. Then it turned to Denwoody, eyeing his share of the sandwich.

"Forget it, kitty," Denwoody said.

Stuart felt as much as heard the low growl coming from the cat. Denwoody, unfazed, took another bite, chewing loudly in the cat's direction. The cat swatted at his leg, then stalked back to Stuart and curled up in his lap, slowly turning back into wood.

Sharpes ignored all of this, his attention focused on something by the wall a little way back the way they'd come. He crouched down, shining his flashlight on whatever it was. Suddenly, he stood up. "Break's over. Let's move."

"You find something?" Denwoody asked.

For an answer, Sharpes held up a stick, a little over a foot long and twice as thick as his thumb. The wood was bleached white, its bark stripped away. Without a word, Denwoody wrapped up what was left of his sandwich, shoved it in his bag, and got to his feet.

"Come on." Denwoody held out a hand to Stuart.

Stuart looked back and forth between the two men. "I don't understand. What's so urgent about a stick? I admit it's odd to find it here, but—"

Sharpes stepped aside, shining his electric torch on what Stuart had tripped over: a pile of bones, clustered at the edge of the passageway. On top of them sat a human skull.

The statue had grown larger during their break. When Stuart bought it from the woman, it easily fit in his palm. Now it stretched from his fingertips to his wrist, and its tail could curl around his forearm.

The sound of claws on stone, scrabbling through the shadows, had chased them through the monastery since they left the passageway with the bones. Before, Stuart had stopped at each opening along the hall, giving the cat statue plenty of time to decide which way they should go. Now, he barely slowed his steps, afraid of giving whatever was behind them a chance to catch up.

And then he stepped through an archway into a long hall that had no openings on either side.

The walls here, like those in the first room, were chiseled smooth, polished enough that Stuart could almost make out his own reflection. But the monks of Tenzin had done more than simply polish the stone. They had carved it, populating it with cats of all breeds and sizes. At first just one or two, no bigger than a housecat, then more the further down the passage they went, some as large as a Bengal tiger. The cats clambered and crawled over one another, sleeping or playing or twining in and around one another.

The statue fell from Stuart's outstretched hand as he reached out to touch one of them. It looked—and felt—not so much like a carving, but as if a cat had leaned against the wall and the stone had grown over it. When his fingers brushed its side, he could hear it growl.

You do not belong here, you do not belong here, you do not belong...

Stuart jumped back, yanking his fingers from the wall as if he'd been burned.

"Everything okay?" Sharpes asked.

"What?" Stuart looked at his fingers, then at the cat carved into the wall. He touched it again, tentatively, but it was just stone. "Yes, I just..." He looked toward the far end of the hall. "I think it's this way."

The passage emptied into a room that dwarfed the one at the monastery's entrance. The carved tableau continued on the back and side walls, the cats growing larger and more numerous. Interspersed throughout, Stuart could see faces, human faces, screaming in terror. Hands reached out, desperate to grab onto something, *someone*, and pull themselves free of the stone.

But it was the far wall that stole Stuart's attention. Here, for the first time, was color. Red enamel. Gold leaf. It covered everything, the walls, the bolster at the top of the ceiling, even the filigree that covered the floor-to-ceiling shelves cut into the stone. On the shelves, long, rectangular boxes were wrapped carefully in embroidered silk.

And in front of it all, a rough stone plinth with a plain wooden box upon it. The Zhang-Ti Sutra. The wisdom of the lost master.

Stuart ran to it. Sharpes and Denwoody came up behind him much more slowly, eyeing the walls and shadowed corners warily.

"This is it!" Stuart breathed. "The Zhang-Ti Sutra! I've found it. I've found it at last!" He slid the top off the box, revealing the ornately scripted pages inside. He picked one up, running his fingers over the calligraphy. Mouthing the words softly to himself, he could feel the power within it. He couldn't understand it, not fully, but he would, in time. He would take the sutra back to England to study, and he would do what his father and so many before him had failed to do—reclaim the power of the lost master!

A low hiss sounded behind him, followed by a strange chittering noise.

Stuart looked over his shoulder. The cat hunkered on the floor, no longer a statue, and glared at him.

"Oh, of course!" He dropped the page and turned around. Sharpes and Denwoody, on either side of him, did the same, hands on their pistols. Stuart waved the weapons away. "No, no, it's my fault. I forgot to thank our guide." Grinning, he took a step toward the cat, hand stretched out to pet it.

The cat hissed again. All around them, the chittering noise echoed from the walls.

Stuart's steps faltered. It occurred to him that he hadn't asked the woman what to call the cat. He hadn't thought he'd need to. "Cat?"

The cat lashed its tail back and forth. The chittering noise grew louder, accompanied now by the scratch of claws on stone as carved cats pulled themselves free of the walls.

This is not for you, you do not belong, this is not for you, you DO NOT BELONG!

Sharpes and Denwoody backed up until they were shoulder to shoulder with Stuart. Both men had guns drawn.

"I—" Stuart stammered, cowering behind them. He didn't know how to propitiate the cat. What did it want? "I—I'm sorry. T-t-truly I am. But I'm very grateful to you for guiding me here."

The cat took a step forward, crouched as if preparing to pounce on a bird.

The tip of its tail twitched, once, twice, then was still. The cats from the walls followed suit, one after another, closing in.

Stuart jumped as a shot rang out. Sharpes' bullet ricocheted off the head of what looked like a puma, not even scratching the stone, and buried itself in one of the silk-wrapped boxes on the shelves behind them. Denwoody maneuvered Stuart so he was between him and Sharpes, then opened fire as well.

With no weapon of his own, Stuart hunkered down between Sharpes and Denwoody. The two men fired shot after shot, turning first one way then the next as they tried to keep the predators at bay, until finally the loud reports gave way to the anemic click of a hammer coming down on an empty chamber.

The cats, unscathed, pounced as one, the eerie chittering giving way to a yowl of anger. They downed Denwoody first, what could only be a sabre-toothed tiger swatting him across the room with one massive paw. The wall opened up where Denwoody hit and stone paws pulled him inside.

"Denwoody!" Sharpes flipped his pistol around, knocking cats aside as he struggled to reach the wall before it closed up again. He made it three steps before another cat, smaller this time, jumped on his back and brought him to the floor.

The cats closed in over him, and he disappeared under a swell of stone.

Alone now, Stuart flailed about blindly with his electric torch. He backed up until he hit the stone plinth that held the sutra of Zhang-Ti. Without thinking, he grabbed the box and hurled it at the cats, hoping to distract them long enough to make a break for the door.

The cats, now an almost serpentine mass, caught the box and ferried it back to the plinth, setting it carefully on the stone.

Then they grabbed Stuart and dragged him into the tableau, his screams echoing on the walls around them.

The sun had just started to dip below the trees when the cat strolled out of the monastery. It hadn't taken him as long to return as it had taken to guide the men to the sutra—but then, he wasn't constrained to the same paths as humans.

Sundha leaned against the cart, waiting for him. She had already taken down the silk covering and re-latched the side. The cat knew this was her name, even if none of the men had asked her. After all, she had made him. How could he not know who she was?

"There you are!" Sundha said. "I was beginning to think you'd be gone all night."

The cat chirruped and rubbed against her legs. Sundha picked him up and scratched him along the side of his cheek, where he liked it best. He stretched his head back and purred.

"You have grown larger since this morning," Sundha said, running her nails under the cat's chin. "I see they fed you well."

He meowed in reply.

"Goat and cheese?" Sundha exclaimed. "That does sound good! A pity you could not get the rest of it. But I am sure you ate enough else to satisfy you, and the other cats will enjoy the treat."

"Are you ready to go?" Sundha asked. "You can ride in the cart, if you like, but you will need to change back first."

The cat wriggled until Sundha let him down, pacing alongside the cart beside her.

Sundha shrugged. "Suit yourself. But it is a long walk, and you are still a small cat."

As if in answer, the cat walked a few feet down the path, then turned around and looked back at her.

Sundha laughed and took hold of the cart's handles. She strained against the cart, struggling to get the wheels turning in the snow-slushed mud. But they did turn, eventually, and she pushed the cart down the path to the village at the foot of the mountain.

"I suppose they tried to take the sutra," Sundha commented when she caught up to the cat. He kept pace beside her, only pausing occasionally to flick snow from his paws.

The cat growled, flicking its tail angrily.

"Yes, well, they usually do," Sundha agreed. "But you have kept it safe for now."

They walked down the path together, side by side, Sundha asking questions or making comments and the cat meowing in reply. Behind them, stones rose up in front of the monastery gate, blocking the way from those who did not belong.

The Ruins of an Endless City

by Lee Clark Zumpe

1.

Samhain, a black Burmese cat with a low tolerance for the tumult of crowded city streets, perched on a fourth-story windowsill in an apartment building overlooking a busy marketplace. The open-air emporium of commerce featured all manner of vendors peddling fruits and vegetables, newspapers and magazines, bratwurst and boiled cabbage, as well as various items salvaged from the lingering devastation.

Though the war had ended seven years earlier, the mottled skeletons of many ravaged buildings still stood. Heaps of bricks and stones had yet to be carted off for recycling. Pillars of smoke still clambered skyward as dwellers sought to expedite waste removal by burning unwanted possessions.

Samhain had witnessed much misery during the course of his protracted lifespan. Nothing he had seen could have prepared him for the scope of cruelty and violence that shattered Europe. Nothing he had experienced could have fortified him against the grief and the suffering propagated by Adolf Hitler and his Nationalsozialist adherents.

From Samhain's perspective, the world had been irreversibly upended. Civilization had begun a downward spiral. This revelation should have caused the cat considerable concern, and yet—Samhain, for the first time in his long life, felt detached and indifferent.

Though the cat would not openly admit it, his uncharacteristic apathy sprang from the personal loss he had endured. Once an advocate of humanity, now he felt little compassion for them.

Humans had always been a narcissistic and self-important lot. Throughout the tumultuous history of this inventive and irresponsible species, its most malicious representatives had traditionally been curtailed in their ability to do harm by the benevolent majority.

Samhain, licking his forepaws, gazed down upon the thronging shoppers and marveled at their obliviousness. Even though burdened by the memory of recent wartime barbarity, they seemed blissfully unaware of their impending extinction. They lacked the perception to intuit the inherent malignancy of their society. Their shortage of insight left them blind to a new upwelling of malevolence in their midst.

The cat had detected ripples of danger undulating through the divided city. Rumors had begun circulating among indigenous cats which Samhain could no longer ignore. Despite his genuine lack of interest, Samhain had resigned himself to the task of investigating the threat.

2.

Delbert Payne sat in a stylish French Art Deco leather club chair sipping coffee and ignoring the morning headlines. The chair of Folklore and Mythology at William Whitley College and a specialist in the field of European esoteric movements, Payne wondered what his students back in Tahlequah, North Carolina, would think of his unexpected summer sojourn abroad.

Some of the students, he reckoned, had lost loved ones here not so long ago—fathers, uncles, older brothers, and other friends and family members had been called upon to subdue Hitler's totalitarian regime. Outside, the residue of that war was omnipresent, from the rubbish mountains on the fringes of the city to the rubble dust that burned one's eyes whenever the wind stirred.

"Professor Payne, I presume?" Gerhard Günther stood in the lobby of the recently resurrected Hotel Kempinski on Kurfürstendamm in the American sector of West Berlin. He offered a warm smile and an outstretched hand to the visiting scholar. "Welcome to West Berlin. I trust your accommodations are satisfactory?"

Günther—a tall and hefty gentleman with fair complexion, blue eyes, and auburn hair—presented a somewhat imposing personage. He seemed conspicuously uncomfortable in this milieu, his gaze shifting from side to side anxiously as he scanned the reception area. His pallid features wore an expression of muffled apprehension.

"Much more than satisfactory, I assure you." Payne, used to his modest apartment located just off campus in Tahlequah, found himself lodging in a five-star luxury suite. "Honestly, it's a beautiful room, but totally unnecessary. If it is costing your school too much, I would be happy with something less sophisticated."

"Nonsense," Günther laughed. Unlike most of the Berliners Payne had met since his arrival the previous day, he spoke English without a hint of an accent. "You may as well enjoy the amenities while you are here. We are grateful you accepted our invitation. You come highly recommended by Professor Willard Jorgenson at Miskatonic University."

Payne nodded graciously, though it seemed to him that he was the one who should be thankful. He had been summoned to participate in the recovery and assessment of a 13th century bestiary and related artifacts. He considered the once-in-a-lifetime opportunity an honor.

"Willard sends his regards. I stopped by to see him in Arkham before crossing the Atlantic." Payne and Jorgenson had worked together on several projects over the last 20 years. Most recently, the pair had partnered to produce a new, concise annotated edition of Jacques Kerver's controversial 10-volume 1717 *Dieux de la lune*. "He would have jumped at the chance to work with the Free University this summer, but health matters are keeping him from traveling these days."

"Then I hope you will pass along my wishes for a swift recovery." Günther glanced at his wristwatch, his muted uneasiness again on display. "I do not mean to hurry you, but we should probably be on our way. Since we last corresponded, new discoveries have been made at the Kreuzbergkirche. The excavation has yielded some surprising materials. I am eager to share them with you."

"By all means, lead the way."

3.

When the sun reached its zenith above the dull gray skies, and the asphalt-colored city buzzed with the clamor of midday traffic, Samhain crept along rooftops tracing a winding route toward Alexandrinenstrasse. On that West Berlin street rested the tumbledown remains of the Kreuzbergkirche, a monastery church for a Franciscan house founded in 1270 and rebuilt or renovated repeatedly over the span of centuries. The building had been destroyed in February 1945, laid to waste during the Allied bombing of the city.

Even prior to its destruction, the Kreuzbergkirche had fallen into disrepair. Abandoned and neglected since the turn of the century, the church served only vagrants and itinerant laborers as temporary shelter. Tabloids ran lurid tales of secret meetings and cryptic cults congregating in the brick basilica in the 1920s and 1930s, often using the unsubstantiated rumors to demonize some ostracized ethnic group. During the years of Hitler's reign, those who sought refuge in the building's shadowy alcoves often disappeared inexplicably.

Samhain, traipsing through the weedy wayside along the moss-covered stones of an ancient wall, understood the history of that place better than any living Berliner. His extraordinary longevity let him observe the rise and fall of the Kreuzbergkirche.

He had seen it in its halcyon days, when it served as a center of veneration and learning. He had watched it deteriorate, too, as the eldest clergy members of its final days died off and its parishioners moved to other, grander houses of worship in the city. Lastly, the black Burmese cat had witnessed the curious sect who gradually took over custodianship of the ancient structure—and of the cache of relics secreted in a subterranean chamber beneath it.

Approaching the rubble-strewn field of the cloister, Samhain stopped to quench his thirst in a trench basin that had once served the lavatorium. He slipped through a crevice in one of the few walls still standing, entering the chapel and continuing his leisurely survey until he reached the area where the sacristy once stood. The room for keeping vestments concealed a staircase down into the darkness. The passageway led to the buried relics.

As expected, Samhain found clear signs that the chamber had been plundered, its contents appropriated.

"Fools," Samhain muttered into the shadows as he journeyed down the stairs.

The place reeked of people. That they had taken care to preserve the interior of the room suggested to the cat that this had not been done by opportunists seeking to profit from pillaged antiques. Their thoughtfulness and their restraint displayed a level of intellectual curiosity. Still, it made little difference: The habitual inquisitiveness of their species coupled with their excessive pride usually set in motion terrible circumstances.

"*Hubris extinguished the hominid*," the cat said, repeating a common adage amongst his kith and kin.

Something moved unexpectedly in the gloom.

Samhain froze in his tracks, recalibrating his eyes and ears. The fur along his spine stood on end and he felt his claws stretching as they readied for an attack.

"Is that you, Samhain?" The voice, though thin and faint, was a familiar one. An Abyssinian cat shambled out of a distant corner, its reddish-brown fur matted with blood. "I hoped you would come. I was not even sure you were still in the city. I didn't know if you survived the war."

"Archimedes?" Samhain darted across the chamber to meet his old friend. "What happened to you? Did the humans do this?"

"No, no," the cat gasped as he collapsed in a soft heap on the cold floor. "My injuries come from a battle not fought on this world. I suppose the humans are to blame, indirectly—but they do not realize what they have done."

"Then it is true," Samhain hissed. "They unearthed the chamber."

"It was only a matter of time. For centuries, the monks guarded the reliquary, kept it hidden away. But humans have short memories. The tales they pass from generation to generation change with each telling until the truth is lost." Archimedes felt an unearthly breeze sweep through the chamber. He wondered if his old friend sensed it, too. He wondered if Samhain could smell the distant mounds of corpses littering the ruins of an endless city thinly veiled by a tapestry of shadow. "My wounds will not heal," the old cat confessed. "My lives are spent. I hope death claims me on this side of the curtain. I do not wish to pass in the Abode of Mist."

"I will stay with you, if you wish," Samhain said. "Archimedes, have they taken everything?"

"Everything," Archimedes said. "The book, the scrolls—even the Tatzelwurm."

"That is unfortunate." Samhain felt a twinge of compassion—the kind of consideration he had not experienced in years. His sympathy for humanity had all but evaporated one harrowing night on Ettersberg hill near Weimar. "They will succumb to its call. Even long dead, the Tatzelwurm's ability to influence them is intense."

"It already infects their dreams with visions of the endless city." Archimedes took slow, shallow breaths. His eyes turned away from his old friend and focused on some invisible horizon. "One by one, they will be drawn here to die."

4.

"This is impossible." Delbert Payne gazed at the contents of the wooden box in disbelief. "This simply cannot be."

"And yet, here it is." Gerhard Günther quickly closed the lid of the box, returning the mummified specimen to its shaded seclusion. "Here we have not only an extraordinary early bestiary—but also biological proof that a creature of folklore truly existed."

Dazed and aghast, Payne took two steps back from the desk upon which his host had revealed the uncanny carcass. His knee-jerk skepticism began issuing a litany of explanations, from extraordinary genetic deformity to elaborate hoax perpetrated by some medieval taxidermist. Even as he sought to disbelieve his own eyes, some other part of his brain less influenced by logic and lucidity reminded him of things he had seen amidst the preserved collections of anatomical specimens at William Whitley College and in the restricted sections of the Miskatonic University library.

The general public had no inkling that for more than a century, scientists and academicians had quietly confiscated and crated up a whole host of inexplicable aberrations and misshapen anomalies—some of which clearly originated outside the terrestrial network.

"You say the illustration in the book matches the...*thing*...in the box?" Payne struggled to maintain his doubt. Seeing the creature's ossified limbs and desiccated skullcap left him dizzy with intuitive repugnance. Its abnormally drawn-out abdomen, snake-like and measuring at least four feet from its forepaws to its hind end, was layered with delicate scales that retained their lustrous sheen and glistened beneath the fluorescent lumiline lamps of the Free University research room. The spiteful expression frozen in its feline face evoked primal fear. "Show me the book," Payne insisted. "Show me the illustration."

"Yes, yes, of course," Günther said. He summoned one of his colleagues and asked her to retrieve the centuries-old tome from the archive. She slipped behind a heavy curtain in the back of the room and reappeared a few moments later carrying the book, her arms outstretched as if to keep it at a distance. "Vielen Dank," Günther said softly. "This is Jutta Wülker. She is an old friend and a knowledgeable scholar."

Even before he had finished making the introduction, Wülker had retreated back to her desk without uttering a sound. In that fleeting instant, Payne discerned a nervousness about her that matched Günther's own conspicuously uncomfortable demeanor. More than fatigue, Payne likened it to some mild form of manic hysteria, as if both suffered from an excessive amount of irritable energy.

"She is tired," Günther said, feeling as though an explanation was needed to account for her behavior. "We are all exhausted. Between completing our excavation at the Kreuzbergkirche and preparing for your arrival, the excitement of this discovery had kept us terribly busy. None of us have had a decent night's sleep in a week or more."

Though Payne heard Günther's justification, it barely registered in his consciousness.

His attention had turned to the recovered manuscript which had dislodged him from his comfortable life in a cozy college town nestled amidst the highlands of North Carolina. The book—magnificently titled *Das Buch der unnatürlichen Bestien*—had lured him across an ocean, through the scarred landscape of Western Europe, and over a thoroughfare meandering perilously through Soviet-controlled territory past Russian checkpoints manned by soldiers wearing the intimidating hammer-and-sickle insignia and clutching even more menacing Degtyaryov machine guns.

The rush of exhilaration Payne felt as his fingers touched the book made him forget how far he was from home, how nerve-wracking his journey had been, and, for the moment, that kernel of nascent anxiety that had gripped everyone who had come into contact with the artifacts. With meticulous tenderness, he opened the book and began examining its contents.

"This far exceeds my expectations," Payne admitted. "So much detail. Such beautiful illuminated pages. So many fascinating entries." The researchers believed the book dated back to the 13th century, characterizing it as either a companion piece to or rival of Konrad von Megenberg's *Das Buch der Natur.* "Lavish illustrations. Poetic inscriptions."

"Here," Günther pointed to a bookmark he had placed in the tome. "The entry on the Tatzelwurm."

Payne quickly flipped through the pages to arrive at the desired entry. As promised, the sketch had clearly been inspired by the organic remains found at the excavation site. The accompanying description provided commonly repeated traits of the mythical creature. It described attributes such as its predisposition for attacking livestock, its highly poisonous bite, and its unusual physical characteristics including short forelegs, a wide snake-like body, and a cat-like face.

Payne took particular interest in some additional details he had never encountered in any other bestiary.

According to *Das Buch der unnatürlichen Bestien,* the Tatzelwurm dwells in the *nilfvegir,* the "mist ways" of Niflheimr. The entry claimed that it uses these pathways to cross the barrier between the world of the dead and the world of the living, from which it seeks to lure unenlightened souls to their doom. The ill-fated victims were said to dwell for an eternity "amongst the sepulchered dead within the rubble of an endless city in a vanquished realm of darkness and mist."

The text added that those "too enlightened" to heed its call would slowly descend into madness.

The ensuing page featured an illustration depicting a sect of monks placing the slain Tatzelwurm in a vault. The passage offered a stern warning to any who would disturb the burial chamber.

"What do you make of this?" Payne's inquiry materialized almost involuntarily. He uttered it with hesitation and uneasiness, unbefitting a scholar of his reputation. He had fallen victim to the tension afflicting his host. "Herr Doktor, have you ever run across anything like this in your studies?"

The lack of an immediate response broke the hypnotic spell the tome had placed upon Payne, forcing him to divert his attention. He suddenly realized that Gerhard Günther no longer stood at his side. The research room had emptied, leaving Payne alone with the both the book and the grisly remains of the Tatzelwurm.

The rush of exhilaration he experienced earlier when he first set eyes upon *Das Buch der unnatürlichen Bestien* now seemed insignificant compared to the overwhelming foreboding gripping him. He quickly made his way across the room to the door.

Much to his relief, he found he had not been abandoned after all. Just outside in the corridor, both Günther and his colleague Jutta Wülker faced two uniformed officials. Günther was calmly relating details of their recent excavation while the Bundesgrenzschutz took notes. Wülker nodded in agreement as she wept into a kerchief.

Payne stood in the doorway for what seemed like an eternity, disinclined to join the impromptu interrogation in the hallway and unwilling to spend another instant alone with the Tatzelwurm. He chided himself for allowing his emotions to run wild. He even found himself making excuses for his rejection of logic, blaming it on his stressful journey and fatigue.

There was no denying it, though; he had been compromised by fear. It was an indistinct and unfounded fear, but it was powerful enough to sap him of his reason. It sprang from a primal cerebral alcove and generated a response akin to utter madness.

When the questioning finally ended, Wülker rushed down the hallway without even looking back at the research room. Günther did not have the luxury of flight.

"You must return to the Hotel Kempinski," he said, his voice sullen. "I am afraid that there will be an inquiry. Our findings will likely be confiscated for the time being."

"What happened?"

"Three days ago, one of the students who worked with us at the excavation site was found dead." Günther's sorrow seemed compounded by a sense of culpability. "He committed suicide."

"That's not your fault," Payne said, immediately regretting his impulsive response. "I don't see why that has anything to do with your research."

"This morning, another student who worked with us shot two acquaintances before turning the gun on himself," Günther said. "It was Wülker's son."

On the short ride back to the hotel, Payne struggled to contain his growing fear. He wondered how long it would be before he would descend into madness.

5.

Shortly after nightfall, Samhain visited one of his favorite cafés on Kurfürstendamm. He could always find a generous kitchen worker willing to share some scraps from the evening's meals. Tonight's menu consisted of half a bowl of cold Gaisburger Marsch (a beef stew), Maultaschen, and Spätzle—all Swabian dishes served to approving diners serenaded by a roving zither-player. The musician's tunes drifted into the alleyway as Samhain cleaned the plates he had been offered. The cat loathed begging for handouts, but it had become a way of life.

Like so many other stray cats foraging for food in West Berlin, Samhain had lost his most recent caretaker during the war years.

One morning in 1938, a group of Schutzstaffel paramilitary forces went door-to-door rounding up citizens for relocation. Samhain's caretaker, a bookseller by trade, had not offered any resistance. He told Samhain—in a tone one might use to comfort a child frightened by a violent storm—not to worry. He assured him that he would be fine and that the world would eventually be free of hate and intolerance.

Samhain had nodded obediently before leaning forward to press his head against his caretaker's wrinkled brow. Both of them understood that the moment of shared affection and appreciation would likely be their last.

Earlier that afternoon, Samhain had lost another longtime acquaintance.

The passing of Archimedes shook the black Burmese cat. Aside from his personal grief, the death had far-reaching repercussions. Samhain and Archimedes were part of a rare lineage—a highborn caste of cats devoted to safeguarding the world from hostile incursions. Once honored—even worshipped in some cultures—by their appreciative caretakers, their numbers had dwindled over the centuries. Few remained in the modern world.

These long-lived cats had given rise to many superstitious notions. Though Samhain and cats of his derivation could not actually boast they lived nine lives, their regenerative abilities led to long lifespans and numerous incarnations. Some managed to live more than 1,000 years, outlasting not only their caretakers but city-states and empires as well. Crossing the path of a black cat could certainly prove unlucky since they were once the preferred prey of extra-dimensional predators.

In the ancient world, Egyptian sages honored their nocturnal vigilance and praised them for keeping the world from slipping into eternal darkness. That same affinity for remaining attentive and wary at night would eventually connect them to witchcraft during a tragic age of ignorance and intolerance.

Samhain lived through that era. He had learned to be cautious when trying to communicate with a human. Still, he could read most of them effortlessly—sense their deportment, deduce their attributes and failings, surmise the nature of their recent undertakings, and infer their intellectual capacity. He could conclude whether a restaurateur would offer him dinner or shoo him away with a barrage of expletives. He could differentiate between the kind-hearted and the cold-hearted, between the generous and the tightfisted.

Most of all, he could sense fear.

The stench of one man's fear alarmed Samhain enough for him to abandon his meal and dart out of the alleyway. He followed his instincts until he discovered an unsettled American shambling along the sidewalk and heading in the general direction of the Hotel Kempinski. Samhain did not have to guess at the source of the man's distress; he could tell he had been in the presence of the Tatzelwurm.

Samhain followed the man through the lobby of the hotel. In an adjoining lounge, a local act performed an unexceptional rendition of "Woody Woodpecker" doing their utmost to sound like Kay Kyser and His Orchestra. The bar buzzed with purposeless chatter and hollow laughter and the sporadic jangle of Deutsche Mark coins. The mix of American military members, foreign dignitaries, and carpetbaggers seeking investment opportunities vexed the cat. Just like the marketgoers he had watched that morning, none of them possessed enough perceptiveness to notice the burgeoning malevolence that threatened to taint their dreams and strain their sanity.

No one noticed Samhain, either.

He walked unseen through the atrium, past the lounge and reception desk, up the stairs and down a corridor populated by more than a few guests. He slipped into the American's room unobserved.

As the American prepared for slumber, Samhain waited. He would reveal himself when the time was right.

6.

Delbert Payne found himself in a pale gray dusk enshrouded by mist.

The rubble and debris at his feet suggested the ruins of an ancient city. He stumbled forward a few paces, tripping over bits of brick and stone as he fought against the pungent haze. After a few moments, he reached a white marble staircase. Ascending it, he gradually reached a height at which he could contemplate his immediate surroundings unimpeded by the thick fog.

He gazed out over the ruins of a seemingly endless city.

The indiscriminate destruction reminded him of Berlin and other European cities, though its scope even exceeded anything that had transpired in the recent hostilities. This city must have stretched a hundred miles in every direction. It must have been home to millions, if not billions, of inhabitants. Their lives had ended long ago, Payne quickly guessed.

"Before the Sumerians built Etemenniguru, the great ziggurat of Ur," Samhain said. "Long before their first settlement between the Tigris and Euphrates, this city perished."

Though he noticed the cat at his feet, Payne looked around to identify the speaker.

"I must be dreaming," Payne said, his eyes finally fixing on the cat. "This is a peculiar dream."

"It is a dream." It had been many years since Samhain addressed a human. Establishing a connection usually required weeks of preparation and planning. He did not have the luxury of time. "But that does not make this unreal. Dreams can be both flights of fantasy as well as windows into other realities. You, Delbert Payne, have stumbled into an accidental twin universe."

"A twin universe in which cats can talk?"

"No," Samhain laughed. "I am from your world. Most cats lack this ability to communicate. I am one of the few with this gift. My name is Samhain."

"I am pleased to meet you, Samhain—although I still believe this is all part of my imagination." Payne again turned his attention to the inhospitable backdrop. "I would like to think I could dream of a more pleasant setting. What is this place?"

"I think you already know, don't you?"

"The world of the Tatzelwurm," Payne answered. "The book called it 'an endless city in a vanquished realm of darkness and mist.'"

"This certainly fits that description." Samhain's fur bristled as an unearthly breeze swept the ruins. It carried the stench of rotting corpses. "It is more than just a city of the dead. It hungers. It aches. It yearns to entangle more unwitting souls. Unsuspecting, they will be drawn here. They will slip through the veil of shadows that separates the two worlds. And it will spread like a plague."

"What can be done to stop it?"

"The Tatzelwurm must be returned to this realm—to the Abode of Mist." Samhain paused. He knew Payne already understood onsequences of such an act. Uttering the words brought him unexpected grief. "Your life will be sacrificed in the process."

"If I walk away, I will likely be driven mad by its influence," Payne said. "Tell me what I must do."

7.

Delbert Payne assured Samhain that he could gain access to the research room at Free University and—assuming the authorities had not yet taken possession of it—recover the box containing the Tatzelwurm. The plan had an infinite number of hitches and hindrances and seemed doomed from the start. The likelihood of failure did not deter Payne.

Even though Samhain shared his lack of faith in the entire enterprise, Payne insisted that they go through with it. Samhain could offer few guarantees beyond madness or death for a man he barely knew. Still, Payne's willingness to surrender his life made an impression on the cat.

Others had gathered at the Kreuzbergkirche early that morning.

A number of haggard men congregated in the wreckage of the church, picking through the debris dreamily, ruminating on the recent past and on its ghastly, unforgivable massacres. They sought to drown out millions of screams in the prodigious silence of a dead city. They sought to lose themselves in the Abode of Mist.

As Samhain waited for Delbert Payne to arrive at the Kreuzbergkirche, his thoughts turned to another human for whom he had a deep admiration.

Although his caretaker had implicitly warned him not to do so, Samhain had almost immediately set out to find him following his arrest in 1938. It took him weeks, but because of the cat's special abilities, and due in no small part to his profound bond with his caretaker, Samhain finally caught up with him in a heavily-guarded facility surrounded by a beech forest near Weimar.

Samhain had no difficulty entering Konzentrationslager Buchenwald. Within the perimeter of the concentration camp, he discovered the pinnacle of humanity's most hideous and monstrous qualities: A fusion of intolerance, racism, bigotry, and perversion had been encouraged and amplified until unspeakable acts became appallingly routine.

Though he found his caretaker amongst the maltreated population, he could not face him in that place. He felt ashamed that he had not anticipated this nightmare. Having spent centuries facing challenges from alternate dimensions and far-flung extraterrestrial empires, Samhain never guessed that members of the species he had vowed to protect could themselves be capable of such violence and viciousness. He never guessed that such a potentially noble race could so easily be swayed into committing continual atrocities.

Unable to save his caretaker or bring a modicum of hope to even one victim, he left that place feeling crushed and alone.

The morning sun shined upon the tops of West Berlin's tallest buildings when Payne arrived. Samhain met him at the predetermined place and led him down the path along moss-covered stones, through the rubble-strewn cloister, past the lavatorium, and into the chapel. Payne had some difficulty navigating the narrow staircase that descended from the sacristy into the long-hidden chamber.

Stumbling in the subterranean darkness, the American nearly dropped the box containing the Tatzelwurm. A moment later, that darkness gave way to sheets of purple and gray mist and distant skies filled with unfamiliar constellations. They stepped into the ruins of that long-dead city, its spectral tenants oblivious to their arrival. In a far-off quarter, some somnolent entity stirred as it lamented the return of its lifeless serpentine acolyte, knowing that one connection to the living world had been permanently severed.

To it, the loss amounted to nothing more than an inconvenience.

An instant later, Payne collapsed to the ground. The box fell and shattered, spilling its contents haphazardly amidst the rubble. Death came quickly but not painlessly; his heart seemingly burst within his chest. In agony, he watched as the willowy, back Burmese cat drew closer, standing faithfully at his side and peering deep into his eyes.

"Good human," Samhain said, as he pressed his head against his caretaker's wrinkled brow.

Payne felt an odd sensation, as if some form of energy had passed through his body. Darkness followed.

🐾 🐾 🐾 🐾 🐾 🐾

Delbert Payne awoke days later to find himself in a hospital bed in West Berlin.

Despite the best efforts of the hospital staff, the cat who had taken up residence by his bedside remained attentive, alert, and thoroughly satisfied—even though he had sacrificed one of his remaining incarnations for the benefit of his new caretaker.

A Glint in the Eyes

by D.A. Madigan

I.

Samwise Gamgee had never begged a wizard for a single damned thing in any of her lives. Not one time, not ever. If a wizard had ever threatened to turn Samwise Gamgee into something unnatural, or accused her of dropping eaves, she'd have scratched that wizard's eyes right out.

Samwise Gamgee was a scrapper. She'd heard her Person say that to her Part Time Person Downstairs many times. She was a scrapper, and she took no shit off anyone, wizard or otherwise.

To be perfectly honest, Samwise wasn't even sure what a wizard was. But she'd heard her name spoken often enough from the loudbox her Person stared at avidly, and heard the other words—wizard, something unnatural, dropping eaves—right around then, as well. She wasn't sure what it all meant, but she knew begging when she heard it in a Personvoice, and she also knew that somehow the begging voice in the loudbox belonged to a Person that had been named after her.

Which was a bit degrading—Samwise felt that if a Person was to share her name, that Person should comport themselves with more dignity. But she shook it off. Persons were Persons, and Cats were Cats, and you couldn't expect something to rise much above the limitations it was born with.

Now, as Samwise Gamgee moved as silently as a well-oiled shadow along the top of the tall picket fence at the back of her yard-domain, stalking a big bright grey cardinal that had made the tragic and mortal error of ignoring Samwise's clearly posted territorial markers, she had no idea at all that she was, in turn, being stalked.

II.

From behind the blinds of the downstairs apartment, Hy'Ia Glarno of the 17th Podding stared out into the backyard, watching the stupid Up-Dweller's felinoid prance along the back-barrier.

Just like the Elder Gods' accursed creature owned the place.

But that was the way of felinoids, Hy'Ia knew. Hy'Ia had done a full cycle of cycles infiltrating the human population of the accursed township of Ulthar, and felt very knowledgeable as to the uppity arrogance of the little Bastlettes. There was something of the divine about them, some eldritch energy that could make any sensitive sentience uneasy...but Hy'Ia didn't care.

What Hy'Ia did care about was, the mission currently assigned to it required stealth. Of course it did, you wouldn't set a shoggoth to a task unless you required something adaptable, something that could blend in, something that wouldn't be noticed, to accomplish that task.

So Hy'Ia had arrived through the ether-entrail, and assumed the form it bore now. The original template of this semblance was currently in the below-ground hole beneath this odd human dwelling pod, crumpled up like an old Mi-Go sausage casing and stuffed behind the machines that first wet fabrics, and then dried them again—and don't get a poor servitor started on the crazy devices humans build!

But when the template started to emit strong and spicy odors, that was when the other humans in this dwelling pod would become aware that Hy'Ia had rendered it non-functional, and an uproar would ensue. As if anyone or anything cared about another non-functional human! But the herd dwellers would make a fuss, and it would be best if Hy'Ia was well away with the vortice-crystal by then.

Otherwise, things might get messy. And the Master Artificers hated mess.

"Kevin, baby," Hy'Ia heard the annoying voice of the template's mate say, from behind it. "Come on in and watch some Netflix with me. Chick says the new season of JESSICA JONES is really good."

Hy'Ia cast one more yearning look at the felinoid on the fence.

That was the body it would need, to get past the screech-wards on the large dwelling pod one over from this one, to scale the outer partition, to slip in through the watching-ports on the upper story.

Well. The felinoid would doubtless be outside later, after the Great Fire Eye slipped beneath the horizon. The felinoid would be out on the fence, screeching and caterwauling its defiance to the Lesser Cold Eye.

And Hy'Ia would be ready to capture it. To embrace it, to crush it, to fully involve itself in all of its structure, to learn its metabolic processes and basic cellular template enough to allow a self-morph into a fully functional duplicate of its body.

A body which could easily scale the vines fastened to the outside of the dwelling pod next over. A body which, even if it were seen slinking into that dwelling through an open viewing-port, would excite no alarums or excursions.

"All right," Hy'Ia said, hating the sound of the human words burbling up through its faux-human larynx, "I'm coming."

It turned away from the window.

On its last mission to the mortal realm, several cycles of cycles ago, it had managed to view the entirety of the first and second seasons of JESSICA JONES.

Now *there* was a human female worthy of shoggoth-battle.

With some anticipation running through its flex-cells, Hy'Ia strode towards the room with the All Seeing, All Speaking Scry-Box in it.

It hoped that the template's mate was making some of that tasty 'popcorn' substance.

III.

Glenn Gerdling stared out his third floor office window, straight down into the back yard behind the apartment building next to his house.

It annoyed him that there was a multifamily rental property right next to his half million dollar, 18 room, three floor Tudor. Although, to be fair, the presence of the apartment building had probably knocked at least a hundred thousand off the Tudor's asking price—but, still. Now that Glenn owned it, if he could just get the goddamn apartments next door demolished, and maybe buy the lot, he could easily double the value of the home he owned. Maybe more than that...but the prick who owned the apartments didn't want to sell.

Well, not for anything reasonable, anyway.

Sometimes there were little compensations. Like for the last 18 months, the downstairs apartment next door had had a pretty hot redhead living in it with her husband or boyfriend...Glenn didn't know, or care, what the actual relationship was there.

What he knew and cared about was that sometimes the hot redhead would do yoga on a blanket in the backyard, in nothing but a leotard. Glenn often worked at home, and there were many occasions when he could stare right out his window at the little slut. He usually broke out the telescope he otherwise kept in a locked lower drawer of the desk, for those occasions.

The irregular eyeful of neighborly T&A didn't exactly make Glenn's heart turn somersaults of happiness about the goddamn rental units next door to him, but it was a positive aspect of the situation, anyway.

You had to be grateful for the little things, Glenn knew.

"Darling," Glenn heard his wife's voice waft to him from out in the hall, "where are you...oh. Here you are!"

Her voice preceding her had given Glenn just enough warning. He'd turned the squeak-free chair around instantly to face his desk, and was apparently studying some papers when Joyce leaned her head and upper torso around the doorway and stared at him.

He could have shut the door, he could even have locked the door, if he'd really wanted to. But ever since that time he'd inadvertently left his Facebook account up, and Joyce had seen all those instant messages from his secretary— well, Glenn couldn't be absolutely certain that Joyce would pick up the phone and dial her mother's goddamn divorce lawyer again, if she came upstairs and found him in his home office, behind a locked door, or even a closed one.

But he was sure she still had all those pictures she'd taken with her cell phone of the pictures Glenn's secretary had taken with her own cell phone and sent to him on Facebook. And if those pictures got turned over to his mother-in-law's goddamn divorce lawyer, well...Glenn wasn't going to be living in his half million dollar, 18 room, three floor Tudor anymore. No he was not.

He'd managed to sweet talk her into giving him another chance. Not just sweet talk, either. He'd had to cry a little, and apologize, and beg. Yes, he'd had to beg. Because if she took him to divorce court with proof that he'd been cheating on her, the feminazi judge would give her everything...Glenn's two houses, Glenn's three cars, Glenn's cherry collection of baseball cards which included the entire set, all 407, of 1952 Topps. Glenn personally knew at least six different collectors whose eyes started turning like pinwheels at the thought of that collection, and while he himself didn't give a flying crap about baseball or baseball cards, he very much enjoyed owning something that other people desperately wanted, and couldn't have.

The thought of those cards going up at auction—or worse, being sold in a yard sale to raise money for breast cancer research, which was probably what his idiot wife would do with them!—and one of those six guys snatching them up and sitting over them late at night, rubbing their hands together and drooling down on to the glass case they were mounted in—it made Glenn physically ill.

No way he could let that happen, so he'd pulled out all the stops with Joyce. He'd really piled it on. The charisma, the big wet eyes, the earnest reassurances that it hadn't been anything physical, the promises that he'd never ever do it again—the silver tongue that had made him Best Regional Salesman for six years running had finally won Joyce back to him...but she'd never quite stopped being suspicious of him.

It was really, really annoying.

But now he smiled at his wife, very lovingly, and said, "Here I am, honey. Did you need me for something?" He put down the papers he'd been apparently studying—this month's American Express bill, in fact, and could Joyce add pages to that little sucker, oh my yes, she could, and did, every single month; it was like she was constantly trying to exceed whatever high-water mark she'd made on the credit card balance the month before—but Glenn never said a word about it, oh no he didn't.

He just wrote the checks, signed them, and mailed them off.

With a sweet, sweet smile.

Joyce blinked her unfortunately rather protuberant brown eyes at him. "I just wanted to see my new locket again. You've got it in your safe in here, don't you?"

She hadn't said 'you didn't sell it to buy drugs and sex toys for one of your floozies again, did you?' but Glenn was pretty certain that's what she was thinking...he was pretty 'fershure' about it, as Joyce would no doubt have put it on one of her endless phone calls to one of her moron sisters, each of whom was fatter than the one before. It was one of the many annoying things in Glenn's life—his ugly wife had four sisters and all of them were just as ugly as she was, and fat, too. What kind of world was it, where you couldn't even fantasize about getting one of your sisters-in-law into your hot tub some night when your wife was out visiting the cancer ward at the local charity hospital? A pretty shitty one, in Glenn's opinion.

Although, if he could have gotten that hot little redhead from next door to drop by sometime...

"Sure, sweetie," Glenn said, agreeably enough, getting up and walking over to the wall, where he pushed aside the framed RAIDERS OF THE LOST ARK movie poster and pressed his thumb up against the wall safe's sensor pad.

(Glenn had never seen RAIDERS OF THE LOST ARK in his life. He'd seen bits and pieces of it, enough to know that the female lead was no Jennifer Lawrence or Scarlett Johannsen, and that was enough for him. The poster was strictly an investment—Glenn had read an article once about the steadily escalating values of old movie posters like this one, and when he'd checked out a few prices on E-bay, he'd been astonished. He'd bought this one in Near

Mint condition for $200 three years prior to this, had a guy he knew do some surreptitious repairs of what few blemishes the poster had had, and then he'd gotten it re-evaluated at New Mint, and it was worth five times what Glenn had paid for it. Glenn didn't give a crap about the movie itself, but he loved gaming the system like that.)

The door of the safe clicked open. Glenn swung it wide, reached inside, and drew out the silver chain with the big gorgeous purple amethyst hanging from it. Seventy-five bucks at a neighborhood yard sale, and even if Glenn didn't work with precious and semiprecious stones every day of his life, he'd have known that was a steal. A big hunk of rock like that, even crudely cut as it was—as is, it had to be worth at least 5K. If he got it properly cut and reset in something a little more appropriate, it could weigh in at a cool twenty-five or thirty thou. Not that he'd told his dumb bitch of a wife that. She just thought it was pretty.

Now she sighed as she took the necklace from him, held it up in front of her neck, turning to look at herself in the reflection from Glenn's glass trophy case along the other wall. Most of the trophies were for golf, but several were for tennis—Glenn believed in staying in shape, and you wouldn't believe how much merch a skilled salesman could move on the links or the courts, either, if you knew just when to strategically drop a game or two, and you didn't have the kind of stupid pride that would prevent that sort of thing.

"Beautiful," she said, staring at her translucent reflection in the glass.

"A beautiful woman deserves beautiful jewels," Glenn replied, the false smile coming easily to his lips after years of practice.

He was wondering, idly, if the silver chain would hold up, should he grab it from his wife and garrote her with it.

No, he thought to himself regretfully. It probably wouldn't...and if it did, then he'd just have to find something to do with her body.

"You're so sweet to me, dear," she was cooing at him now.

IV.

In the first floor apartment next door, a shoggoth of the 17th Podding closed its (merely two—how did these humans even *see*?) eyes and summoned to the forefront of its multi-leveled sentience an image of the vortice-crystal it had been sent to recover.

Purple, roughly hewed, with glimmering sparkles deep within that would merely look like flaws to the ignorant eye, but that were actually the nascent Gateways, waiting to be activated. Hy'Ia had little sense of aesthetic judgment, but regarding the image now suspended within the forefront of its mind, even a shoggoth could see that the vortice-crystal was a lovely thing indeed.

Had it known that the crystal was at that very space/time integer being held in front of a human female's throat as that human female preened in a reflective surface, Hy'Ia might well have simply leapt out of the nearest viewing-port, fountained its malleable form straight up the opposite dwelling-pod's outer barrier, slammed in through the third floor viewing-port, and snatched the crystal out of the ape-paws holding it. And then, quick as a night gaunt, flick away again, down the building's wall-mounted water tube, back into the sub-hole, back through the ether-entrail, back to the Plateau, and a doubtless very pleased Master Artificer.

But Hy'Ia did not know that. It only knew that preliminary scrying done the night before indicated that the vortice-crystal was securely locked in a cold iron box, and that cold iron box lay behind barriers that were shriek-warded.

It was the shriek-warding that troubled the shoggoth most. Shoggoths had been made in the wastes of the Plateau, and mostly dwelt there, or in the cold and lightless depths beneath the eternal ice. They were sensitive to loud noises—and the peculiar device-generated howlings of these mortal shriek-wards were a torment, even at a distance. Up close, Hy'Ia was not certain it could keep from relapsing into its natural shape and form, subjected to such sonic barrages. Or focus well enough to rip the cold iron box open while its hateful ferric properties burned Hy'Ia's substance.

But there would be times, Hy'Ia was sure, that the crystal's human would take it out of the cold iron box. If Hy'Ia could assume a form agile enough to get into the chamber with the cold iron box without activating a shriek-ward, and small enough to hide within, it could wait until such an event occurred.

Then, the quick as thought snatch, and away to the ether-entrail.

A somewhat contrived and overly complex plan, for a shoggoth—but Hy'Ia was rather more intelligent than the average servitor.

It was sure it could bring it off—but first, it would need that accursed felinoid.

V.

Samwise had gone inside for quite a little while. She had suffered her Person to lay hands upon her for a time—her Person was well-trained in Ear Scratching and Chin Rubbing, and had long ago learned to steer well clear of Samwise's belly fur.

But then her Person had settled down in front of the loudbox again. Samwise had curled up on the end of her favorite soft perch (graciously allowing her Person to sit at the other end) for a time, until she was certain that the loudbox was not going to call her name any time soon (Samwise knew this, because she had not heard any of the 'Bilbo,' 'disturber of the peace,' or

'ProudFEET' noises). Then she got up, leapt onto the windowsill that faced the shingle-slope leading to the rear yard-domain, and then leapt again, out onto the shingle-slope itself, and thence, into the yew-tree and from there, down to the night-shadowed ground once more.

Samwise had a sense that something bad had intruded into her domain... something much less appealing than the bright grey cardinal had been. Something that Samwise would have to sort out. It was, after all, her domain. Her Person and her Part Time Person lived and slept here, and as annoying as Samwise's Persons could be on occasion, still, they were Samwise's, and Samwise had to protect them.

Samwise was unsure...was the bad thing she sensed lurking in the wild roofless region of her domain, or in the walled-around/roofed-over area? She didn't know. She just knew, something had arrived that was wrong, and bad, and it was up to Samwise to get rid of it.

Nose to the breeze, ever scenting for prey, Samwise Gamgee went prowling.

Yet, even with all her feline senses sharply attuned to anything out of the ordinary, Samwise still did not notice the snake-like tentacle, slithering through the grass of the back yard towards her...

VI.

Jenny had been sitting on the tiny back porch to the apartment, reading under the small porch light. Nothing great; she wouldn't have money to buy any new books until her next payday, and Kevin had still not paid off that thirty bucks he'd racked up on their library card when he'd lost that coffee table book about 50s hot rods. So she was just rereading something trashy she'd pulled out of the trade-in box...some sci-fi wet dream romance about a guy and a girl battling man-eating aliens in an office building. THIS SLAUGHTERHOUSE EARTH was what it was called, and it was corny as all get out, but still pretty entertaining. She'd enjoyed reading it the first time, and although she'd tossed it into the box to trade in for credit next time she went to Half Price Books, still, she was enjoying rereading it now, too. Maybe she should put it up on the permanent shelves.

She'd just gotten to that first really hot sex scene where Megan blows Lloyd in the stairwell after they've escaped from the conference room, when something gave a horrible yowl out in the back yard.

She'd jumped up, and looked out there and...what the hell? Some kind of boa constrictor, attacking Samwise?

Without giving it a thought, Jenny tossed the book aside, jumped up, grabbed the rake Kevin had used last week on the gravel in the driveway and never put away again, and ran out into the yard. Yep—it was dim over here, out of the light from the porch, but still, that was definitely a big snake, wrapped around the upstairs neighbor's cat Samwise, trying to squeeze the life out of it. A long section of the snake's body could be seen trailing away in the grass. Good, she didn't want to hit poor sweet Samwise—

Five whacks with the heavy metal rake, and the snake was in at least two pieces, and the one not wrapped around the cat was slithering away like lightning. Jenny turned to check out whether poor Samwise was still alive or not—

The other snake-section had let go of the cat and was whipping away through the grass even faster than the first one. Now that was crazy. Snakes couldn't do that...could they?

The cat rolled back to its feet, then shook itself out, as if it had gotten wet.

Stared up at Jenny for a second, a glint in its eyes, almost as if it were grateful.

Then, with a single bound, it leapt away, vanishing into the darkness.

Jenny shrugged...then turned, and walked back to the porch. She propped the rake up against the stair-rail, picked THIS SLAUGHTERHOUSE EARTH up again from where it had fallen, walked back up the steps, across the small porch, and into the apartment kitchen.

"Kevin," she called out, "you will never believe what just happened in the back yard..."

VII.

In the bedroom, Hy'Ia stared morosely between the blinds, out the open rear-facing window, into the back yard.

It had withdrawn the tentacle it had extruded after the feline, and reshaped it back into the semblance of a human arm. That arm ached rather a lot, from the savage beating its template's human mate had dealt it with that cold iron implement.

Hy'Ia walked across the room, lost in thought, absently rubbing the aching appendage. The felinoid would be wary of it now, and time was growing short. It would need—

In the other wall, there was also a window. This one looked out to the side, toward the dwelling pod where the vortice-crystal was currently secured.

Without thinking much about it, Hy'Ia peered out through that window.

And noticed, up above, in the window of the chamber where the vortice-crystal was—the hateful human who had acquired the crystal, staring out at... something.

What?

The template's mate?

Very few other shoggoths could have reasoned the way Hy'Ia did at that point, but Hy'Ia had spent a great deal of time infiltrating human societies. It knew more than most about human behavior.

And for a shoggoth, it was very clever.

Was the template's mate unusually attractive for a female human?

Thinking about it...Hy'Ia suspected it might well be. It had those bumps in front that human males enjoyed. The odd cellular filaments that grew from its outer braincase were lengthy, and often shiny. Its limbs were very symmetrical, even for a human. And although it was crippled as all humans were by its lack of eyes, still, the two it had were bright and well formed.

Well, then. If this were true—and if the hateful next door human were, indeed, attracted to its template's mate...*ia!* This was a nutrient stream of a different texture entirely.

It would not even need to render the female dysfunctional. Carnal intercourse would allow an intimate enough examination for a passing duplication, and the creature had displayed no objections to such to date...Hy'Ia rather felt the creature had tried to initiate such earlier, while they had been 'netflix and chill'-ing. Hy'Ia had not been interested then, and had rebuffed the advances. The Plateau did not get HBO, and Hy'Ia had been enjoying the newest season of JESSICA JONES.

But tonight...ah, yes, tonight would be a different matter.

Tonight, both Hy'Ia and the template's mate would get what they wanted.

Hy'Ia started, then, as it heard its template's name called by the human female.

"I'm in here, babe," he called out in response. "What's so unbelievable?"

VIII.

Glenn Gerdling stood in front of his open safe, wishing he could breathe, and wondering how the hell he had ever gotten into this godawful situation.

He remembered, of course, the knock at the front door, ten minutes after Joyce had left for the non-profit she had founded, to raise money for breast cancer research. He remembered groaning as he'd gotten up off the couch to go to the door, certain that the dumb bitch had forgotten something and had to double back to get it—just when he'd been about to call that good-looking single mom he'd run into at Whole Foods the weekend before this.

So he'd said, "Who is it?" trying to keep the annoyance out of his tone as he'd walked across the front room.

And felt the whole day turn around on him, when he'd heard: "Your next door neighbor."

In a pleasantly feminine voice.

He'd opened the door and there she'd been in all her red-headed hotness... wearing a leotard, too, by God, although she'd pulled on a pair of blue jeans as well. Gorgeous red hair falling down in brushed, full bodied waves to her freckled shoulders, great big delectable hooters sitting up high and firm and proud on her chest, huge green eyes in that gorgeous face with those wide full lips...

She had blinked at him, and smiled, and said, in an oddly uninflected tone, "May I borrow a cup of sugar?"

He'd let her in, of course he had.

And then, somehow, she'd wrapped something around his neck—something that felt hideously alive, viscous, and pulsating, as thick as a rope, cold and slimy and gross—and said: "The vortice-crystal is above us, in a cold iron box. Take me to it."

And he'd brought her up here, led her up here, actually, like a dog on a leash. Opened the safe for her. Watched, horrified, as something like an octopus tentacle—but with eyeballs on its underside, instead of suckers—had undulated over his shoulder, into the safe, and come out with the amethyst necklace.

Holy shit, was something like that wrapped around his *throat*?

And that was when he'd heard the cat start to yowl behind him.

IX.

Samwise Gamgee stood on the windowsill, staring into the shiny-room. The Bad Thing that had tried to get it last night was in here now, with some other Person Samwise didn't care about. But Samwise cared about the Bad Thing very much. It had invaded Samwise's yard-domain, tried to murder Samwise—and now, from what Samwise could smell, it was trying to pretend to be Samwise's part time Person Who Lived Downstairs.

The Person who had helped Samwise drive the Bad Thing off last night.

Bad Bad *Bad* Bad Thing.

So now Samwise Gamgee opened her mouth, and a *yowl* emerged—a yowl that was a declaration of war, a battle cry, and a prayer to the ancient gods that favor cats, all rolled into one.

And the thing about that is, as all shoggoths and other arcane entities know, there is something of the divine about cats. Where humans are ill-shaped, loutish things, short-lived ape-mutations brought about by random radiations cascading through brutish genes, cats are the handiwork of the Gods themselves. They carry a spark of godhood within them.

And so, when Samwise Gamgee cried out *Raaaaaaaaaaaaaaaaaaaaaa* from the brightly sunlit windowsill, it should have come as no surprise to, well, at least Ky'Ia of the Seventeenth Podding, that the Sun God answered her.

The glint of fury in the feline's eyes grew to a solar glare—and flashed across the room, twin beams of golden, searing power, to strike its target.

In its passage, it reflected from the many rolling ocular orbs along the tentacles that Ky'Ia had extruded, to become a glint in those eyes as well—a glint of sheer raw terror.

For the twin beams from the ululating cat's eyes did not strike the shoggoth.

Rather, they struck deeply into the vortice-crystal hanging from the shoggoth's eldritch grip.

There were 17 crudely hewed facets on the outside of the sizable chunk of purple gem.

Inside, there were orders of magnitude more.

The holy beams of Ra struck deep into the crystal, bounced around—

and then, a Gateway opened.

A shimmering in the air that Glenn could barely see, through the tears in his eyes.

A shimmering, through which blew a warm breeze carrying the scents of spice, and worked silver, and saltwater, and the sounds of crying gulls and whispering wind and slapping, cracking sails.

An inhumanly beautiful hand extended from the shimmering, its flesh tinted blue, each of its six fingers nimbly articulated by an extra knuckle.

It grasped the vortice-crystal, and yanked it away, back through the shimmering Gateway, while at the same time, a sibilant voice, with all the depth and power of earth, air, and sky within it, cried out in an archaic tongue a spell of banishment—

And Hy'Ia of the Seventeenth Podding screamed as it fell away, into the whistling cold darkness of...

...the Plateau of Leng.

Once again.

Returned, with no vortice-crystal to show for it.

Still stinking and shimmering with the hideous warmth of the god Nodens.

With nothing at all to show for its mission, to justify the energy expended in sending it to the mortal realm...

Something flopped, and writhed, and gasped, at the end of one of Hy'Ia's appendages.

It rolled its eyeballs in that direction.

Well. Apparently, it had brought the mortal who had once possessed the vortice-crystal along with it.

So the Master Artificer would have a new mortal toy to play with, for a time..

That was something, anyway.

Hy'Ia lifted Glenn Gerdling up by the throat, examining its spoils.

Glenn Gerdling hung there in the screaming black cold of the Plateau of Leng, a shoggoth's eldritch tentacle about his neck—and sincerely wished that he would die.

But it would be cycles and cycles before his wish was granted.

X.

Samwise Gamgee curled up on the kitchen linoleum, in the spot of bright, golden warmth created by a sunbeam streaming in through the window over the sink. Dust motes danced in the hot yellow light above her head, and in the way of predators, she was aware of their languid movements, but she felt too satisfied to care.

She had driven off the Bad Thing. Her domain was secure, and her Persons—full time Upstairs Person and part time Downstairs Person—were safe once more.

Her part time Downstairs Person was sad, because that other Person who had lived there with her for a time had somehow broken itself. Samwise was not sad, that other Person had been an annoyance that never fed her or petted her, and who had taken up far too much of her Downstairs Person's time and attention—but Samwise wished she could do something to make her Part Time Person feel better again.

Maybe she should let her Downstairs Person pet her for a while.

But it was so warm and comfortable here in the sun...

With a sigh, Samwise got up, and padded down the stairs, and went in through the partially open door, and paced down the hallway, tail twitching, and into the slumber room and over to the big soft sleep furnishing where her Part Time Person was lying with the wetness on its face, making the sad snuffling noises.

Samwise leapt up onto the bed, and nudged her Downstairs Person with her head, and suffered it when the Person grasped her, and hugged her, and cooed at her.

Sometimes, you just had to put up with stuff, for your Person's sake.

A Field Guide to Wanderlust

by Joseph S. Pulver, Sr.

My window-ledge block: motor traffic (slow even at rush-hour); wash on the line (flaps when the breeze dances in its sprite shoes); potted plants; radios clash; occasional birds I'd like to have to lunch; butcher—OK Sam; baker—Perrier Pellegrino; lighting retailer—Eastside Lighting Décor; night comes, the 11pm despondency deepens.

Me. Parked 6th floor. Never counted the yawns between the cans of tuna, but they added up.

Mid-March. Partly sunny Tuesday, pre-soap operas in full bloom. A (taxicab-yellow) salmon (well oversize, feast for twelve or more adults with immense appetites), who I would later discover, carted around the name, Nemo. *There.* Quietly swimming down the street, ease of his passing, might have been Maurice Chevalier strolling Paree's byways in *Gigi*. Claiming to be an escapee from a Brobdingnagian vat of Drambuie, the enormous salmon swam by my boring window to the boring street of ordinary world and mundane passersby.

Paused. "Good day to you, sir." Smiled. What a glow. Mouthpiece was twice as wide as his head.

I sat up, not formally, loose affable. "Hey. Please, pardon me, but…ah, how do you do the out of water thing?"

"Always rebellious when it comes to restrictive strategies, laddie. A congenial co-schooler who took me under his fin and had a way with ingenuity was a practitioner. It brushed off," the salmon said.

Bored and chaffing at the four years stuck in my boxy apartment, outside yanked. "You roam; leaving familiar to pursue traces, sounds fascinating," I said.

"Profound. Provocative, when offered. Views of the faraway keep my wanderlust fueled. The time and space of consciousness cause me to circulate from garden to garden. There's room in the current if you have the mind for moving."

He talked...and talked...and intoxicated by his thumbnail travelogues and charming theories, I signed up, leapt off the ledge to follow him. I couldn't help myself (he'd hooked me at first sight). He was too fascinating and had certainly stripped off my own incuriosity. No more shared rooms of plenty for me, as we traveled faraway from those certainties, that stifling boring comfort. No stray out Tom-cattin', built for that comfortable sofa not for speed, the paths were odder than my aged house partner's displays of bedeviled imagination.

I had traveled some in the last few months, mostly from one floor to the next; Gillian (Miss Holroyd to her customers) closed the book, quenched the candle, and the bell no longer rang, and Aunt Queenie, as sweet a bumbler as you'd care to have tea with, powers and memory slipping away, began spending hours alone with old miseries. Home, it seemed of late, was only a place to do time, and I now found myself seeking new music, other keys, fruitful vines not rooted to wretched idleness.

Nemo, and yours truly, Pyewacket, in tow. Down the street, my street in the neighborhood. Forward, but not straight, rise, arc left, *zippity-zip* nose down for a story or two, circle back, and on a dime rocket straight-up for seven floors. Window environments altered form and magnitude; rectangular—round, oval—diamond. What was contained in windows changed; boy, maybe 5, with his Teddy bear, became a giant in a top hat with a monkey hopping on his shoulder; woman watering her houseplants transformed, she was naked and dancing around a moonlit blaze with her naked-sisters; sofa turned into a spider, lamp-table into a purple serpent chasing his long tail; Miss Lonelyheart, after surgically removing her heart with a butter knife, put on her tombstone dress and closed the lid on her coffin-bed.

Out and about.

Abroad. The headed-out-of-town type.

Zip. Swoop.

"Headed a—where?" I asked.

"To *The Frolic* in Oasis. Big goin's on. Promised Dharma a game of Chance & Necessity."

Food follows fun in a cat's dreams, had to have a seat at the table when Nemo pulled into Oasis. Game (caviar, turkey, ham—) afoot, I was ready for the dance.

Better part of morning and afternoon bursting with high sun we cruised along; your friendly neighborhood sure-paws doing quite well for an FNG.

Quick as an *up yours*, somebody turned off daylight. Dark as a witch's backside; odor of the thing, too. Owls cued to fresh fish and cat-kabobs skipped the mouse-patrolling and lit after us.

Beeline for the lights on the horizon. Old joint, grey moat to ironbar windows to towers, castle. Door closed. Big, green-neon keyhole. Nemo looked at me for help. No key, not even an all-purpose kitchen instrument. Mouth and eye full of sorry, I shrugged. With a stiff, extended fin Nemo knocked. Twice. Nuthin'-and-nuthin' echoed.

Owl talons closing in.

City cat, I'd read owls are solitary, bunk. Whole parliament (silent as death and taxes) was on our six in full-zoom. Timepiece of my *this life* said 2 minutes to endtimes. Ferocity and sharpness of those talons was all the revelation I needed.

"Open sesame!" Didn't do squat. "*Sésame, ouvre-toi.*" Nope, nuthin'. "Sesame, open!" Another big zero.

"That all you have?" I asked.

"Ogglu!"

If that was another of his words of power, the lock remained untroubled by it.

"I think some type of course change is in order here," I said.

The daredevil barnstormer wore a 12 ft. long and 14 in. wide, white silk (100%, of course) aviator's scarf (handmade by Tibetan monk who also dabbled in the mystic arts). Using mind-magic, Nemo, with a mojo-phrase (*Asazobaehbalaldit Octicu Nahta*) of potent enchantments, could make pockets appear on the scarf. From them, articles of assistance were removed; they often came in handy.

We were desperate and his pockets were not providing helping hands.

"Could you hurry? Try something else."

"*Nahta balaldit.*"

The door lock did not unlock.

Nemo finally pulled out his gris-gris bag. "Satan's claw foot root, no." Dropped it.

"Reasons for waiting dust. No. No." Back into the bag it went.

"Make her hair look funny feather—that won't work."

4th pull from his bag, had a slip of paper in his fin. "Yes. Will. Has to." Yelled, "*Abracadabraxas!*"

Door (hopefully leading to a winning enterprise zone) welcomed us by opening.

Inside. Did not resemble the fortress outside promised. No suits of armor lining the corridors, no longswords hanging on the walls, no armory or strapped security guards.

Inside. Door between our fear and the appetites of our pursuers. Trying to normalize our breathing. Every hall and corridor, there were no rooms, floor to ceiling was lined with file cabinet drawers, each labeled but in no understandable order.

We faced SECT (slid it open, an array of multi-colored insects pinned to an outlandish map), ORRGALOOO (a small red lump of thick hard mud), RNK (a grotesque grey sculpture size of a tall man's fist. My vision blurred looking at it, heart-rate kicked up to panic-speed), DRAGON (we didn't open that one), THOKAI (no clue and was not chancing it), BLUE, TAP-TAP, TAINTED, PLATO JACKSON, NARRATOR, ANTS, GREED, RIGHTS, CARE, UNRESOLVED, HYDE, CRYSTAL MEMORY, SISTERS, PLASTIC, CONCAVE, SAILS, LIMP, HAUNTED, DEBRIS.

LAKESIDE. "That's where Oasis is," Nemo said. Opened the drawer with a fin and hit the water with an excitedly vibrant splash before I could utter a word. Captain, my Captain, gone.

"Zemo! Wait, I can't."

I'm not good with water. I stood alone on the shoreline.

Afternoon died in the arms of twilight. I climbed a lakeside tree and continued to wait. Moonlight lit my tree and the lake. Next day I remained at my station, hoping for my guru's return . . . Day 4: this was getting me nowhere. Sky became a collection of shadows lacking emotional peace. Bird was rapidly getting away from a peal of thunder. Leaving this wrecked ship was the right idea; I followed the sailor.

Solo I roamed.

Heard things that frightened me. Saw things outside my understanding, shied (or ran like hell) away.

Didn't know where I was bound, but I hoped fun and pleasant were going to be involved.

~~~ Welcome to THIS PLACE POP. 437.

Monochrome. Muddy fields to the south. Tornado & Hurricane duo had whipped it up and left a decorator's nightmare. Was sure I'd lose a life or 3 here.

More bad weather brewin' above, I decided exit was the only reasonable course. No Greyhound bus depot. Train (reptile car, green-furred hyenas, elephant car, Hippogriff and Uchchaihshravas and Peryton, thing that looked like a muse-maddened 4-year-old's idea of a dragon with an aria-belting vulture perched on its shoulder) pulled into the station. Pounced aboard. Conductress, a former runway model of some repute, didn't ask for a ticket or travel documents when she sashayed by.

Coal smoke and steel wheels thunderin' on steel tracks we headed out of town, left what was left of the disorder. Slow-train serpentining through relentless lack of fertility. Seven days not one damn improvement, I, without a word of good-bye to Miss Sashay, caught an extraction that was headed south.

~~~ Wind talkin'. Yes, clouds, too, the heavy kind. No exorcism handy. Fingerpost announced: ZOMBIETOWN. Was. A marathon of nightmares; guts, blood, and guts ripped open full-stench, here to everywhere. Worries and unhappy pulled out with the meat. Crunchin' bone on boulevard corners, lappin' up spurtin'-plasma in the parks, mindless thing diving out a dreamhome window with two legs (one in its jaws and one for later). Off with its head and into a belly had occurred many, many times. One zombiething was going at a woman's chest with an ice pick, in search of her heart I suspected. Dumb (scabbed, scarred) to Dumber (bleeding from several bites and slashes), "Give it here!" Dumber to Dumb, "You give it here." No rhyme no planning no king or principal director. Horde hunger; at their chore no plate or spoon involved in the process/chaotic mess *notshutoffable.* And they had dog *and cat* on the bill of fare; back on my little New York City block we had a stock reply— FUCK THAT! Dumb #72 grabbed my tail. Mightily opposed to disfiguring parts of me, (my claws don't do the losin' end of predatory and his opinions on gratification were not mine), took a chunk outta Dumb's nose with my left and raked his eye with my right. His iron-grip rebelled against the pain induced by my razor-sharp complaint, lessened as he backstepped and I was liberated.

~~~ Forest, the dark and extremely-spooky kind that frightens anyone who functions at levels the rational identify as reasonable, beyond the reconfigured cornfields: every moonlit hut sat on bent and gnarled trees that looked like deformed chicken legs—psychosis was the lamplight here, it ate your nerve-ends. Witch-shack windows were wide and screams poured out.

Scaredy-cat me. Reek of burning meats—to my olfactory appliance there were more than one or two unsavory (to feline tastes smaller than that of lions or tygers) varieties on the menu—had me probing the woods for departures. Set my heart-sights on one to my left, but the huts began to amble and saunter, blocking all exits. Doors and windows opened and the repulsive heads of old hags popped out, calling and yelling to one another.

Baba Yaga 1: "Got me a girl of three. Fat one she is." Perhaps in an asylum what followed would be termed laughter.

Baba Yaga 2: "All I nabbed was a damn dog. Old thing, more bones than etables."

Baba Yaga 3: "Yaga's snagged twins—boys. Fatties. Onions, taters, toads, and twin fatties, boiling well, my pot is belly-pleasing!"

A sharpened branch of fire-black hardwood pierced my tail and I was hanging upside down. Other end of the broom-spear was a hunchback menace out of a fairy tale, the kind that weren't meant to soothe children at bedtime. Only had one eye, black and oozing watery puss, and some rampant pox had not been kind to her face, if it had ever been fair. The wispy clumps of thin-hair topping her gruesome features were little nests, disheveled by a drunk madman who one can only believe was in the middle of a berserker tear-it-up, and each tuft was filthy-greasy and full of stout, bone-white spiders glistening like dew-spritzed maggots.

Baba Yaga 4: "Baba's skinning knife will be most glad to ready your meat," the witch promised me, her tone gleeful.

Her knife arced, sliced—deep. Off with my tail.

Out came my claws! Caught #4 below her one functioning eye, and yarned—four nicely-scored furrows opened on her cheek and my claws twisted as they raked her swollen and horribly-bent nose. I flicked the chunk of meat that came off into her screaming maw. Hissed, "Eat that, witch!"

Baba 1: "Can't even dead a cat, Baba. You're not fit to measure secrets."

Baba 4 turned, perhaps to sling a foul retort, and I, spinning half-a-spin and arcing upward, got another shot at exposing additional facemeat. Target acquired and zapped, I completely ripped open her nostril, which hung in two bloody flaps.

Baba 3 joined Baba 1 in assaulting Baba 4. "If you could catch anything other than crawlies you wouldn't have such a scrawny ass...and maybe you could get a ghoul to give you a poke."

Baba 1: "Only poke she can get is a branch stub in her ass!"

Baba 3: "Ghouls, Baba? Even lesser demons avert their eyes, and the last psychopath that passed through our wood, while he was enjoying the cold my tit offered, told me he wouldn't put his sadistic anywhere near her cooter."

#4 was crying, steaming storm and fume, and bleeding, and her sisters, near bent double with cruel-abrupt hilarity, were not giving me any notice; saw an opening between their chicken-legged abodes and ZAP made it out, bloody, tailless, but breathing.

~~~ Winterlude, Vermont: broken...spells, teacups, promises, them bells, what was on the way UP. Hellhole-backwater of savagery grinnin'-ugly. Prowlin' for eats I got nabbed by two freaks with a disposable lighter and a clear-glass

fruit-jar of inferno-strength gasoline. I'll skip the novel of *fires of Hell* pain and leave it at, burned alive.

Wound up at the Doors of Perception where Nick Drake and Jim Morrison were sharing a dual-stemmed hookah pipe.

"Looks like he has a few left in him, Jimmy," Drake said.

"Heart and hearty, yeah, I have to agree," Morrison said, exhaling smoke-ships scented with cinnamon and clove.

Nick said, "He'll need a makeover."

"Yup." Morrison reached into a carpetbag (that might have been last in use the day after the Alamo was invaded by blood-red calamity), hauled out a foxtail. "Belonged to Jimi. He'd be pleased to have it find a nice home." Tossed the tail to me.

Drake opened his painting box, looked at his colors and bestowed a furry new coat on me. "This should make you brighter. You'll present well at tea ceremonies and duck ponds. Help you avoid Minotaur's waltzes, too."

The pair set aside their smoking device and out came needles and red thread, which Morrison said was, "Lifeblood and wind. Always does the trick. Comes with a few, too."

I didn't understand a word they whispered as they tailored my new skin.

"Looks ready for unsullied procedures to me," Morrison chimed.

Drake held out a mirror. "See. You're all *purr-D* now. Word of caution though, won't give you any extra traction in the rain." Grinned.

Pretty? In my travels I'd acquired a few new identity facets; I could walk on air, I had a Cheshire smile that could produce "smaller" magics, and now, my fur had gone from Siamese coloring to red with uncommon green striping. And there been a change in my claws; each set of paw-claws was a different color, as each set was now empowered. Didn't have the array of magic Nemo's scarf possessed, but they, I was certain, might be handy for a clueless adventurer who was bound to be forced to deal with bothers. Wasn't sure I'd call my new hide pretty, but, sartorially speaking, it was a proper fit and the comfort level was snuggly.

Morrison: "Hey, kiddo, do your souls a favor and stay away from cowboy movies. Furries and bullets don't mix well."

Both waved, smiled, mumbled some mumbo-juju and sent me back to terra-somewhere without an immigration form.

~~~ 2nd coming: with a "Land-ho!" stepped over the line between death and life.

Nightside of the city—civilization, with and without reason. Dry, quiet street. Kind of air I knew.

Woman, smelled like she exhaled shrimp. Stopped. Lit a cigarette. Saw me. "Pretty kitty. *I love kitties.*"

New tail, figured I was a charmer; Jimi was. Might play it for some fine dining. Rubbed her ankle and purred.

Mistake.

Bad girl.

Shoulder-slung, oversize black bag-purse became a cage. And I was in it.

Lady did not look like a Baba, but I should have asked what she loved cats for.

Swayed when she walked. My purse-cage wasn't what you might call comfortable.

Yeowlin' set to miserable I was in her bag for Bast knows how long.

Shook me out of her bag plopped into a cage. Hauled in, caged in a wire-coffin. Corner table in a rathole tavern-clubhouse, called the Den of Death. Dark. Deteriorating.

Decades ago it was called the Bamboo Klub, strip joint, 44 double Ds, sweaty palms, and overpriced beer (cover charge—4 drink minimum).

Old blood stains on the floor and cigarette smoke (loaded with slow-galaxies of dust motes). Gin and burn-marks on the chessboard-Linoleum. Stripper pole/mirrored disco-ball. Pot of old coffee behind the 60 foot bar. Framed photographs of exorcists and a painting of St. Echo's on the wall with a bison skull and a fading poster for the brakepad factory (closed 22 years ago). Signed photos of touring A-list strippers who appeared in those wilder days.

By the front door four bulletholes in the bar where "11am" Wayne Lawrence was murdered by his eighth-timed wife. Jukebox crying an old pop heartbreaker from the 60s.

One pool table, three dart boards. B&W TV over the bar on a high stand with a stuffed red fox.

Penny Greystocket, an aspiring super villainess (Miss Delusion), was showing me off to her fellow baddies in The Legion of Terror; Obeler Gutter a.k.a. Dr. Chemistry, The Lottery, Lady Blood, Blackstorm, Fang & Claw, Insanity, Queen Cobra, Captain Lunar (four doubles beyond lit), War Wolf puttin' the moves on Frequency, The Enchanter looks at The Merman who's looking at Tomorrow Girl like she's cheating at stud, and two dozen more in every tint and magnitude and costume an old Jack Kirby 4-color chronicle could accommodate.

Monstrous hulk name of Lumbering Jack rose from his (sizzling) electric chair, walked over. Bent way down. Looked in the cage. "I likes kitties. Soft and all furry."

Enter Leslie Ballard, The Zombie Empress. "*Cat?* Where?" Had me in her sights. Full-tilt covet.

Rushed over, no Lightning Man ever moved so fast.

Love-eyes locked.

Tears.

Her beloved feline-sidekick, Gargoyle, dead and gone three months back.

"You're perfect. I'm going to call you . . . *Eddington*. Wait until you see your new home. It will be fresh albacore for you every night."

"Stick your nonsense up your ass, Bitch. Cat's mine. I found him. I'm going to train him to be my familiar," Miss Delirium hissed.

"Yours? That would be a *no*."

Clusters of impolite words were exchanged. Bitch—I saw him first you brokendown-*cunt*—You are a totally-fucked wannabe—Your continent-size ass is about to inhabit a chunk of oblivion.

"Cat-fight," The Cannibal Ape shouted. Clapped.

Claws came out. Raked. Right cross to a recent rhinoplasty. Elbow compressed a boob. Haymaker/kidneypunch/liver-shot/low-blow. Head was dangerously-tilted backward. Hair was pulled out. Zombie-talon extended, pretty mouth bled. Armbar. Knee-smash. Heard a bone break, a good size one. Scream. "*Totally-fucked*, bitch!" Leg-lock. Spit! Rollin' and tumblin' on the dirty floor.

Weapons were drawn.

Fists were ready to riot!

Papa Macabre offered The Scarf 3-to-1 odds on The Zombie Empress.

"5-to-1 and it's a deal," The Scarf said. Waved a pair of Franklins at him.

Butcher desires wanted grab and twist-arm till bust. Rip out an eyeball, or stick a chair leg up a twat would have been welcome, too.

Lumbering Jack opened my cage. Stroked me. Walked to the door and opened it. "This is not the place for you, my little friend. Go. *Be fast*."

Nuke on my six would not have added a thing to my zippy. Halfway to the corner—

Jerusalem and Bog, Fuckedville, USA. Locals call the corner Lion's Head, and roar it did (all sewers and slaughterhouses do). Cooking oils and curried-to-burn and garlic and various kinds of BBQed and stir-fried meats (cheap/outlawed/two-days-past out-of-date/snake-lizard-bug). Min Wu's and Thu Ba's glared at each other from conflicting corners. Open door to Kellermann's Star Burger pushed its nose-twisting stink into the street right at Mister Ytsu's Rusty Taco neon offerings.

Too-much any meat is on the menu is too-much for this less-than-9lives. Ain't no way (in any multi-verse or alternate dimension) I'm a stuffed dumpling ingredient.

Up—Up—and (with twenty-seven ten-pound dollops of extra *go, cat, go*) far away!

~~~ Ill-fated for felines or women or families or anyone who had a heart of goodliness were The Robots of Kylashum—32 foot tall brutes, who, driven by their *mort techniques*, sought a workforce to grease their service lines and distribution mechanisms. The diabolical whimsicalities of their weapons and the Night Demons they had allied themselves with produced revulsions no cat should see. I, horror-struck and not pausing to blink, hit *go, cat, go* again.

~~~ Marathon of oldfolks (who do not remember It or When well these days) alone timid desperate forgetting or forgotten (medicinal schedules—laughter—the life-partner who spoon-feeds them). Pained, few good moments, fewer prayers. Who'll fall off the carousel next; falling is easier than wobbling these days. Death smiling, holds out his cold hand for a companion in his next funeral tango. Building (eight floors) was full of them. 4B. Cat, old timer, in the window, locked in with Guadalupe Page (DEAD 4 days 13 hours). I opened the window, urged him to jump—he had one life left. Didn't stick around to see if he engaged with opportunity.

Not a good way to start a day.

~~~ A red river shore, shack town—Littleway—ruined by fire: folks pressin' on, cartin' carpet bags of threadbare dreams as they left hellish sights (many without heads) behind. Center of it all, newly erected, tower, cage, of cats—*filled with cats*, old, small, female, tabbies, city cats, hellminded-ferals from the Wildlands—and rolling out of the barbed-tips of a pair of curved chimneys, set on top like demonic horns, the stench of burning flesh and fur. I have a fear of water and of being burned—alive! I also have a very large dislike of cages. Seeing members of my feline family locked-down and on the way to who-the-fuck-knows-what-fiendish-ending, got my angry dialed-up to asplode. Not having a rocket launcher at the ready, I decided to pick the simple locks, a skill I had acquired from Nemo.

I set to it; my mouth silent, my claws furious.

Cats out of the cages runnin'. Made like a herd member and did the same.

My end-of-the-line was an immense mirror, easily the size of a great lake, that reflected Eternal Night. On its stage, a naked witch-queen (conjuring death blizzards from the scar-sigils on her body), vampires, and mind-lords, dark gods and maggots (feasting on what the mind-lords shattered), (grunting and barking) masters of the grave (stirred by the gruesome appetite in their heads, claws rooting 'round in the blood-soaked black soil for meat-treats), played blood games. Fearing snatch and over, I stepped lightly—until zig and zag and bat-outta-hell were required. Midnight (its edges frayed) and the

Borderland just beyond—no pussyfooting, I was quick to split the towering shadows of deadliness.

~~~ Under a confusion of wandering stars in a swamp of celestial-soup/twinklin' below dragonhead-nebula roarin' up/solar system of hundreds of iceberg tombstones wizzin' and bangin', pinball was never this poppin'/gas giants and dwarves/blackstars/deathstars/deathrealms/life, mine, in FEAR of dead again—you should have seen me running to safeguard my fur.

~~~ Slept in an alley (Los Angeles, not far from the river and a long-dormant railroad hotel) with a skeletal, elderly dog. Meager from trash cans was served. Napier, who lived with 'an adorable cat' when was young and very fond of felines, asked about the road, wondered if I ever missed home, and told me he wished there were a reset button. Added, some nights (many of them WET) he wished for an OFF switch for the containment suit he was inhabiting. Two scabby and scarred rats popped up, and made *mine*-eyes at the half a baloney (no cheese/extra onions) sub my dinner partner and I had dug up. I mentioned fang and claw, and (with no flux of maybe) enthusiasm vanished in the dust of an identity crisis, the rats bugged out. Napier thanked me; seems most nights he lost what bits he came upon to the never-tentative poachers.

Two nights later, in an alley 2 alleys from Pho Vo's Saigon Spiceshack, where I'd scored some spilled take-out three nights in a row, Napier expired. Wasn't leaving him for a role in ingredients, dragged him to a garbage pile and buried him best I could.

Maggots. Rats. Knew they'd come. *Might have been better if I'd left him for Pho Vo's wok.*

~~~ (Outside a hard stretch of scrub-and-nuthin'-territory called Athens Ridge) Watchtower: drifted too far—stepped off the last train. John Q. Negotiator (ex lawyer/ex-politician/fulltime liar and known vainheart with his thumb ready to drown any honest man type) that couldn't cut a deal, in chains. Gallows in the square, ready it was, to release all the sins dammed up in his soul. Summer day, thunder comin' down off the mountain. Vultures had settled in, waitin' on post for the vittles. T-shirts and cotton candy and hot dogs and beer were being sold. Whole families had buckboarded in. And the midnight stars over at the Rose of Cimmaron Saloon were havin' such-a-deal—any *explicit undertaking* 5 bucks. Made my way around. Avoided a young girl wanted a pet. Avoided a Chinaman who was wantin' what he felt was an overdue helpin' of din-din. Front porch of the sheriff's avoided getting' my fine long-tail squeezed under half a dozen rocking chairs.

Noon struck. Funeral executioner skipped prayers...Neck SNAP!

Hootin'! Clappin'-and-ajumpin' up-and-down! CHEERSssssssssssssssssS!

Shoutin' frabjously. Old lady in a Sunday-meeting pill-box hat fainted. Trio of wanderin' dogs, sizable brutes untidy-in-the-extreme—homeless by their demeanor, howled. Gravediggers toted the carcass away, the vultures were sorely pissed; circled over and dropped droppins on the pair. I vaulted up on the roof of the Empire Saloon for a nap, grabbed a few winks. Moon came out and there was that Chinaman, snuck up the backstairs and had his choppin' cleaver ready to skin the fine fur off my 3rd life, me and garlic and rice in a pot—told him that was a No Sale. Lickety-zippy hopped right the hell outta Watchtower. Kept goin'. I'm not big on dustbowls.

~~~ Came out of a forest; old, dark. Sun was high. Splendid rock perfectly contoured for napping, sat in the middle of a glade of flowering shrubs. Settled in; cleaned my paws, cleaned my ears and whiskers. Nodded off. On the rock across from mine sat a man in green boots and leggings. Green tunic and cloak. Grinned, said his name was Loki. Voice like a soothing drug he offered me employment, I think. Twenty minutes into his linguistic maze I still had no clue what he was about or proposing. 'Bout ready to say, "sorry, Charlie," noise—roar and a bellow and a howl and several barks, sliced out of the brush. Loki lost his glee and finger-snapped—*PTOOF*, vanished. But I faced new anxieties, monstrous to behold. 13 beasts, bodies half big game cat/half hulking bear, headed with crocodilian Anubis heads. Huffy, growling, gently grinning jaws (on the nearest) dripping with unsavory fluids, its twin was sharpening its teeth.

"Ah, a fellow traveler. How *charming*," tectonically slow. Old man in black robes, prop in a magic show, suddenly there. Pulled up a rock and sat. Lit a bone pipe with the tip of a glowing-finger. "Sit," he told his beasts. They did, instantly. "Wandering between the cold stars—you'd be shocked to hear how boorish they can be, the seemingly ending desert sands, and dark twisted streets wind or rain or 3am, I so seldom get to sit. Taxing for a gent my age." Lightly slapped his knee, winked. "I understand why men enjoy their creature comforts; there are times I'd enjoy a stuffed armchair and ottoman, a warm hearth, and a brandy. So many things pile up in The Circus. Wouldn't you agree, Pyewacket?"

Strange man, terrible beasts, and he knew my name; I looked for an out.

"Hearsay and bias, subjective bullshit. Plato, Nietzsche, the struggles imagined by the drunk on the street corner, all noise, snapping at our throat. Change the tenor I say. Light and breezy. Tell the magus and the ploughman to shut it for an hour or two. Wouldn't you say? And Loki, doublecross and venom, what a waste of matter. Murder and murder and slit throats and broken hearts. *Broken hearts.* Smashed dreams. Larceny. Liars. Creation, tradition. The collapse. And over it all, a halo of flies. A river of darkness runs through it. Sad. Always been. Seen it; darkness at play. Watcher, messenger, that's my role. I was born to it. No one ever asks, do they?"

"I noticed you. I need a number 14 and thought you might like to sign on—see it all. Regular feedings. *Cadabaraxas—Zo*, can fix you right up. Make a new beast out of you."

"And who might you be?"

"Endless apologies for not introducing myself. I am Nyarlathotep. Known here and there, as the Wicked Messenger, Messenger of the Old Ones, the Crawling Chaos, trickster, wrongly Ratatoskr to some, but I understand the comedic aspects of the appellation. The Faceless God, the Dweller in Darkness, the Black Pharaoh, the Seeker from the Stars. There's a woman in Sheboygan, she was rather young—15, if we're counting—when I met her. To this day she calls me, the Apple Stealer." He brightened, looked pleased and guilty, grinned, and shrugged. "It was a lonely night, one in a very long string, and rather chilly and soft charms can be so...*mouth-watering*. What can I say, she unzipped so nicely; there was no pussyfooting on my part."

I thought the Wicked Wanderer was going to pitch a fit of merriment, but all he did was produce a glass of brandy and continue on.

Dead and Bardo.

Spiders and the myth of angels.

Cookbooks. "If your taste runs to it, there's a very large bookstore in Paris, nothing but."

Pox.

Ambition and exit wounds.

Nyarlathotep downed the last sip of his brandy. "Decided to sign on? Marvels await."

A few might, but between marvels, assuming great they'd be, I had it figured metaphysical filth and monsters and furnaces swirling with darkness was most of the trek. Was betting 9lives would not cover the incidents we'd clash with. Lied small: "Kinda had it in my mind to find my way back to the homestead. Miss my sofa and the windowsill. Can of tuna and a nap been on my mind, so, thank you, but I'll have to pass."

He rose, adjusted the hem of his robe, adjusted his sleeves. His gaze testified to him being unused to rejection. "Your loss."

His beasts at his heels, Nyarlathotep began to stroll off, whistling an odd, discordant melody.

"Answer a question, if you would?"

He stopped and turned.

"Might you know in what direction my home lies?"

"Just to the left of that wandering star. You'll feel it as you draw closer." With that he was lost in a rain of blurry stars.

I began to softly paw my way toward the star.

~~~ Beyond the starry horizon: woven briars where they ran out of barb wire. High water; levy broke, hard rain—the drowning kind. Most folks had all they could take of these strange and shredded days of tombstone blues and weren't up for staying another day.

One evening, the hardass kind you'll leap to snatch-up any distraction that offers release from crude and/or crushing, I was nursing my tombstones. The conductor I followed (some years back) from Queenie's apartment window to *adwentoursomme*, swam by. He was full of different, as he'd been at sea in an ocean of Courvoisier and his metrics (and coloration) were off (he'd even lost his Cheshire smile).

"'Board! Next stop, someplace *wonderful*." Nemo the salmon broadcast.

After all the to's and fro's and not so gently back again's and swipes of demon-black darkness, stabbing and fouling everything they could paw and mangle in the colorful inklings in my head and real-as-dead-all-around, how could I resist a place advertised as "someplace wonderful"? My curiosity ('bout the size of some critics' heads) ready, willing, and (still) able, and widest (Cheshire) smile fully displayed, I followed.

Before we could engage in old home week—

There was a rabbit—scruffy, white, and sixteen shades overwrought...and a hole—that was expanding rapidly—

I landed with a thump, and as I righted and dusted off...things up and got *brilling.*

First thing I heard didn't come with anything that sounded merciful or accommodating. "OFF WITH HIS FURRY HEAD!"

In the End There is a Drain

by Tim Waggoner

"Daddy, why did he go?"

Dwayne glanced up at his daughter's reflection in the rearview mirror. Hannah was strapped into a forward-facing car seat, swinging her legs, the backs of her heels thud-thud-thudding onto the seat. It was dark out—the sun set early this time of year—but enough light filtered into the Prius from the streetlights outside to enable him to make out Hannah's face. She was tilting her head back and forth, as if she was matching the rhythm of her feet, which sounded loud as a jack hammer to him. He already had the beginnings of a headache after watching an animated movie about talking flamingos with Hannah and several hundred other children of various ages, all of whom couldn't keep quiet throughout the film. It had been the longest ninety minutes of his life. It hadn't helped that the damn thing had been in 3-D. He always got headaches from 3-D.

He wasn't sure what she was asking.

"Do you mean why did Fernando fly away at the end of the movie?"

"Yeah."

"He finished helping that family of flamingos, and he left to find someone else who needed his help."

At least that's what he *thought* had happened at the end. But at that point, his head had been pounding so hard that he could barely think. His headache had lessened somewhat since they'd left the theater, but it still bothered him. He wanted to tell Hannah to quit kicking the back seat, but he didn't want her to feel as if she was doing something bad. *Go, Go Flamingo!* had been the first movie she'd seen in a theater—her first *big girl* movie—and he didn't want to say anything that might tarnish the experience for her.

"He should have stayed," she said. "It was sad."

Dwayne wasn't sure what, if anything, to say to that. The ending *had* been sad, at least to a four-year-old, and it was okay for Hannah to recognize that. Healthy, even. Part of him wanted to protect his child from experiencing anything negative, including uncomfortable emotions. But parents had a duty to prepare their child to live in the world the way it was, not as they wished it would be. Maybe he should provide some context for—

"Daddy!"

Hannah's cry of alarm shocked Dwayne out of his thoughts. He looked in the rearview and saw that she was pointing forward, eyes wide, mouth open in horror. He looked out the windshield in time to see the cat. It sat in the road, legs tucked underneath its body. It was a calico, small and delicate, probably no more than a year old. It turned its head to look at the Prius as it came, headlights starkly illuminating the animal. The cat didn't move, didn't so much as twitch a whisker. It seemed completely relaxed and calm, and it watched placidly as four-wheeled death bore down upon it.

Dwayne had two simultaneous reactions. The first was confusion. What the hell was a cat doing sitting in the road like this, and why wasn't it hauling ass to get out of the way? There had to be something wrong with the animal. His second reaction was to feel a profoundly disturbing sense of recognition, as if he had seen this cat before. Not merely another calico but this exact same one, although he had no idea where he knew it from. He only knew that the feeling of recognition made his stomach churn with nausea, and his head began pounding harder, to the point where he started seeing flashes of color in his vision.

He checked the left lane for oncoming traffic and saw a pickup coming toward them. If he swerved to try and miss the cat, there was an excellent chance they'd get into an accident, and he couldn't risk that. He remembered something his father had told him when he'd been learning to drive. *If it comes down to your life or an animal's when you're on the road, you choose yours. Every time.*

Dwayne took his foot off the gas, ready to press the brake. He couldn't jam the pedal all the way down. If he did, their car could swerve, and they might hit the pickup. But if he could manage to slow down a little, give the cat a few extra seconds to get out of the way . . . But Dwayne had run out of time, and more to the point, so had the cat. Dwayne felt the impact through the steering wheel as well as the floor. He was surprised that hitting such a small, frail-looking animal felt like slamming into a bowling ball. Adrenaline jolted through his system. His headache diminished and his nausea vanished—at least for now—and he looked at Hannah in the rearview. Tears streamed down her cheeks, and her hands were balled into small fists, as if she wanted to strike out at something but there was nothing close enough to hit.

Dwayne's foot remained off the accelerator, and the Prius began to slow. *Too late now,* he thought. He wasn't sure what to do next. He thought he should find a safe place to pull over and go back to see if the cat was still alive—although its survival seemed doubtful given how hard they'd hit the poor thing. But what if it *was* still alive, hurt and suffering? Although if it was, he wasn't sure what he could do about it. He supposed he could get the tire iron out of his trunk and use it to put the cat out of its misery, but he didn't know if he could go through with it. Hannah wouldn't see him do it. She wouldn't be able to turn around in her car seat and look out the back window, but she was smart and would probably guess what he did. He didn't want to traumatize her further. His primary responsibility—his *only* responsibility—was to his daughter. What had happened to the cat was a shame, but it couldn't have been avoided. Something had to have been wrong with the animal to make it act so strangely. Maybe it had been sick or had already been injured. Whatever the case, there was no way in hell the cat would live much longer, assuming it wasn't already dead.

Get Hannah home, he thought. *It's all that matters now.*

Yes. Get her home, try to calm her down, and help her process the horrible thing that had happened.

That decided, he pressed down on the accelerator again, and the car began to pick up speed. Hannah whimpered softly in the back seat.

"It's okay, sweetie," Dwayne said as he continued to drive. "It's okay."

Dwayne was twelve. His family lived only a few blocks from the middle school he attended, so instead of riding the bus, he walked. It sucked when the weather was bad—when it was pissing down rain or it was freezing out—but overall, he liked it. He enjoyed having some quiet time to himself in the morning and afternoon.

There was only one problem with walking: passing the Cat Lady's house. Cat Lady wasn't her real name, of course, but that's what all the kids in the neighborhood called her. Most of the adults, too. According to his mom, the woman's real name was Mrs. Figueroa. Dwayne didn't have anything against her personally, but her property was a *mess*. The yard was overgrown with long grass and thick weeds, and her small one-story house was falling apart. Shutters hung at awkward angles, flanking grime-streaked windows of cracked glass. The siding was a pale yellow, and the color reminded Dwayne of diseased mucus. The roof sagged in several spots, and there were a number of shingles missing. As her neighborhood nickname implied, she had cats. *Lots* of cats, and she kept her windows open just far enough so the animals could come and go as they pleased. You could always see a half dozen cats, maybe more, prowling through the miniature suburban jungle that was Mrs. Figueroa's yard, and even if you couldn't see them, you knew they were there. You could hear grass rustling, the sound punctuated by the occasional meow. Every time Dwayne passed by—even when he made sure to walk on the other side of the street—he had the feeling that dozens of small inhuman eyes were watching him. But that wasn't the worst part. No, the worst part was the *smell*. The air was heavy with the harsh tang of ammonia—which he supposed came from cat pee—but beneath that was another scent, a thick greasy odor like rotting meat, along with a curdled sourness that reminded him of spoiled milk. The stink was so strong that even across the street, Dwayne would hold his breath as he hurried past, wondering—as he did every day—if it was possible for a person to be stanked to death. If Mrs. Figueroa's house hadn't been located on the most direct route to Dwayne's school, he might've chosen a different path. But he was twelve-going-on-thirteen, and he was too old to walk farther than he had to because some crazy old woman lived like a pig.

But one morning in early March—chilly but not too cold—a two-man construction crew was tearing up the sidewalk opposite Mrs. Figueroa's house. The sidewalks were old around here, the concrete chipped and broken, and evidently the city had finally decided it was time to replace them. Unfortunately, this meant Dwayne had to use the sidewalk in front of Mrs. Figueroa's house.

The odor of decay was so strong around her property that Dwayne felt like he was walking through a semisolid wall of stink. His exposed skin started itching, as if the foul air were eating away at the surface of his flesh. He told himself he was imagining the sensation, and began walking faster.

He heard a rustling in the grass close by, and he jumped backward when something small and furry dashed across the sidewalk in front of him. As the cat—a calico—reached the middle of the street, a car—driven no doubt by a parent in a hurry to get his or her kid to school then head off the work—struck the animal. There was a *thump*, a high-pitched yowl, and the car passed over the cat and kept going.

The cat lay on its side, a thin coil of intestine protruding from its burst belly. Its head was twisted at a sickening angle, and Dwayne knew its neck had been broken. He hoped the animal had died instantly, but that hope was shattered when he heard the animal meowing pitifully.

The traffic didn't let up. Cars continued zipping by, all of them swerving to avoid inflicting any further injury on the cat, but none stopped or even slowed. The two men working on the other side of the street had witnessed the accident, but it hadn't seemed to faze them, and they continued to work. The next driver that attempted to swerve didn't do so in time, and the two wheels on the passenger side rolled over the cat, first the front tire, then the rear. The cat didn't yowl this time, but more guts were squeezed out of the animal's stomach, along with a significant amount of thick gray fluid. Dwayne had no idea what the stuff was, but it was *gross*.

At first, Dwayne had been numb with horror at what he'd seen, but now he felt a strange calm settle on him. Without making a conscious decision to do so, he dashed out into the street.

He ran to the calico cat, bent down, and picked it up. He carried the animal back to the sidewalk, the exposed organs dangling from its body cavity and dripping that weird gray muck onto the ground. The cat's injuries were fresh, but they were far from the only things wrong with it. There were bald patches on its body, and the exposed skin was riven with fissures through which more of that thick gray substance oozed. The smell was awful, a stomach-churning stench of rot that seemed to coat his nasal passages with a greasy film. Worse than that, though, the cat didn't *feel* right. It felt squishy in his hands, like it was only a flesh bag filled with that sickening gray muck.

Revulsion gripped him, and he wanted to hurl the cat into Mrs. Figueroa's yard, but he resisted the impulse. The cat had already suffered enough indignities, and no matter how disgusting the animal's corpse was, he didn't want to subject it to one more. So when he reached the sidewalk, he knelt and gently placed the cat in the yard.

Some of the gray gunk had gotten on his hands, and the areas where it coated his flesh felt hot and tingly. He would've wiped his hands on the grass, but he couldn't bring himself to touch the vegetation growing in Mrs. Figueroa's yard. Instead, he wiped his hands on the sidewalk to get off the majority of the stuff, and then he stood and wiped the remaining residue on his pants.

"I saw what you did."

He wanted to run, but a hand fell on his shoulder and bony fingers tightened, holding him in place. He held his breath, too afraid to speak.

"Her name was Nala. She was one of my favorites."

The woman's voice came from close to his right ear. Her breath was cold on his skin and smelled of the gray gunk that had oozed from Nala.

"You feel guilty for what happened, don't you?" A deep inhalation, a slow release. "I can smell it on you. But you should rejoice. Your actions have hastened Nala's union with the Magna Mater."

She turned him around to face her.

He had never seen Mrs. Figueroa before, didn't know anyone who ever had. Her face was lined with deep wrinkles which reminded Dwayne of the fissures in Nala's skin. Her nose was crooked, as if it had been broken sometime in the past, and her lips were so thin they were almost nonexistent. Her teeth were crooked, but they were a startling white—*like bone,* he thought. Her gray hair was a wild, unkempt mop, and her eyes were large and filled with a shining intensity.

"Have you heard of the Magna Mater?" she asked.

Dwayne managed to shake his head.

"It's Latin. It means Great Mother."

He heard rustling in the grass, coming from numerous directions. Small forms slunk between the weeds as a dozen cats—maybe more—approached.

"She's inside us," Mrs. Figueroa said. "She's part of us from the moment we're conceived, and she remains with us until we're nothing but old bones and dust. She speaks to us constantly, but most don't hear her. Some of us do, though, and we *listen.*"

Cats emerged from the grass, padded onto the sidewalk and gathered around them. There were more than a dozen—*way* more—and they filled the sidewalk for ten feet in both directions, and their numbers spilled onto the street. All the cats had bald patches like Nala's, and gray gunk oozed from fissures in their skin. They were eerily silent as they watched Dwayne with their inhuman eyes.

"Cats know," Mrs. Figueroa said. "They *listen.* You ever want to see the truth—the *real* truth—look into a cat's eyes."

"I have to get to school," Dwayne said, and then added a plaintive *"Please."*

Mrs. Figueroa gave no indication that she was aware he'd spoken.

"Most people do everything they can to postpone the Mother's embrace, but by doing so, they only prolong their own suffering. But to those who understand, she grants the mercy of the Benefaction."

She removed her right hand from his shoulder, reached toward her face, and touched her bent, swollen-knuckled index finger to her left cheek. She pushed, and the finger slid through one of the lines in her flesh, disappearing all the way to the knuckle. She rooted around for a moment, and when she withdrew her finger, Dwayne saw it was coated with gray slime. She extended the finger toward his face, as if she wanted him to examine it. The stink was so fierce that he thought he might vomit.

"The Benefaction helps us grow closer to the Mother. We honor her by becoming one with her blessed decay." The woman's eyes gleamed with madness, and gray muck oozed from the spot on her cheek where she'd inserted her finger.

Dwayne was on the verge of panic now. He looked toward the men working on the other side of the street. Maybe if he could get their attention, they would realize something bad was happening to him, and they'd come over to help him. But the men were no longer there. It was too early for lunch. Had they gone on a coffee break? Had they seen Mrs. Figueroa leave her house and been so creeped out by her that they'd decided to leave? Or had they been helping her? Had they set up a fake work site to purposely divert him to this side of the street so she could finally get her hands on him? Had they heard the Mother, too?

The cats began making *mmmrrrr* sounds deep in their throats.

"It's a lot to take in all at once, I know," Mrs. Figueroa said. "But when you taste the Benefaction, you'll understand."

She smiled and moved her finger toward his mouth.

The thought of the old woman sliding her muck-covered finger past his lips and depositing the gray sludge onto his tongue was more than he could bear. Sheer animal panic took hold of him, and he yanked free from her grip with such force that he stumbled backward and fell on his ass. Cats scattered when he fell, darting off in all directions. Pain erupted in his tailbone and shot up his spine, but he barely noticed it. He crab-walked backward several feet to gain distance from the woman, then he sprang to his feet, turned, and ran like hell, Mrs. Figueroa's laughter following behind him.

He took a different route home that afternoon. It took ten minutes longer, but it was worth it. His mom was there, and he told her about his bizarre encounter with Mrs. Figueroa. She didn't quite understand all the details, but she understood that the woman was crazy. That night, she told her husband what had happened to Dwayne, and he called the police to report the incident. Social services quickly became involved, and Mrs. Figueroa was declared incapable of caring for herself. A judge ordered her to be taken to a hospital for a mental evaluation, but before she could be removed from her home, she sealed her head in several layers of plastic wrap and suffocated herself.

One night, he overheard his parents taking about her death.

They say she had a smile on her face, his mom said.

Dwayne had no trouble believing it.

After Dwayne's encounter with Mrs. Figueroa, his mother started driving him to school so he wouldn't have to walk past the woman's property, but one morning she had an early dentist appointment and couldn't take him.

"I don't want you going past That Place," his mother said. That's what she called Mrs. Figueroa's now. *That Place.* "Take a different route, okay?"

He promised he would, but it was a lie. After what had happened to him there, how could he resist revisiting it?

When he arrived, Dwayne couldn't believe how drastically the place had changed. The lot was empty, like Mrs. Figueroa had never existed at all. But despite the town's best efforts to clean up the property, the air still smelled like ammonia and rotting meat.

The town had brought in a bulldozer to level her house, and no sign of it remained—even the foundation was covered. The earth had been turned over, like a farmer's field prepared for planting. Dwayne doubted anything would ever grow again in this diseased soil, not even weeds. The bulldozer had left behind rocks and chunks of broken roots, along with scattered bits of broken bones, remnants of the cats Mrs. Figueroa had buried over the years, he assumed. He wondered what had happened to her living cats. Some—maybe most—had run away, but the ones who hadn't? He supposed animal control officers took them somewhere, probably to be euthanized.

Gazing upon the empty lot, Dwayne felt guilty. Mrs. Figueroa might have been looney—and sick with some kind of weird disease that made gray muck ooze out of you—but she hadn't deserved what happened to her. And it wouldn't have happened if he'd kept his mouth shut. His mother told him that it had only been a matter of time before something like this occurred. *Better now, before she hurt anyone,* she'd said. *She hurt herself,* Dwayne had replied. His mother hadn't been able to respond to that.

He stayed on the sidewalk, reluctant to set foot onto the contaminated ground. Sure, he was wearing sneakers with rubber soles, but he didn't want to take any chances. He was several yards from where Nala's corpse had disappeared, and while he didn't want to examine the location any closer, he started walking toward it anyway. Why, he wasn't sure. Morbid curiosity? Or was something else drawing him forward, something even darker? When he reached the section of sidewalk in front of where he'd put Nala, he stopped. The ground here looked the same as in the rest of the lot, and he figured Nala's body had either been removed by workers or had been buried even deeper by the bulldozer. Whichever the case, he was relieved not to see it, and he was about to continue on his way when he noticed what looked like a tuft of black fur poking out from the dirt. There was a broken branch lying in the gutter nearby—another leftover from the lot cleanup, he guessed—and he picked it up. It was only a foot long and thin, but he thought it would do the job. He returned to where Nala was buried and began using the stick to excavate the cat's corpse. The soil was loose, which made the task easier, and after only a few minutes, he'd managed to expose most of Nala's head.

The animal's mouth was partway open, and a small greenish-gray tongue lolled from the side. Needle-sharp teeth were visible, and like Mrs. Figueroa's, they were a startling bone-white. The worst part was that Nala's eyes were open wide, and lines of crusty muck trailed from them, as if the animal had been trying to expel the Benefaction from its body as it died. Flecks of dirt stuck to the eyeballs' surface, but despite how disgusting the eyes were—or maybe because of it—he couldn't look away. He remembered what Mrs. Figueroa had said.

You ever want to see the truth—the real *truth—look into a cat's eyes.*

Mrs. Figueroa had said that the Magna Mater lived in everyone, that she was some kind of dark force that slowly ate away at everything that lived until there was nothing left. If it was true, then he—along with everyone else— carried the seeds of their own destruction from the moment they exited the womb. He'd become so obsessed by this idea that he barely ate or slept anymore, and his grades were starting to suffer. His mother and father were beginning to talk about sending him to see a child psychologist, but he knew no doctor could help him. There was only one thing that could: *knowing.*

Despite his misgivings about the soil, he stepped onto the property and faced Nala's corpse. He got down on his hands and knees and lowered his head toward Nala's, holding his breath so he wouldn't have to smell the stench of the animal's rot. He focused his gaze on both of the cat's eyes and leaned in close so he could *see.*

He remained in that position—not moving, barely breathing—for nearly three hours before a neighbor finally noticed him and called the police.

After the police brought him home, he told his mom that he had no idea why he'd been staring into the eyes of a dead cat in the empty lot where Mrs. Figueroa's house had once stood. He slept the rest of that day, through the night, and well into the next afternoon. When he finally woke, he climbed out of bed, staggered to the bathroom, peed, flushed, and then washed his hands. As he did, he watched the water circling around the drain before it went down, and he remembered.

In Nala's eyes, he'd seen an unfathomably vast gulf of darkness, not merely the absence of light, but a darkness that was its own thing, real and tangible, and it filled Forever. At the center of this darkness was something he wouldn't have thought possible: an object that was even darker. It was the absolute embodiment of nothingness, of emptiness. A name for it flashed through his mind then. The Big Dark. But around that emptiness, light swirled, and he understood that this light was everything that ever was or would be. All existence—all space, all time, and everything and everyone within—had only one purpose: to satisfy the eternal hunger of the Big Dark. Together, the hole and the light rotating around it were called the Gyre, and the Magna Mater was one of its servants. She helped to break down reality, like a mother chewing food for her infant so that the child could digest it more easily.

That's all we are, he thought. *All we were ever meant to be. Food.*

He turned off the water and screamed until his throat bled.

It took a while to get Hannah settled, but after she was finally in bed and sleeping, Dwayne's wife wanted to have "words" with him in the kitchen. She accused him of driving recklessly, of not paying enough attention, of traumatizing their little girl due to his carelessness.

"It's your duty as a parent to protect her from things like this," Kate said.

He wanted to smile at her and say *Honey, you don't know what trauma is,* but he knew it would only make things worse, so he remained silent. Eventually, Kate's anger dissipated, although it didn't go away completely, and she went to bed, leaving Dwayne sitting in silence at the kitchen table, alone with his thoughts. Kate was right, of course. He *had* failed to protect Hannah. But that was because he hadn't prepared her to understand the true nature of reality. And if she didn't understand it, how could she face it?

He understood then what he had to do. He rose from the table, removed his car keys from the wall hook by the door to the garage, and departed.

"Hannah? Sweetie?"

Dwayne sat on the edge of his daughter's bed and shook her shoulder gently. She didn't wake right away. She'd had a difficult night, and her mind and body needed rest. But he persisted, shaking her a bit harder, until finally her eyes opened and she gazed at him blearily.

"Daddy?"

"I'm sorry for what happened tonight. I know it came as a shock to you. I want to make sure you never feel like that again. I want to show you something. Because once you know the truth—the worst thing that ever could be— something like hitting a cat will be no more remarkable to you than taking a breath."

He bent over to pick up the dead calico from the floor. He'd gone back to the scene of the accident to retrieve the cat. Was the animal Nala reborn or a different animal entirely? He supposed it didn't matter. He held the cat before Hannah so she could look into its unseeing eyes, and as she did, her own eyes widened and she began to tremble.

Dwayne smiled as thick gray tears began to slide slowly down his cheeks.

finis

In November of 2009,
two of the most amazing beings in
the world entered my life, in the form of two
young cats named Zeddicus and Graymalkin Shireman.

2008   2018

In April, 2018, cancer stole away my precious
Graymalkin far too soon, and with her,
it stole half of my heart...